A DIFFERENT KIND OF JUSTICE

The final Sarah Beaufort mystery

While visiting her mother in prohibition New York, a series of murders grab Sarah Beaufort's attention. But while she's as inquisitive as ever, Sarah is determined not to get involved. Until, that is, her mother's maid, Morna, disappears following a date with a wealthy gentleman of dubious connections. When Morna's date is found brutally murdered in a house of ill repute in the guise of a nightclub, and with Morna still missing, Sarah can't help but become involved

A DIFFERENT KIND OF JUSTICE

A Sarah Beaufort Mystery

Linda Sole

Severn House Large Print
London & New York

This first large print edition published 2010
in Great Britain and the USA by
SEVERN HOUSE PUBLISHERS LTD of
9-15 High Street, Sutton, Surrey, SM1 1DF.
First world regular print edition published 2008 by
Severn House Publishers Ltd., London and New York.

British Library Cataloguing in Publication Data

Sole, Linda.
   A different kind of justice. -- (A Sarah Beaufort mystery)
   1. Beaufort, Sarah (Fictitious character)--Fiction.
   2. Serial murder investigation--New York (State)--New
   York--Fiction. 3. United States--Social life and
   customs--1918-1945--Fiction. 4. Detective and mystery
   stories. 5. Large type books.
   I. Title II. Series
   823.9'14-dc22

   ISBN-13: 978-0-7278-7819-9

Printed and bound in Great Britain by
MPG Books Ltd, Bodmin, Cornwall.

Prologue

'No! I told you what happened, he raped me!' the girl screamed as the man took the flatiron from the kitchen range. She knew it was hot, because she had been using it to press the sheets she had washed the previous day. 'No, Pa – please don't do it. Please...'

'But there was someone before him,' her father said. 'Give me your lover's name or you'll be sorry!'

'No, I won't ... I can't ... Pa, don't do this...'

'Tell me his name!' the man said, holding the flat surface of the iron just a few inches from her face. She could feel the heat even from that distance and the fear coursed through her, because she knew he was drunk. 'Tell me the name of the bastard who made you a slut or I'll burn your face. You will never disgrace me again! I'll make certain of that!'

'No, Pa,' she said trying to pull away from him. 'I can't tell you his name. Besides, it doesn't matter. The child died and...' She got no further for he was pressing the hot iron to her cheek. 'Pa—!' The word ended in a scream that seemed to echo endlessly in the small room.

The pain was so bad that she fell in a daze to the floor, the stench of burning flesh rising into the man's nostrils. He gagged on it, turning away to vomit on the floor she had scrubbed only hours before. A wave of shame rose up inside him as he saw her crumpled body lying there; only now was he aware of the terrible thing he had done to his own daughter. She was all he had left in the world, for the others were gone, dead and buried. As the realization of his crime struck home, he fell to his knees beside her, his tears bursting out noisily as he sobbed, mingling with the mucus from his nose.

'I'm sorry, Lucy,' he wept. 'I didn't mean to do it...'

Her eyelids fluttered and she moaned but her eyes didn't open. He got to his feet, suddenly overcome with what he had done to her. Her face looked so red and puckered and he knew that he could never put right the wrong he had inflicted.

'I'll get help,' he muttered. 'I'll get help...'

Lucy was stirring as he rushed from the room. She opened her eyes, feeling the unbearable sting of her scorched flesh. Dragging herself upright, fighting the pain and the nausea, she looked round the kitchen. It was clean and neat despite the poverty she had endured since returning to her father's home, but she would keep it so no longer.

She went to the water jug and splashed some on her face, welcoming the cooling sensation though in another moment the ruined flesh was stinging more than before. She had heard that butter was good for burns, but there was none in the house – had been none for days, because money was short.

She went round the room, picking up a few things, tying them into a bundle, because she would stay here no longer. She had no idea where she would go, but she would not be here when her father returned...

One

'Have you got all you need?' Cathy Marshall asked as her husband came downstairs carrying the one medium-sized suitcase he had owned for as long as she could recall. 'Is that all you are taking? You will be away a long time, you know.'

'I am not sure I should be going at all,' he said. 'All the way to America to judge a couple of cat shows. It doesn't seem right when you are staying here.'

'We've been through all this before,' Cathy said. 'I don't mind you going, Ben, truly I don't. Besides, my sister is coming to stay with her twins and you know you don't really get on with her husband. And you know you wanted to make sure those cats you sold to the American lady were all right.'

'Yes, I did,' Ben admitted, because his wife had put her finger on the real reason he had agreed to go. 'I never should have sold them to her.'

'Well, I am sure she is looking after them,' Cathy said. 'I think it's a good thing I packed another case for you though.'

'You didn't!' Ben smiled and shook his

head. 'I might have expected you would look after me – but I wish you were coming with me, love.'

'You know you wouldn't feel comfortable leaving the cats to someone else all that time. Look on the bright side, Ben – you might see Sarah Beaufort when you are in New York. If you do, give her my love.'

'Yes, I shall,' Ben said and kissed her on the mouth. 'You are so understanding, Cathy. Most wives would be complaining about their husbands going off on a trip like this, but you haven't said a word.'

'That is because I really don't mind,' Cathy told him. 'I don't get to see my sister often. She is having a big operation, as you know, and I'll be looking after her while she recovers. Her husband will take the twins back with him, but they will come and stay with us for a few days when she's on the road to recovery. I shall hardly be alone at all.'

'Well...' He heard the doorbell ring and knew that his taxi had arrived. 'I suppose I should go. I'll send you a telegram when I get there.'

'All right. Now have a good time, and don't worry. I'll look after the cats.'

'Don't overdo things, Cathy. You know what Jane can be like, and the twins are little monsters...'

'Stop worrying about me and get off. The ship won't wait if you're late.'

10

'Well, at least this time I shan't be testifying against a crime boss,' Ben said, because the only other time he had been to America was when he was working for Scotland Yard and had been instrumental in tracing a criminal the New York police had been trying to find. 'I'll bring you a present back, Cathy love.'

'You had better,' she said, and laughed. 'And make it something expensive!'

'Oh, I will,' Ben promised. 'I'll ask Sarah to help me choose it if she's still in New York. I haven't heard she is back, so I don't know...'

'Get off then,' Cathy said, pushing him out of the door. 'Have a good time, love, and don't get into any trouble.'

'Some chance,' he said, and smiled. 'You have a good time too.'

He smiled to himself as he settled back in the taxi. It would be nice if he happened to bump into Sarah when he was in New York City, but she might be on her way home for all he knew.

'How are you, Mrs Beaufort?' Lady Meadows said when her maid showed the visitor into her sitting room. 'I am so glad you could come. I have been hoping for a little chat for a while now.'

'You are thinking about Larch and Sarah, aren't you?' Amelia said as she went to sit down in the large, comfortable wing chair by

11

the fireplace. 'I had a letter from Sarah the other day, but she didn't mention Larch.'

'That is because he would hardly be there yet,' Lady Meadows said. 'I know he intends to go and see her as soon as he is in New York, but he was going to Boston and somewhere else first to call on some friends he met when he was travelling the year before last.'

'Oh, I see...' Amelia broke off as a maid brought in the tea trolley. 'I thought Sarah would be home again long before this, but she seems to be enjoying herself out there.'

'Well, it is her mother's home now, isn't it?' Lady Meadows' hand hovered over the pot. 'Do you like your tea with milk or cream?'

'Milk please...' Amelia said. 'Yes, I know she would be welcome to live there, but I was hoping it was only going to be a short stay.'

'Yes, well, between you and me, Amelia, I think the only reason Larch accepted the invitation to show some of his paintings in New York was in the hope of seeing Sarah. I believe he means to ask her to marry him.'

'Ah...' Amelia accepted her tea. 'I was pleased she went, because I wanted her to get away from all those nasty goings on here – but I hope she says yes and comes home with your son.'

'So do I,' Lady Meadows said, and smiled comfortably. 'I am looking forward to being a grandmother one day.'

'And I shall be a great-grandmother if they get a move on with it!'

The two ladies nodded their heads in perfect agreement.

'At least while she is out there having a good time she isn't getting involved with any of those nasty murders,' Lady Meadows said. 'Try this seed cake, Amelia; it is very good if I do say so myself...'

The house was one of the few nineteenth century mansions still in regular use by its owners. Since the beginning of the twentieth century, many of the wealthiest residents had given up on Newport, Rhode Island, and moved on, renting their homes to people who came for the yachting. But the old van Allen mansion had been recently taken over by newcomers. Some folk remembered the grace and charm of the old days, remembered the quality and the visiting royalty, when foreign princes had been seen on their yachts in the bay, guests of elite American families; those who remembered turned their noses up at these new people. They called them parvenus, the new rich, but what they truly meant was that they were vulgar. They flashed their money, spending it on fast cars, expensive clothes, jewellery, and huge yachts – and the parties they gave were loud, the guests leaving in the early hours, drunken, racing their car engines as they zipped along roads that had been meant for a quieter age.

This particular party seemed to have been going on for days, jazz music playing so loudly in the grounds that it could be heard by neighbours day and night. The whole house blazed with lights, and no one had bothered to draw any curtains. The man watching from outside could clearly see what was going on, the appalling behaviour of men and women high on drink and possibly opium too. He wandered in through the front door, which someone had left wide open, his eyes moving scornfully over empty gin and bourbon bottles lying abandoned on the floor. What good was the law on prohibition when people like this had no problem in getting what they wanted? His stomach turned as he saw the remains of food and dirty dishes scattered everywhere, used glasses upturned, sometimes lying smashed amongst a pool of what had been inside before the glass was knocked over.

It was nothing short of an orgy, the man thought as he heard a burst of laughter and saw a half-clothed woman embracing a man while others watched and called out encouragement. He turned away, a snarl of disgust on his lips. People like this didn't deserve to live. They were the scum of the earth, wasting money, tossing it away as though it grew on trees. Had they any idea of what it was like to live in the real world? Did they know that in the squalid tenements of New York there were men and women struggling to make enough money to feed their families?

His expression hardened as he realized that these people wouldn't care if they did. These were the here and now people, live for today in case you die tomorrow. None of them deserved to live. And if he had his way, before the night was out some of them would not. He had come here to ask for a favour, to beg for the job he had lost months before, because it was his last hope, but what he had seen had made him angry. He was finished with begging! In future he would take!

Sarah heard the grunt that came from behind the newspaper her stepfather was reading at the breakfast table. She smiled, because she had fallen in love with Philip Harland in the nicest way. When she arrived at his beautiful house here in New York, she had been prepared to dislike the man who had stolen her mother, leaving a big hole in her life – and hurting her beloved father. However, Philip was a dear man and she had not been able to dislike him, particularly as he so obviously doted on her mother.

'Something wrong?' she asked as he looked up. 'In the paper, I mean?'

'There was another murder,' he said and frowned at her over the top of his gold-framed spectacles, which perched precariously on the end of his nose. 'They started when

15

you were at the ranch, Sarah. The first were in Newport, at the old van Allen residence. It had been taken over by some newcomers – rich but no class. I think the man who bought it made a fortune out of making armaments. His son was a playboy. By all accounts he held a lot of wild parties there until one night a man walked in and shot the son and half a dozen others.'

'A mass shooting?' Sarah said, horrified. 'Why would anyone do such a thing?'

'The police have been trying to find out. They thought it must be robbery, because some silver was taken, but if it was the thief didn't know much about his business. There were far more precious things to be taken – a fortune in jewels.'

'Wouldn't a thief have wanted to get in and out as quietly as possible?' Sarah asked, wrinkling her brow in thought.

She was looking very pretty. Her skin had taken on a pale golden tan after some weeks at her stepfather's ranch in Louisville, Kentucky, a light dusting of freckles over her nose. Her reddish gold hair had recently been cropped in the latest style and curled in the nape of her neck. She wasn't sure yet if she liked it, but her mother had taken her to one of the fashionable stylists when they returned to New York, insisting on buying her a whole new wardrobe from Bloomingdale's and Macy's. They had visited the new store on Seventh Avenue, which had been

16

opened a couple of years earlier in 1924 and was an amazing shop.

'You have to indulge me, Sarah darling,' Mrs Harland had said when Sarah protested that she didn't need so many new things. 'It may be ages before I see you again...'

'A professional thief would almost certainly have waited to break in when the house was empty,' Philip observed, his grey eyes serious as he looked at her across the table. 'That is what has been puzzling the police I imagine. There have been three more similar shootings since, all of the victims the playboy sons of rich men. Stuff has been taken from the house on each occasion, but never the most valuable. The police seem to think the killer has a grudge against his victims, but they can't link them as yet.'

'A grudge – yes, that seems a logical explanation,' Sarah agreed. 'Do the police have any clues at all?'

'According to the papers they are completely in the dark,' Philip replied, and grinned at her. 'At one time the crime here was horrendous, but for the past few years the police have had much better control. They seem baffled over this though. You'll have to give them a hand. I know the officer in charge of the investigation. Shall I give him a call and ask if he wants you and your friends to help him out?'

'Don't you dare!' Mrs Harland looked at her husband sharply as she sat down at the table. 'Sarah came here to get away from all that nasty business last year, didn't you, darling?'

'Yes and no,' Sarah said, considering. 'I was a bit shocked when Ronnie Miller knocked Mr Ashton out with his spade. I thought he was going to...' She shuddered as she remembered the strange light in Ronnie's eyes. For a moment the great daft lad had looked as if he meant to chop his victim's throat with the sharp edge of his spade. 'He stopped when I told him, though. We thought he might have killed Simon Beecham during the Beecham Thorny murders, but I'm not sure now that he did. Gran told me in one of her letters that he had died in his sleep. Poor Ronnie! He didn't have much of a life.'

'It sounds as if he might have been a danger to himself and others,' Mrs Harland said. 'So perhaps it might be for the best.'

'Yes...' Sarah hesitated and her reply was lost as Mrs Harland's maid entered the breakfast room carrying a small silver salver with a buff-coloured envelope. She presented it to Sarah. 'For me – a telegram? Oh ... I hope it isn't bad news.' She was immediately thinking of her beloved grandmother.

'It's all right, Miss Beaufort,' Maura told her with an engaging smile. 'The boy said it's not bad news. Sure he'd know, so he would.'

Maura Trelawney was a recent immigrant.

18

She had come over from Ireland to seek her fortune on the stage, but so far this was the best job she'd managed to find. Sarah had taken to her as soon as they met, because they both had similar ambitions.

'Thank you, Maura,' Sarah said, tearing the envelope open, her heart beating faster despite the girl's reassurance. She gave a little cry of surprise. 'It is from Larch, Mummy. He has been asked to show some of his paintings at the Arlington Gallery. He is already in America and he arrives in New York the day after tomorrow.'

'Well, that is nice for you, Sarah,' Mrs Harland said. 'Thank you, Maura. We're not ready for you to clear yet.' She pulled a face at her daughter as the girl left. 'You can't find good servants here, and she's worse since you started talking to her about going on the stage. I am sure she spends half the day dreaming of becoming a star on Broadway.'

'I think she wants to be in the movies – talking pictures, she told me. They are going to be the big thing of the future, I think. She is very pretty. You must admit that, Mummy?'

'I suppose so. She might as well leave for all the good she does here.' Mrs Harland frowned. 'Are you pleased your friend is here, Sarah?

'I'm not sure,' Sarah replied honestly. 'I was cross with him when I discovered he

19

was the angel who put up the money for that show I was in, in London. I thought they had taken me because I was good, not because Larch told them to.'

'I am sure they wouldn't have done so if you couldn't sing,' Philip said, folding his paper. 'Well, I have to go. What are you ladies intending to do today – more shopping?'

'We don't spend all our time shopping,' his wife told him. 'I have invited some friends for lunch – and Sarah has been invited to a party this evening. Bradley is taking her, don't you remember?'

'Ah, yes.' Philip nodded. His son was a year or so younger than Sarah and had just finished his education at Harvard. He was taking a few months off before making up his mind whether or not he wished to join his father's business. 'Where is that son of mine this morning?'

'He came in late last night,' Mrs Harland replied. 'I think he must be sleeping. I didn't wake him. Did you want to see Brad for anything?'

'No, let him sleep in if he wishes,' Philip replied. He got up and kissed her cheek. 'I may be late myself this evening, but I will let you know when I'm sure.'

'Of course. As long as you keep this weekend free. You know we've asked friends, because Sarah doesn't have much longer with us before she goes back to England.'

20

'I hadn't forgotten,' he said, smiling at Sarah. 'We have to celebrate, my dear. Not that I am glad you're going. I wish you would make your home with us, but we've discussed this and you know your own mind.'

Mrs Harland looked at her daughter as he went out. 'He means it, Sarah. You know he likes you a lot, don't you?'

'Yes, and I love Philip, Mummy. But I only came for a visit, and I've been here six months. Daddy wrote to ask when I was coming back, and Gran asked me too. I've had a lovely time. You and Philip have spoiled me terribly, but I want to work for a bit longer. I think it is time I went home and looked for another job.'

'You wouldn't consider working here? Philip knows a lot of people. I dare say he could help you find something.'

'Mummy! You know I don't want that,' Sarah said. 'It would be the same as Larch paying for that show. I only want to be a professional singer if I am good enough to do it on my own. Otherwise, I might as well take my allowance and do the social thing at home.'

'Sorry.' Mrs Harland gave her a rueful smile. 'I just wanted to keep you here a little longer, darling.'

'I know.' Sarah got up and embraced her mother. 'I shall come and visit again, I promise, but I can't live with you. I don't want to live with Daddy all the time either. At least, not until I've given singing another try. I have to prove I can stand on my own two feet.'

'I do understand,' her mother said. 'Your father always tends to want to dominate others – but it wouldn't be like that here. You are so pretty, Sarah. I am sure you could get a part in a picture, sing in it too the way things are going.'

'Yes, perhaps,' Sarah said. 'I have to go back for lots of reasons, Mummy.'

Her mother avoided looking at her. 'Well, I have to talk to Hannah about lunch. Can you amuse yourself for a while?'

'Yes, of course. Do you mind if I ring for a taxi? I have something I want to do in town.'

'Do whatever you like but don't forget we have guests for lunch.'

'I'll be back soon,' Sarah promised.

She left the room immediately after her mother. She didn't want to say anything to anyone yet, but she had an audition that morning. Not for a show here in New York but on a cruise ship that went back and forth between America and England several times a year. It might be a way of keeping in touch with both sides of her family; if she got a couple of weeks onshore at either end it would be just the thing.

She'd seen the advertisement in her stepfather's newspaper a couple of days previously and made the appointment immediately. There were bound to be loads of other girls auditioning, of course, and she probably wouldn't be lucky. So rather than have to explain afterwards, she was keeping the whole thing to herself.

'You should have asked Mrs Harland,' Hannah said, looking at the Irish girl severely. 'You know she has guests coming today and I need you here to help me. I am not sure that I can let you have a couple of hours off.'

'Please,' Maura coaxed, her soft, lilting voice persuasive. 'I'll do all the clearing up afterwards, and if Mrs Harland complains I'll tell her you had no idea. Sure, I'll be back before you know I'm gone – and it's a chance for me, so 'tis.'

'Go on then,' the cook said, frowning as the girl ran from the room. 'But don't blame me if they give you the push!'

Maura wasn't listening. She flew up the back stairs to her room, locking the door as she hurriedly stripped off her uniform and put on the dress Miss Beaufort had given her. It was classy, well made and expensive, and Maura knew it would make more of an impression than anything else she owned. She really wanted to get this job on the cruise liner, because it would be one way of going to England. She had believed America was the land of dreams and that the pavements were lined with gold ... well, she hadn't quite believed that but everyone had urged her to come here, because they said with her looks and voice she would make a fortune. Unfortunately, no one had wanted to give her a chance, and listening to Miss Beaufort talk about the friendly seaside shows she'd taken part in, Maura believed she might have more of a chance in England. She couldn't afford the fare, but if she could work her passage, even as a chorus girl, she would go.

She looked at herself in the dress Sarah had given her and smiled. She didn't look like herself, more like a lady. She held her head up as Sarah did, and practised some expressions in the mirror, then giggled. The resemblance was remarkable, though she didn't think Sarah had noticed it herself. A lot of it had come from practising Sarah's mannerisms. Maura knew she would make a good actress if she got the chance. It would be all right until she opened her mouth to talk, because she hadn't got rid of her accent yet – but maybe they would be impressed with her singing and wouldn't need her to answer many questions.

He stood watching as the girl came out of the house and got into a taxi. As yet he didn't know much about her, except that she was a part of the family. There was a son, he knew that, the English wife and this girl ... He'd seen the wife smiling and laughing with the girl, and he believed she must be the favourite. To make the biggest impact she was the one who must die.

It wasn't going to be as easy to pull off as some of the other killings he'd done. He had just walked into the first house, and seen what was going on – what beasts they were – and he'd shot them down where they stood. He had felt like laughing as he saw the disbelief and then the fear in their eyes. The last one had wet himself, begging to be spared. *He* had no mercy. None had been given to *him* when he'd begged. He had lost everything, even the will to live. Until the moment he had realized that he had power over these people he hated he had simply wanted to die. Now he was cold inside. The only time he felt anything was in the moment before he killed ... the second when he held the power of life and death in his hands. It gave him a moment of pleasure.

His lip curled in a snarl, because he hated them – the filthy rich. It was what people said often as a joke, but he knew it was true. They had more than was good for them and they believed they could treat others like dirt, using them, taking what they wanted and then discarding them. But he was taking his revenge for the harm they did, these wealthy people – he was making them suffer. He picked his targets more carefully these days, because he wanted to be sure that he caused the maximum pain. Taking their possessions didn't hurt them; it didn't make them weep through the bitter nights as he had wept. They simply went out and bought more. They thought themselves invincible, protected by their money – but money couldn't protect them from him. He thought of himself as an avenger ... the giver of death ... judge, jury, executioner. It was a different kind of justice.

Ben glanced out of the taxi window at the noisy streets of New York and wondered if he was completely mad. What on earth had possessed him to come here? He had almost made up his mind to refuse but Cathy had persuaded him that he would be a fool to pass up the chance of judging a prestigious cat show in America.

It was the idea that he might find a new cat worthy of breeding with his own stock that had finally made Ben say he would come over. He had wished a thousand times on the voyage that he hadn't let himself be persuaded, because he'd felt ill for some days. The sea had been choppy for a couple of nights and he hadn't been able to keep a thing down, but he was beginning to feel better at last.

He looked out of the window again as the car was forced to stop because of the press of traffic, catching sight of a girl wearing a stylish grey dress. For a moment he thought it might be Sarah Beaufort, though when he looked again he saw he was mistaken. This girl's hair was a slightly different colour, darker red, and when she turned to look at him he knew it wasn't her, but there was definitely a likeness – something about the dress seemed familiar. Of course Sarah couldn't be the only one to have a dress like that, but it had looked rather like one of hers. He smiled as he sat back in the car again.

Ben was thoughtful as his taxi drew up in front of the hotel. It might just be worth looking Sarah up, having a word. She was a lovely girl and he'd enjoyed working with her on the investigations he'd taken on the previous year. Cathy said he ought to set himself up as a private investigator, but following errant husbands didn't appeal. Yet there was no doubt that working with Sarah and Larch Meadows had been interesting and he had found things a bit dull of late...

'Sarah,' the middle-aged woman with frizzy ginger hair beckoned to her. She was in charge of the press of girls backstage waiting their turn, and seemed to chain smoke, lighting up as soon as she stubbed out her last cigarette, her fingers yellowed by nicotine. 'They want you now, darling. You've got your music, haven't you?'

'Yes.' Sarah looked at her, a flutter of nerves in her stomach. 'It's a song I did on stage in England by Irving Berlin—'

'Just tell the guy on the piano,' the woman

said, looking bored. 'Sing when he gives you the nod and stop when they tell you they've seen enough.'

'Yes, thank you.'

Sarah felt like telling her that this wasn't her first audition, but the woman wasn't interested. She didn't seem to rate Sarah's chances much and that made Sarah feel that she was probably wasting her time. Judging from the other girls, she wasn't what they were looking for at all. Most of the others auditioning were wearing stage clothes and a lot of make-up. Her street dress looked too reserved – too English.

She walked on stage, gave her music to the young man at the piano. He grinned at her in a friendly way, which made her feel slightly better.

'Don't look so scared, beautiful,' he said. 'Just sing in tune if you can and you'll be fine.'

Sarah nodded, feeling her confidence return. She could certainly sing in tune. She took her place centre stage and waited for his signal, deciding that they could only say no. And then the words just seemed to come, flowing as if she had never been away, was back in the successful show in London she had loved, before the horrible murders and the revelation that Larch had been their financing angel. She lost herself in the music, forgetting that she was supposed to watch for a signal to stop. When she finished the song, she became aware of the silence and her stomach clenched. They hated her!

'What did you say your name was?'

Sarah blinked and looked at the man sitting out front. 'It's Sarah – Sarah Beaufort. I'm sorry if I went on too long.'

'You didn't, honey. You were fine.' He got up and came to the front, staring up at her for a moment. 'English? You look English and you sure don't sound American.'

'Yes, I am English.'

'Have to be with that accent. Yeah...' He hauled himself on to the stage, walked around her, looking her up and down. 'Been over here long, Sarah?'

'Six months. I am visiting relatives.'

'Now you want to go home, right?'

'Well, yes, and no,' Sarah replied. 'I thought it would be nice to spend some time in both England and America ... if there was a turn-around of a week or two between cruises it would enable me to visit both my families.'

'Yeah...' He nodded and grinned. 'I'm Sam, Sam Garson – and you may be what we've been looking for, darling. Class, that's what we want for this show. The clientele are filthy rich – you know the sort, Sarah.' He pulled a wry face. 'We can't take some of these girls on a cruise like that; they would probably get drunk and throw up on customers – what are you like at sea?'

'I am fine,' Sarah said. 'I wasn't ill at all

29

coming over. Some of the other passengers were but I didn't suffer from sea sickness once.'

'Yeah, right, figures...' Sam said. He ran his fingers through his hair, which was black and curly, his eyes a deep blue. Sarah noticed the tiny scar at his hairline, the only blemish on an otherwise almost too handsome face. He was wearing a pinstriped suit and crocodile skin shoes, a large diamond ring on the little finger of his right hand. 'You wouldn't run out on me when you got home, Sarah? Some girls work their passage and then jump ship the other side. English girls wanna come here; American girls wanna try their luck in England. It means we have all the bother of looking for another singer.'

'No, I wouldn't leave without giving you notice,' Sarah said. She held her breath as he looked at her for what seemed an age. 'I know you are looking for singers ... are you considering me for the chorus?'

'What do you take me for, Sarah? I ain't that crazy, darling. A girl like you doesn't work for peanuts. You would have three solo spots in the show – how does that sound?'

'It sounds wonderful. I didn't think you would want me at all.'

'I know talent when I see it,' he said. 'OK, give Ellie your name backstage and be here in the morning. We start rehearsal eight thirty sharp. Be late and you're out.'

The charm switched off so suddenly that Sarah was taken aback. She walked off stage wondering what had hit her and whether she had stumbled into some sort of a madhouse. Ellie would probably tell her it was all a big joke.

'He liked you.' The middle-aged woman with ginger hair came up to her, looking down her list. 'Sarah Beaufort. I marked you with a tick because I thought he might. You know the terms? You have to do at least one trip there and back – fifty dollars a week, paid when you get back.'

'Oh, I didn't realize that bit,' Sarah said, and looked thoughtful, because it didn't seem quite normal. 'Not that it matters so much...'

'Last two cruises we lost the main singers for the show after the first trip,' Ellie told her in a bored tone. 'Sam says he won't hire girls who might run out on him this trip.'

'Well, I suppose that is fair enough,' Sarah said. 'But what about girls who need money in the meantime?'

'You can get a fifty-dollar sub up front if you're desperate. Sam ain't a hard man.' She laughed suddenly. 'Taken you by surprise, ain't it? Sam always did have a soft spot for English ladies – he spotted you right off. Watch him, because he can be dangerous for a girl like you, but I think you've got more sense than to fall for him, even if he is a looker.'

'Oh yes, I shall be careful,' Sarah said. 'Besides...' She shook her head, because she didn't want to say too much.

'Got a boyfriend, have you?' Ellie nodded. 'Stands to reason, a girl like you. You'll have no trouble from Sam if he knows that...'

As Ellie went off to tell the next girl to get ready, Sarah saw a face she recognized. Maura was sitting on her own at the far end of the room. It crossed Sarah's mind that she might be trying to keep out of the way, because she was almost certain that her mother hadn't given the girl time off. However, she went up to her, smiling to show that she wasn't going to find fault.

'I've been told to come for rehearsal in the morning,' she said. 'You haven't been called yet, have you?'

'Just my luck,' Maura said. 'Hannah will skin me alive if I don't get back soon. She didn't want me to come at all.'

'It is only fair that you should have time off for auditions,' Sarah told her. 'But it might have been best if you'd asked Mrs Harland first.'

'I thought she might ask me to leave,' the Irish girl said truthfully. 'Sure, I know I should have asked, so I do – but it was a chance. I want to get to England. I think I might stand more chance of a decent job over there.'

'Well, you might,' Sarah agreed. 'I'm not sure. Everyone thinks of America as the land of opportunity and there are some wonderful shows over here, Maura. Besides, I thought you wanted to be in films?'

''Tis what I want right enough, but until I can get a job in a show there's little enough chance of it, Miss Beaufort.'

'You know you can call me Sarah, at least when Mummy isn't around,' Sarah said. 'Look, I have to go. I wish you luck, Maura. I shan't tell anyone I saw you here. Let me know how you got on when you can.'

'I will that,' Maura said in her lilting accent. 'And 'tis a good girl you are to keep me secret.'

'It would be fun if we were on the cruise together,' Sarah said. 'Good luck. I shall see you later.'

'So you will, Sarah.'

Sarah nodded and walked on, going swiftly down the stairs. She saw a cab passing the theatre and hailed it instantly. She would have to hurry or she would be late getting back for lunch, and she wanted to change her dress.

Louise van Allen stroked the beautiful cat, listening to its purring and thinking how lucky she had been to meet that nice Mr Marshall at the show she'd attended in England. He had sold her two kittens, both of which had turned out beautifully. She was looking forward to seeing him again later that day. It might take her mind off the thing that had been bothering her for a while.

Her husband said there was nothing to worry about. Their son Jonathan often went away for weeks on end without bothering to get in touch, but Louise had an uncomfortable feeling that something was wrong – something more than usual. She wondered if he knew what she had done, but then she told herself it was impossible. He had gone because of a row with his father over that incident. Her face screwed up in an expression of distaste. She didn't want to think about that at the moment. Like most other things she disliked, she pushed it to the back of her mind and stroked the cat's fur, letting its purring soothe her. There was no need to worry just yet.

It wasn't the first time Jonathan had sulked after a row with his father, but this was different. Gerry didn't know it, but she had always bailed her son out of trouble in the past. She had her own money and what Gerry didn't know, he couldn't stop ... but he would be angry if she told him she had given Jonathan a thousand dollars in cash before he left. That had been eighteen months ago, and she knew her son – a thousand dollars wouldn't have lasted this long. So why hadn't be been in touch?

She knew he didn't want to work for his father. He had a small musical talent – at least his father called it small, despising him for being proficient at nothing but tinkling with a piano.

'If he wanted to be a concert pianist I could accept it,' Gerry had told her. 'But he isn't serious about his music anymore than he was his business studies at Harvard. Admit it, Louise, that son of ours will never amount to anything much.'

Louise hadn't answered. She didn't talk to Gerry more than need be these days. He called it the silent treatment and it made him angry. He had lifted his fist to her once but he hadn't hit her. She knew things ... things that he wouldn't want anyone else to know. Gerry was involved in things that weren't quite legal. Oh, it was all wrapped up in clean linen and presented to the world as all above board, but she knew that some of his money came from a source that he wouldn't want his political friends to know about.

It wasn't the fact that her husband was involved with unsavoury people that she could only term gangsters that made her despise him, Louise thought as she stroked the cat. She hated him because of the business with that girl ... a young girl who had worked for them.

Gerry didn't know that the girl had told her what he'd done to her – what he did with the other girls he had working for him at one of his whorehouses, or 'nightclubs' as he called them. As far as Louise knew the other girls were content to sell themselves for

35

money, but this girl hadn't been ... so he had raped her. Only she'd escaped from him, and she'd run away, disappearing into the night – but not before she had told Louise things. Louise had never heard from her since, but then, she wasn't likely to get in touch after what Gerry had done to her – what *she* had done to her! But Jonathan couldn't know about that ... she pushed the thought from her mind. If her son had guessed that the girl he had quarrelled with his father over had been sent off without a penny in her pocket he would be furious ... but he couldn't know.

Louise had never told her husband that she knew his dirty little secrets. For the moment it suited her to remain Mrs van Allen, but that was for Jonathan's sake. Gerry ate too much, smoked far more than was good for him, and goodness knows what other vices he had. She hadn't slept with him for years, and as long as he stayed away from her room she was content to keep things as they were. If Gerry tried to cut Jonathan out of his inheritance things might change, but for the moment she would allow him to believe himself safe.

She picked the cat up, rubbing her face against its soft fur. Gerry thought she was the meek woman he had married and treated like a doormat from day one. He would get a surprise one day.

'Where is Jonathan, my sweetie pie?' she

crooned against the cat's fur. 'It's time he rang me, told me he wanted some more money...' The cat's contented purring made her smile. She lifted her head to listen as the doorbell rang and she heard her maid admitting a visitor. 'That must be that nice Mr Marshall ... come all the way from England to see you, my precious.'

Two

'I'm sorry, Mrs Harland,' Hannah said later that morning when summoned to the drawing room to explain why the preparations for lunch were late. 'I should never have let her go, but she said it was her big chance and I didn't want to seem mean – so I said she could have a couple of hours. I can't do everything on my own, not with so many guests.'

'This really is too bad,' Mrs Harland said. 'We shall have to let her go – and I quite liked her.' She sighed. 'These young girls are all the same. I shall look for someone older next time, more responsible.'

'Is something wrong, Mummy?' Sarah asked, coming into the room at that moment. She had changed into a light cream linen dress and looked cool and fresh, like a breath of spring air. 'Can I do anything to help?'

'I have ten guests arriving for lunch at any minute, Sarah, and the dining table isn't set. Hannah can't do it...'

'I'd best get back, Mrs Harland, or the soup will spoil...'

'Don't worry, dearest,' Sarah said, and kissed her mother's cheek. 'I'll see to the table, and I'll help carry things in so that Hannah doesn't have it all to do.'

'That will look very odd,' Mrs Harland said with a frown. 'It really is too bad of Maura to take time off without asking – just to go to an audition.'

'Well, she ought to have asked,' Sarah said. 'But it can't be changed – besides, I help with the table and serving when Amelia has guests. Just put it down to my odd English ways.'

Mrs Harland laughed, her humour restored. 'I've always been thought of as slightly odd because of my English ways so perhaps it won't matter. Did you have a good time, darling?'

'Yes, I did. I shall tell you about it later, before I go out for the evening. Have you seen Bradley at all this morning?'

'He surfaced a few minutes ago but went straight out,' Mrs Harland said. 'Philip doesn't know but I am a little worried about him. I'm afraid he is getting into bad company.'

'Surely not?' Sarah arched her brows. 'Bradley seems to have his head screwed on the right way to me. I know he likes parties and sometimes drinks a bit too much, but that is only natural in someone of his age, isn't it?'

'Is it?' Mrs Harland shook her head. 'I

really don't know where he gets the stuff. Prohibition was supposed to curb drunkenness.'

'It doesn't work, Mummy darling,' Sarah said, and wrinkled her smooth forehead in thought. 'It seems to me that it makes things worse. Gangsters see it as a way of making huge profits and the alcohol they produce isn't regulated, which only makes it more lethal – and them richer and more dangerous. There are hundreds of speakeasies where it can be bought, and I am sure Bradley has his own sources.'

'It is such an odd law,' Mrs Harland said. 'It is illegal to manufacture and sell alcohol but not to drink it or have it in your possession – so it doesn't stop young people getting hold of it and drinking it.'

'I agree with you,' Sarah said. 'Philip was speaking this morning about those awful shootings – the Playboy Murders, as the press are labelling them, but there are gangland shootings all the time. You only have to read the stories about Al Capone. I mean, I know all that is in Chicago, but the same goes on here, Mummy – and it is no wonder because they must be able to make so much money from the sale of illegal alcohol. I don't think it makes sense at all, do you?'

'No, I don't,' her mother agreed. 'But if we don't make haste we shall never have that table ready in time...'

★ ★ ★

Sarah was dressing for the evening when someone knocked at her door and then Maura slipped in. She looked at the dress Sarah was wearing, unable to disguise her envy.

'That is a lovely dress, Miss Sarah. It must have cost the earth, so it must.'

'Yes, it was expensive,' Sarah replied, feeling slightly guilty as she realized that it had probably cost her mother more than she paid this girl in six months. 'It was a going away present from my mother – only I shan't be leaving as soon as I had expected, and I shall come back again when the ship returns.'

'I shall be coming with you,' Maura said, a gleam in her eyes. 'Sam gave me a job in the chorus – and I've got a date tonight. I wanted to ask if you would lend me something of yours. If you have an evening dress you don't wear any more?'

Sarah hesitated, because it wasn't always a good idea to lend things to other girls, but she had started it by giving Maura one of her day dresses. She thought about the evening clothes in her wardrobe and then realized there was a dress she didn't much care for, because the colour didn't suit her. She and Maura were similar in colouring, but Maura's skin was paler, her hair a slightly darker red, and it would probably suit her.

'Yes, I do have a dress you can have,' she

said. 'And you can keep it – but what about shoes?'

'I've got a nice pair of strappy sandals,' Maura told her, her eyes shining. She gave a cry of pleasure as Sarah took the green dress from the wardrobe and draped it over her arm. 'But that is beautiful so 'tis – English isn't it? I haven't seen anything like it in the shops here.'

'It's Worth actually,' Sarah said with a smile. 'The colour is a bit hard for me, but I think it will suit you. Anyway, you can take it and see if it is what you want, Maura.'

'You're so kind to me,' Maura said. 'Mrs Harland was angry with me. She says I'm to work a week's notice but I told her I'm leaving tonight. I shall come back for my things tomorrow afternoon after rehearsal.'

'Oh...' Sarah wondered if she was being taken advantage of by the Irish girl. It wasn't a very nice thing to do, leaving her employer in the lurch, but on the other hand she didn't have much choice if she wanted the job. Sam had made that perfectly clear. 'Well, I shall see you there in the morning I expect.'

'So you will,' Maura said, and grinned at her. 'It's going to be lovely working with you, Sarah, so it is...'

Sarah smiled but didn't say anything. She had an idea she might find it a little too much if Maura made a habit of borrowing her things, but if she did it too often Sarah would just have to say no. She turned back to the long cheval dressing mirror, looking at the dress she was wearing once more. It was a narrow sheath of silver and shimmered in the lights of the chandelier, with a low dipping neckline. She was wearing a pair of dangling diamond and pearl earrings her mother had bought for her recently. Remembering a diamond and pearl pendant that her father had given her a year or so earlier, she opened her jewel box and looked for it. When she hadn't found it after several minutes of looking, Sarah closed the box with a frown. She knew it had come with her from England, because she had worn it on the way out here – but it certainly wasn't here now.

She couldn't recall wearing it at the ranch, but she thought it had been in its box then ... so it must have disappeared since they returned to New York. Surely Maura hadn't borrowed it without asking? Sarah frowned, because it made her feel uncomfortable. She didn't want to blame the Irish girl without good cause, and perhaps she had left it at the ranch after all. She would ask her mother to telephone and enquire if the housekeeper had found it. But it would have to wait for the morning, because Bradley would be waiting for her downstairs...

Maura waited until she was out of the house before she fastened the pendant around her throat. She hoped that Sarah wouldn't notice it was missing, but she hardly ever wore it. Maura hadn't seen her wear it once. She seemed to prefer her pearls, which were far more expensive than this trinket. Maura knew she ought to have asked about borrowing the pendant, but she hadn't expected that Sarah would lend it to her – she hadn't been sure about a dress. If Sarah had already left the house when she went to her room she would have borrowed something without asking. She doubted whether she would have dared to take this, though, because it must be one of Sarah's best evening gowns. The fact that Sarah had given it to her made her feel worse over taking the pendant earlier, but she had so wanted to look nice this evening for him...

At first Maura had thought she wouldn't get in the show at all. Sam had told her to wait backstage, because there were several girls he was considering. When she'd been told she was in she could hardly believe her luck – and she was convinced it was down to the dress she was wearing. Sarah's dress! It made her look like a lady, something she wasn't, not really, even though she liked trying to look as if she were.

She was sure it was because she was wearing Sarah's dress that *he* had asked her out that night. She had been leaving the theatre when he turned up, almost bumping into him in her hurry. He'd grabbed her arm, steadied her, his eyes bright with laughter, and then he'd told her how beautiful she was – and he'd asked her out.

Maura hadn't hesitated, because he was obviously a rich man. He was quite a bit older, but she didn't mind that in the right man. She thought he might come from a wealthy background, because he spoke a bit like Mr Harland. He was American, not English.

'I would like to take you somewhere nice,' he told her. 'You are too beautiful to be working as a showgirl ... what did you say your name was?'

'Maura Trelawney.'

'That would be Irish then?'

'So it would, sir – and what would your name be then?'

'Everyone calls me Michael,' he said, a gold tooth gleaming as he grinned at her. 'I think you and me are going to get along just fine, Maura. Just fine...'

She was excited as she hailed a cab and gave the name of the nightclub where she was to meet Michael that evening. She had never been to a posh club before and dressed in Sarah's gown she felt as if she were really a rich lady going out with her gentleman friend...

Sarah looked doubtfully at the silver hip flask Bradley had just taken from his pocket and offered to her. It wasn't that she was a prude, but if she was going to drink alcohol

45

she would have preferred wine.

'What is it?' she asked. 'If it is that awful hooch you had the other night, no thank you. I would prefer fruit punch.'

'I'll put a drop of this in the punch if you like,' Bradley said. 'It's good Irish whisky, Sarah, not hooch, promise you.'

'And where did you get that?' she asked, a teasing smile in her eyes. 'Or shouldn't I ask?'

'You can ask but you won't get an answer,' Bradley told her with a grin. He was a tall man, dark-haired with a thin, pale face. It was true that he drank more than his father would like, but Sarah thought it was just a fad – a stage he was going through. She actually liked him a lot, and thought his father was wise not to try and bring him to heel too soon. After all, Brad knew that he was going to inherit a fortune one of these days so why shouldn't he have some fun for a while?

'Not that it's a huge secret. The police know where it comes from and they know who brings it in, but they take a cut and turn a blind eye – until someone does something foolish and they have to make a raid. Even then, they usually take a backhander and let the hoods go. It's only when they get wind of some really dangerous stuff that they close it down if they can. Some of that illegally brewed stuff is pure poison. Drink too much and it will kill you.'

Sarah nodded. 'I can't see the point of it, Brad. Surely prohibition makes the gang-land warfare even worse because there must be a lot of money changing hands. It is the reason for a lot of the shootings going on.'

'Yeah, I expect so,' Bradley said, and took a swig of the whisky. 'Have you had enough of this? It's deadly dull here this evening. Why don't we go on to a nightclub?'

Sarah hesitated, because she had been en-joying the party. She had met some friends and danced with several young men, but she could see that her stepbrother was bored. It couldn't hurt to go on somewhere else, she supposed, providing it was decent.

'I shan't come to a speakeasy with you,' she said. 'But if you mean a proper night-club, yes I'll come.'

'Great. You're a sport, Sarah. When my father said you were coming to stay I thought you would be a drag – but you're OK.'

'Thank you, and I like you too, dear brother,' Sarah said, and laughed as she saw the wicked gleam in his eyes. 'You know, I rather like having a brother, Brad. It isn't much fun being an only child, is it?'

'Isn't it?' He cocked one eyebrow at her. 'Depends on your point of view. I rather like being a rich man's kid...'

'Oh, you're teasing me,' Sarah said. 'I'm not sure you do like it really, Brad. What do you actually want to do with your life? Philip hopes you will take over his business one day – but what do *you* want?'

Bradley gave her an odd look as they went outside. He hailed a cab and opened the door for her, following her inside. 'To be honest I'm not sure,' he said when they settled back against the seats. 'If I knew I'd tell the old man, but I haven't made up my mind yet.'

'All right, I shan't pry,' Sarah said. 'I know it isn't my business.'

'I would tell you if I knew,' Bradley said. 'I really haven't made up my mind yet.'

Sarah nodded. She didn't quite believe him, but knew when to keep quiet. If Bradley wanted to tell her what was on his mind he would. She was sure that something was bothering him but she had no idea what it might be.

Maura looked around her as the door closed behind her. She was feeling a little hazy, because she had been drinking whisky and she wasn't used to it. After the second one she had begun to lose track of what was happening, and she wasn't sure how she had got here.

She stared at the man who had begun to take his clothes off, her fuddled mind reacting to something that just wasn't right. This wasn't what she wanted! She had come for a bit of fun, but this ... suddenly her fear made her wake up to the danger she was in.

'No,' she said. 'No! I'm not going to do this! I won't!'

'You will do as you're told, you little bitch...' he said menacingly, moving towards her. 'I've got plans for a girl like you...' He grabbed hold of her, his hand at her throat. 'You'll learn it's best to do as I tell you...'

The way he said it made Maura realize what he really thought of her. All the flattery and the promises he'd made as he fed her the liquor were lies. He wanted to use her like a whore – and from the look of this room it was the first stepping stone to something else, because this was a whore's room.

'No!' She looked frantically for something with which to defend herself and saw a heavy metal ornament on a table close by. Picking it up, she struck out at him as he came nearer, catching him a blow at the temple. It felled him, sending him crashing to the floor, the blood seeping from his wound. She turned and rushed to the door, tugging at it for a moment before she realized it was locked. He hadn't taken the key out. He must have been so sure she was out of her head with drink that he'd been careless. Maura turned the key and opened the door, running down the stairs. She was too frightened to leave through the club so she went out of a side door into a dark alley. She began to run instinctively, her mind whirling in confusion. Was he dead? Had she killed him? He deserved what he got, but she didn't want to hang...

She ran round a corner and straight into a man. He grabbed her by the arms, steadying her. She looked up at him, recognizing him at once.

'What's going on?' he asked. 'Hey, I've seen you before – you were at the audition.'

'Yes...' She gasped. 'A man ... he tried ... I hit him. I don't know if he's dead ... I may have killed him...' She gave a sob of fear. 'They will hang me if he's dead ... won't they?'

'Stop being hysterical,' the man said, giving her a shake. 'Who saw you with him?'

'People at the nightclub. He took me upstairs. I didn't know what was happening ... and then I suddenly saw him taking off his things.'

'And you hit him? Well, you'd better come with me,' he said. 'It may be that he's not dead, and if he is it will take the cops a long time to work out who did it – if ever. Most of them are not very bright. I'll look after you until you're over the fright. Tell me ... what do they call you?'

'Maura. Maura Trelawney.'

'Well, Maura, this could be your lucky day,' he said. 'Trust me. You will be fine now you're with me. I know what those bastards are like ... rich pigs that take what they want from girls like you. If you ask me, he got what he deserved.'

'I ought to go home...' Maura put a hand

50

to her throat, gasping as she realized that she had lost the necklace she'd been wearing. It must have come off – perhaps when she was struggling with him. 'I've lost Sarah's necklace ... she will never forgive me ... I took it without asking and now it has gone.'

'Well, you can't go back for it if he's dead,' the man told her. 'Besides, it's best if you disappear. If they know you were with him, they will look for you and if they find you – you will go to prison for the rest of your life...'

Maura stared at him, feeling hopeless. She was trapped, because who was going to believe a girl like her? She had taken Sarah's pendant without asking, and she'd gone to a nightclub with a stranger. They would say she had been asking for trouble, that she was no better than a whore – and they would put her in prison. They might even hang her...

Sarah was up early the next morning. She dressed in a simple linen dress with a dropped waistline, and some court shoes with Cuban heels, because she wanted to blend in as much as possible with the other girls in the cast. Most of the clothes her mother had bought for her were far too expensive, but she'd brought this from England. It was a dress she'd worn the summer she had been in the London show. She had booked a taxi to take her to the theatre, because she wanted to be sure of being on time and she wasn't completely sure of her way yet. Once they got into rehearsals she would probably start walking, as she had in London.

As she got out of the taxi and paid her fare, she saw a billboard for a newspaper, and the headlines caught her eye. There had been a murder the previous evening at a nightclub. She felt a chill of apprehension for a moment, remembering that she had spent an hour or so at a club with Bradley. She wondered if it was the same place, though it probably wasn't because there were a lot of clubs all over New York.

She put the headline from her mind as a group of girls came along the pavement towards her. They were chattering and laughing, and one of them grinned as she saw her.

'Hi,' she said. 'I'm Katie – you're Sarah, aren't you? I heard you sing yesterday. I wasn't surprised Sam picked you for a solo spot. I've worked with him before and I know he likes classy girls.'

'Should I take that as a compliment?' Sarah asked. 'I just want to be the same as everyone else.'

'Well, I've got a solo spot as well,' Katie said. 'So maybe that makes me classy too?' Her eyes were filled with mischief.

'I am sure it does, for what it's worth. From what I saw he doesn't suffer fools lightly,' Sarah replied, and received a grin.

'You'll do, honey. Sam is a real tyrant to

work for. It doesn't matter who you are, he'll work you to death to get the best out of you – and if you don't come up to scratch soon enough he'll boot you out. A word of warning – don't go out with him! He's a love 'em and leave 'em kind of guy.'

'Ellie told me we don't get paid until we get back?'

'Yeah, that's the new rule, but kick up a fuss and you'll get some of it. I told him I wasn't going to work for nothing. He agreed to pay me for the first trip when we get there – but don't tell everyone, because he'll have my ass!'

'Oh...!' Sarah was a little taken back at her plain speaking, but since Katie was a friendly girl she decided to accept language that would have horrified her grandmother had she heard it. 'Right, I'll keep it to myself. Ellie said he might pay a week up front if anyone needed it. If we have a couple of weeks' turnaround some of us might.' She wasn't going to say she didn't because it might seem as if she were pretending to be better than the others, and she didn't want that to ruin her chances of making friends.

'Yeah. You just have to know how to work Sam,' Katie said. 'I ain't frightened of him and he knows it. 'Sides, I could get a job anywhere. I've worked all over in vaudeville and he knows he's lucky to get me.'

'Why did you audition for this?' Sarah asked as they went into the theatre.

'I needed a change,' she said. 'There's this guy ... he had been bugging me for months, see. Kept asking me to go out with him, but he gave me the creeps. He's got money and he flashes it about, comes to the theatres and hangs about after the girls – but if they're daft enough to go with him...' She shrugged. 'Some never learn about that sort.'

'One of those, is he?' Sarah said, shuddering as she remembered what had happened to one of the girls she'd worked with the previous summer. 'What happens to them?'

'They don't come back,' Katie said. 'I don't know why – maybe they can't...' She frowned. 'I warned the others not to listen to him, but one girl went with him...'

'Do you think she's still alive?'

'Oh, I don't think he murders them,' Katie said. 'There's no money in that ... No, they probably end up in whorehouses for the rich clients he provides.'

'Do you know that for certain?'

'I'm pretty sure.' Katie frowned. 'One of the girls got a message to me – she said she was shut up against her will. I took it to the police and that's when he turned nasty, started threatening me.'

'So that is why you decided to try the cruise ship.' Sarah nodded. 'It is probably a good idea.'

'Yeah, I thought so. I saw him outside the theatre yesterday, but he didn't see me. He was talking to one of the other girls...' Katie frowned. 'She looked a bit like you ... wore a dress like yours...'

'That must have been Maura,' Sarah said with a frown. 'She was a maid for my mother but she wanted to sing so she took time off and came to audition. She gave in her notice yesterday and ... she asked me for a dress because she was going out on a special date...'

'I hope she didn't go with him,' Katie said. 'If she did that's the last any of us will see of her.'

'But she had landed a job as part of the chorus...'

'Well, let's hope she turns up this morning,' Katie said. 'If she doesn't...' She shrugged. 'She'll be one of his girls until she can't work anymore.'

'No!' Sarah swallowed hard, feeling slightly sick. 'She was so excited...' Her stomach felt hollow, because it was just like Esther all over again. 'Surely someone could find them ... the girls he takes?'

'Maybe, if anyone cared,' Katie said. 'The cops think we're all whores anyway. This is a big city, Sarah. What does it matter if a few girls go missing here and there? Besides, he probably has half of them on his payroll.' She saw the disbelief in Sarah's eyes. 'That's the way it is here. I ain't saying no cops are straight, but a hell of a lot of 'em are on the take.'

'That's what Bradley said about the illegal hooch last night...'

Katie nodded. 'It's big money, Sarah. What are a few missing girls when there are big dollars to be made? Anyway, forget I said anything. Maura will probably be here and then there's nothing to worry about.'

Sarah nodded, but she had that uneasy feeling at the base of her neck as she looked round at the girls gathering backstage. Maura wasn't here and Sarah was afraid that she wasn't coming.

'Ah, there you are, darling,' Mrs Harland cried as Sarah walked in at half past three that afternoon. 'I told Mr Marshall that I wasn't certain when you would be back, but he said he had nothing else to do so he waited and kept me company – and it has been very interesting too. He has told me so many things that you didn't...'

'Ben!' Sarah cried as she saw him. She felt a rush of emotion, because it was such a relief. 'I am so glad you're here. It's like a miracle. I need you and here you are, right on cue.'

'That sounds ominous,' Ben said. 'I came over to judge a cat show and look at Mrs van Allen's cats – Bella's kittens – but you look as if this is serious. You had better come and sit down. I can sense that something has happened.'

'First of all, I have to ask Mummy something...' Sarah looked at her mother. 'Do you know if Maura has been back to fetch her things? She said she was coming this afternoon after rehearsal – but she didn't turn up.'

'Didn't turn up? Why? I thought that was why she wasn't here – because she had given in her notice to join that wretched cruise?'

'No, she didn't come,' Sarah said. She looked at Ben. 'Last night Maura borrowed a dress from me because she had a special date – and I think she took a pearl and diamond pendant of mine to wear. She may have intended to return it, but she didn't ask ... but that isn't important! Katie told me that she saw Maura talking to this awful man who abducts girls for his whorehouses – or nightclubs, as he calls them—'

'Sarah!' Mrs Harland looked shocked. 'You mustn't get involved in anything like that ... it sounds dangerous.'

'Only if you are stupid enough to go with him,' Sarah said. 'Katie wasn't – that is why she decided to leave her job at the theatre and go on the cruise. This man got nasty with her because she asked about one of the girls who did go off with him and hasn't been seen since—'

'Slow down, Sarah,' Ben said. 'You're going too fast for me. You look pale – do you have any sherry, Mrs Harland?'

'We can't get it here often,' she replied. 'My husband has some whisky I believe. We keep it out of the way because of the prohibition, but I think it is in the sideboard. I'll get it...'

Sarah watched as her mother left the room. 'It's like Esther all over again,' she said in a hollow voice. 'I know something has happened to Maura – but I don't think she is dead. I don't feel it, Ben. She may be being held against her will. I don't know...'

'It has shaken you,' Ben said, concerned. 'But it is very unlikely to be the same as Esther – at least, I hope it isn't. We don't want that sort of thing happening again.' He frowned. 'It is why your family hoped you would give up the stage, Sarah. These things do happen.'

'Only if you are stupid enough to go with men like that,' Sarah insisted.

'Yes, perhaps you are right,' he agreed, smiling at her, because she hadn't lost her spirit. The colour was coming back into her face. 'What do you want me to do?'

'Could you inform the American police and see if they will begin an investigation into her disappearance?'

'Well, I could try,' Ben said. 'It is a bit soon yet, because she has only been missing a few hours. I shall probably be told that they haven't got time to look for every girl that goes missing. It is a big city, Sarah, and there are a lot of young women.'

'That is what Katie said the cops would say.'

'Sarah, language, my dear!' Mrs Harland said as she brought in a silver tray with a small glass of amber colour liquid. 'Drink this and it may make you feel better, though I hate the stuff.'

'I will sip it because it may help,' Sarah said. 'I have been worrying about Maura all morning – because of what happened in London, I suppose. But Ben is right. She hasn't been missing long. She may still be with her friend. I can't be sure she went out with the man Katie saw her talking to.'

'She may have had a boyfriend,' Mrs Harland said. 'I didn't encourage it but a girl like that takes no notice of the rules. If she took your pendant she isn't worth worrying about!'

'I liked her,' Sarah said. 'I would hate to think of her locked up in—' She saw the look on her mother's face. 'Well, you know what I mean. I don't mind her taking the pendant but I am worried about her.'

'Well, I shouldn't want any harm to come to her,' Mrs Harland said. 'But it is her own fault, Sarah. She should never have gone off with a stranger like that, you know.'

'I know,' Sarah agreed. 'It was a foolish thing to do – but someone like Maura does not have the advantages I've had. She would not necessarily have understood the dangers.'

'She understood them,' Mrs Harland said. 'She just thought it was worth the risk for a night out and the chance of something more. He may have offered her a gift or something.'

'Yes, perhaps,' Sarah agreed. She turned her soft eyes on Ben. 'You will help me find her?'

'I'll do what I can,' he agreed. 'We should try the police first – but if they aren't interested we might engage a private investigator?'

'Oh yes,' Sarah cried. 'I feel so much better now that you are here.'

'It is very odd,' Mrs Harland remarked. 'Your telegram said that Larch Meadows would be here tomorrow, Sarah. It is almost as if it were meant to be ... isn't it?'

'Yes.' Sarah looked thoughtful. 'Philip joked when he said he knew the man in charge of looking for the Playboy Murderer – but he might be able to help us too.'

'Surely the two aren't connected?' her mother said.

'No. I didn't mean that,' Sarah replied quickly. 'Oh, no, not at all. I am sure there is no connection whatsoever. Someone who has a grudge against rich people is committing those murders. Whoever he is, he wouldn't be interested in snatching girls for a whorehouse.' She glanced at her mother. 'Sorry, Mummy, but you can't pretend those places don't exist, because they do.'

'I am well aware of that, Sarah, but we don't have to talk about it.'

'But we should,' Sarah said, her eyes blazing with sudden anger. 'Don't you see, it is because people like us refuse to talk about these things that depraved men can get away with their nasty habits! If we made a fuss about girls disappearing into those places, the authorities would have to sit up and take notice.'

'Well...' Mrs Harland curled her lip in distaste. 'Some women ... some of them actually want to work and live in that way, Sarah.'

'Yes, and if they do that is their business, I imagine. But girls like Maura do not! She was so excited about getting the job – about being on the cruise with me. I can't bear to think of some awful man taking her away just because she was silly enough to say she would go out with him!'

'Sarah is right, you know,' Ben said. 'It isn't a nice subject for your drawing room, Mrs Harland, but it goes on and unless some of us stand up, it will continue. If a girl chooses that way of life it is her affair, though it still isn't legal; but she ought not to be forced into it.'

'I agree of course, though New York has had its fair share of ladies prepared to stand up for their rights. You may have heard of the suffragist Dorothy Day – and of course Henrietta Rodman who has done a great deal for the rights of women, but I understand your feelings, dearest.' Mrs Harland looked as if she wished she could disappear through the floor. Turning to Ben, she said, 'I am concerned because I do not want Sarah to put herself in danger.'

'I agree with you there,' Ben said, and smiled. 'But I know Sarah. If I don't make sure that someone investigates this sordid business, Sarah will start an investigation herself...'

'You wanted to see me?' Mrs van Allen stared down her long nose at the police officer her maid had just shown into her drawing room. 'I think it must be my husband you wished to speak to, Detective Hudson. I am afraid he isn't here at the moment.'

'It was about your husband...' Detective Hudson cleared his throat, feeling decidedly uncomfortable in the over-formal room. He didn't much like women like this, and he wished himself anywhere but here. Someone had to tell her, and it seemed he had drawn the short straw. 'I am very sorry to be the bearer of bad news, ma'am – but your husband is dead.'

'Dead?' Her eyes bulged. She looked indignant, shocked – but not particularly distressed. Hudson felt better. 'How? Where?'

'He was hit over the head to stun him ... and then someone used a knife...' He saw her eyes widen. She found the news distasteful but she wasn't about to start crying. 'His throat was cut, and his body was slashed in several places, almost as if the murderer was in a frenzy of hate.'

'Was it a robbery?'

Hudson considered telling her a white lie but the cold stare in her eyes made him decide to give her the full blast. 'He was in a bedroom at a nightclub. He was seen to go up with a young woman. When he was found some hours later a necklace was discovered – diamond and pearl. It was in his hand, torn from her throat. We think they were struggling and she hit him...'

'Yes, I see.' Mrs van Allen was calm. 'That doesn't explain the slitting of his throat or the other cuts.'

'No, ma'am, it doesn't. She may have done it as revenge for something –' he frowned, because in his mind the theory didn't fit. 'Usually, in a crime of that nature the killer would flee – but this was done in cold blood.'

'Yes, I see. Well, I shall expect you to solve the mystery.'

'Yes, ma'am. We will surely do our best.'

'See that you do. Was there anything else?' She stared at him down her long nose, the picture of an autocrat: wealthy, demanding, expectant.

'No, ma'am, not for the moment.'

'Very well. You may call again if you have more news.'

'Yes, ma'am.'

Hudson walked from the room, feeling as

if he were a tradesman dismissed for poor service. She was one proud, cold bitch! He wouldn't like to be married to a woman like that one!

Not a flicker of regret in that proud face. No tears for a husband of thirty years. If he didn't know it was almost impossible, he would think she had committed the murder herself!

Had he been able to see Mrs van Allen's face as the door closed behind him, her look of satisfaction would have chilled Hudson to the bone.

Louise smiled as she touched her hair and glanced at her reflection in the gilt-framed mirror. So she had outlived him after all – and now she had everything. At least until Jonathan returned. It was all for him. He was her reason for staying in this house with that animal. Now she was free and as soon as her son returned he would have all the money he desired.

Surely he would come, because his father's murder would be splashed over the papers. She only hoped that her husband's nasty little secrets didn't come out now that he was dead. But even if they did it wouldn't matter because she would have her son back. Once Jonathan knew it was safe to return he would come home to her.

'Yes, I understand your problem,' Philip Harland said as he listened to Sarah and then Mr Marshall that evening. 'The police are too busy to investigate the disappearance of girls, unless they have special information to go on – but I do have a contact who might listen. His name is Hudson – Detective Robert Hudson. I know he has a lot on his plate at the moment, but I did him a favour once and if I ask him to put Maura on the books he will ... I can't guarantee a full-scale investigation, but at least they will keep her in mind.'

'Well, I suppose that will be something,' Sarah said, and sighed. 'Maura hasn't turned up for the rest of her things, but of course it is still only a few hours so we may be worrying for nothing.'

'If she liked this man she went out with she may have moved in with him,' Philip said. 'You shouldn't worry too much, Sarah. She may turn up yet.' He looked at Ben. 'Is this your first time over here, Mr Marshall?'

'No, I visited a few years back on police business. Not this time, though. I came over to judge a cat show. Mrs van Allen invited me. She bought a couple of kittens from me when she was in England and I wanted to see them – make sure they were being looked after.'

Philip nodded, his gaze narrowing. 'When did you last see her?'

'Yesterday? Why?'

'She had bad news today. Her husband was found murdered at a nightclub. He had gone upstairs with a girl and they think she may have hit him. Apparently there was a struggle and she hit him with a heavy object...' Philip cleared his throat. 'Bit of a nasty business. It seems his throat was cut after he was knocked out.'

'Philip, please dearest,' Mrs Harland said. 'You will give Sarah nightmares.' She glanced at her daughter. Sarah looked a bit pale. 'You mustn't be upset, dearest. Philip shouldn't have said anything.'

'I'm not upset,' Sarah told her. Her eyes were thoughtful as she focused on her stepfather. 'What makes the police think it was the girl that hit him?'

'Oh, they have a piece of evidence – a diamond and pearl pendant was found in his hand—' He broke off as Sarah gasped. 'What is it? What have I said?'

'Maura borrowed a pendant of Sarah's without asking her permission,' Mrs Harland said, looking disturbed. 'Sarah, you don't think ... no, it couldn't be, could it?'

'I think it might, I really do,' Sarah told her. 'I have a feeling at the nape of my neck. It might have been Maura who hit him. He probably tried it on and she hit him; the pendant must have come off in the struggle – and then she ran. Maura wouldn't have slashed his throat...' She saw her mother's expression. 'I am sorry, Mummy, but you have to talk about these things. It helps, doesn't it, Ben?'

'Yes, it does.'

Philip intervened after a look at his wife's face. 'Shall we discuss this again after dinner, Sarah? Your mother doesn't like this sort of thing and we shan't distress her. The three of us can talk in my study. As a matter of fact I shall give Hudson a call and see if he has time to visit. I won't tell him why until he gets here.'

'Thank you,' Sarah said, giving him a grateful smile. 'Ben doesn't have any connections here and I think we shouldn't try to do this on our own. If it was just Maura going missing I would have taken the option of a private investigator, but there is a murderer involved now – and a particularly nasty one by the sound of things.'

'Leave it until after dinner for your mother's sake,' Philip said, and put down his drink. 'I think we should go now or Hannah will be giving us notice...'

'Don't say that, Philip,' his wife begged. 'I've already been on to the agency to send us another girl, but I couldn't replace Hannah.'

'It was merely a joke, my dear,' Philip said, and smiled at her gently. 'Come along, everyone. Hannah has made one of her famous pot roasts and I am famished.'

Maura looked up eagerly as the door opened and *he* came in. He had been gone for hours and she was hungry and angry, because she didn't like being shut up in this bedroom alone.

'Where have you been?' she demanded. 'Sure, I thought you were leaving me to starve, so I did. I want to get out of here. I should have been at the theatre today. Sam will give me the push, so he will – and Mrs Harland won't take me back after the way I went off. And I've lost Sarah's necklace—'

'Stop whining and listen!' he said, the threat in his voice making her draw back in alarm. 'The police are looking everywhere for you, Maura. If you leave here they will arrest you within hours. They've got a good description of you and it is in all the papers. You killed him. He's dead and that makes you a murderer. Your only hope is to stay here until things quieten and I can get you away somewhere.'

'He can't be dead,' Maura said, and gave a whimper of fear. She put a hand to her throat, feeling it tighten as if a rope were around it. 'What will they do to me? I only gave him a little tap. He was going to rape me ... it was self-defence.'

'What good will it do to tell the police that?' he asked. 'They will never believe a girl like you. Men like that have friends in high places. They won't let you blacken his name. You'll be locked up for years before you ever get a trial and you'll get the death penalty.'

Maura went white. She was trembling with

fright. She retreated to the bed, sitting on the edge, hugging herself as she tried to stop shaking. Her eyes were huge, the pupils dilated as she stared at him.

'I don't want to go to prison. I didn't mean to kill him. Please ... I don't want to die.'

'Then you must do as I tell you. Are you going to do that, Maura?'

She nodded, fear robbing her of the power of rational thought.

'You have to stay here until I tell you it's safe to leave. I'll bring you food and water to wash. I'll get something for you to wear, but you have to trust me.'

Maura looked at him. 'What shall I do afterwards?'

'We'll think about that when the time comes,' he said, and smiled at her, becoming the friendly man she had thought him when they first met. 'I like you, Maura. Be a good girl and you will be safe with me. I don't want to hurt you. I like you – but I have to keep you here for your own good. Do you trust me?'

'Yes,' she whispered, her voice hoarse with emotion. 'Yes, of course I trust you. Why shouldn't I?' In her head another voice was warning her that something was wrong but she shut it out. She had to trust him because she didn't know what else to do.

'You'll be all right,' he said, and his smile was warm, comforting. 'You're not alone now, Maura. You've got me. I'll take care of you. I'm going to get you something to eat and then you can sleep for a while. Nothing can harm you now that you have me to watch over you.'

Maura ran the tip of her tongue over lips that were suddenly dry. She had known how to handle the other one, because even though he was a dirty old man she'd understood what he wanted. She wasn't sure about this one. His mood could change suddenly, as she'd already discovered. When he smiled she liked him, but there was another side to him ... one that frightened her.

She would stay here for a while, because she had no choice. Her panic had eased a little now. New York was a big city. If she could get out of here, she could probably find a way of losing herself. There was no one she could turn to for help, unless Sarah would help her. She might be angry because the pendant had gone, but she was kind. Sarah might know what she ought to do, but she had to get away from *him* first, and something told Maura that wouldn't be easy. He was determined to keep her here for reasons of his own. As yet she didn't know what they were, but she didn't believe that it was just for her sake.

'Well, you can certainly take a look at the pendant,' Detective Hudson said. His eyes narrowed as he looked Sarah over. On the face of it she was a nice English girl and not the sort to go upstairs with a man like Mr van Allen, but you could never be sure. He would keep an open mind, even though she had an alibi from the Harland boy. Families like these were close knit and they might all be in this thing together. If it was her pendant she would remain on his list of suspects until the case was solved. 'If you come into the station in the morning I'll get someone to show you.'

'Would you mind if I came in the afternoon about three?' Sarah asked. 'I have rehearsal in the morning and if I don't turn up I shall lose my place.'

'The afternoon might be better. I can be there myself.' Hudson looked at her hard. 'You say Maura Trelawney was supposed to be at rehearsal this morning but didn't turn up?'

'Yes, that's right,' Sarah said. 'She was very excited about being in the show. It was her first and Sam – he's the producer – had picked her provisionally for the chorus. We are all of us under probation until rehearsals are finished and then he will make his final choice.'

'So she knew she would lose her job if she didn't turn up?'

'Yes, she did,' Sarah replied. 'I know she would have been there if she could. I don't feel she is dead – but I do feel she is in trouble.'

'Why should I take notice of your feelings

in the matter, Miss Beaufort?'

'I don't suppose there is any reason,' Sarah told him honestly. 'I expect you think I am a foolish girl who ought to mind her own business and keep out of police investigations, sir – and I can't say I blame you.' She smiled at him, her eyes suddenly filled with laughter.

Hudson blinked. She was a pretty girl but not remarkable until she smiled. He didn't know why but all at once he believed every word she said – and that was a first. He had learned the hard way to distrust everyone. He damped down the feeling of unwilling admiration.

'If you think this is some kind of a joke, Miss Harland...'

'Oh no, not at all,' Sarah said quickly. 'I was laughing at myself – not you or the work you do. I admire the police. I am a great fan of Mr Marshall; as you know, he was with New Scotland Yard.'

Hudson turned towards the Englishman. It was Marshall's reputation that brought him here as much as the request from an old friend.

'I heard about an investigation you helped out with some years back, sir. We had been looking for that particular crime boss for a long time. Your information helped us to root him out.'

'It was just a matter of Anglo / American cooperation,' Ben told him. 'You can trust

Miss Beaufort, Hudson. She has been of great help to me with a couple of cases I worked on. She has a special intuition, which I trust – of course you must use your own judgement. This is your patch, Hudson. I wouldn't dream of interfering – and nor would Sarah.'

Hudson turned back to look at the girl. He wondered if he was having the wool pulled over his eyes. Yet his instinct was to trust her. She was very appealing when you thought about it, and he wasn't so hard bitten that he couldn't appreciate a young woman's charms.

'Well, I shall keep an open mind for the moment,' he said. 'But I should be pleased if you will come in tomorrow afternoon and take a look at the necklace. I'll list Miss Trelawney as missing – and that picture you have of her will be useful.'

'Yes, my mother thought it might,' Sarah said. 'It was lucky we had one, but Maura was helping out with a children's party for the orphanage that my mother supports and she happened to be in the picture the press photographer took. I know it isn't clear, but it may help.'

'Well, I shan't take up more of your time,' Hudson said. 'Goodnight, Miss Beaufort – Mr Harland. Mr Marshall...' He paused and then made up his mind. 'Marshall, I have another case I would appreciate your thoughts on – unofficially, of course. If you could spare me a few minutes of your time?'

'Yes, I would be glad to,' Ben said. 'We could have a drink somewhere now if you wish – I was about to leave for my hotel.'

'I'll give you a lift,' Hudson said, feeling pleased. 'It's just something that has been bugging me. A fresh mind might help.'

'Of course. Talking always helps.' Ben smiled at Sarah. 'Goodnight. Try not to worry too much. We are doing all we can, Sarah.'

Sarah met Katie as she arrived at the theatre the next morning. The American girl looked at her, sensing the anxiety she was trying to hide.

'Still haven't found her, huh?'

'No, Maura didn't come back for her things as she said she would.' Sarah kept the events of the previous evening to herself, because she couldn't reveal information she knew was privileged. 'I can't help thinking she is in trouble, because she was so excited about being picked for the show.'

'Yeah, it's rotten luck,' Katie said. 'But just because I saw her talking to that guy it doesn't mean it was him she was meeting that night. I know I told you about him, but I didn't mean you to worry.'

'No, I know,' Sarah said. She understood that Katie was trying to lift her spirits and smiled, deciding to put Maura's disappearance out of her mind for a while, because if she didn't she wouldn't be able to concentrate on her work. 'I wonder what Sam has in mind for us today.'

'Oh, he'll grind our noses into the dust as usual.' Katie grinned. 'He's not too bad really...' She hesitated and then looked oddly shy. 'What do you think of Eddie?'

'The piano player?' Sarah hadn't thought much about him at all. He wasn't particularly remarkable, just a sandy-haired young man with a friendly smile. 'Oh, he seems nice. I've hardly spoken to him – though he did tell me not to worry that first morning.'

'Eddie is the best thing about this job,' Katie said. 'We had a coffee together yesterday. I really like him.'

'Oh, I see.' Sarah laughed as she saw the look on Katie's face. 'I hope it goes well for you. Will he be coming on the cruise?'

'Yes. He is a part of the show. He has been with Sam for nearly a year now.' Katie's pretty face went pink as she saw the teasing smile in Sarah's eyes. 'I liked him as soon as we met. In this business you meet a lot of men you can't trust, but Eddie is different.'

'Yes, I am sure he is if you like him,' Sarah said. 'Oh, look, here come some of the others...'

A party of eight girls from the chorus came up to them, and they were swept along with the chattering flock towards the back of the stage, where Ellie was waiting with her clipboard.

Sarah was caught up in the excitement of preparing for the show, forgetting the nagging worry at the back of her mind. She saw Katie talking to the piano player. He noticed her and sent an engaging grin her way, coming over to her as Ellie sent most of her flock on stage to start rehearsing some dance steps.

'Katie told me you were a friend of the girl who didn't turn up yesterday,' Eddie said. 'You mustn't worry about her too much, Sarah. It happens a lot in this business. Girls hear about a better job – or they get cold feet and decide they can't face the idea of singing on stage after all. She'll turn up safe and sound one of these days.'

'Yes, I expect you are right,' Sarah said. 'Katie tells me you are coming on the cruise with us?'

'It is a part of my job,' Eddie said. 'You'll start rehearsing with the band in a day or so, but I do a piano solo – and even on board you'll need me for rehearsals. Besides, I'm here to help you all with your problems.'

'I see...' Sarah nodded. She agreed with Katie; he was rather nice. 'I had better go, Ellie is looking annoyed. I think she wants us both on stage.'

'Perhaps you might like to go for a coffee some time, Sarah?'

'Oh, yes, if Katie is coming too,' Sarah said. 'But not today – I am expecting a visitor this afternoon.'

'Someone special?'

'Yes, he is,' Sarah replied, a smile touching her mouth. 'A really good friend.'

'Well, that's nice for you, Sarah. Enjoy your visit.'

'Thank you, I shall.'

She left him and went to Ellie, listening to what was required and yet at the back of her mind thinking how nice it would be to see Larch again. It seemed ages since their quarrel, and now she thought about it, she understood that her friend had only been trying to help her achieve her ambition to sing on the stage of a London theatre. Yes, it would be lovely to see Larch again. She hadn't realized until this moment how much she had missed him.

He watched as Sarah left the theatre and got into a cab. He knew her name now. He'd heard one of the other girls call to her. Damn it! Didn't the rich bitch walk anywhere? He had thought she would be easier to get to than the playboy son, but maybe he should switch back to his original plan. Maybe he should just go in there when they were all having dinner and shoot the lot of them!

It had been instinctive the first time. They'd had it coming to them for the depraved way they were behaving! Since then he had picked his victims with more care, but somehow the thrill of killing had become dulled. His hatred still burned deep in his guts, eating at him so that he couldn't rest. But simple death wasn't enough any more.

He wanted to inflict pain, to make his chosen ones suffer. The way he had suffered ... watching his wife sicken and die, his children taking the sickness from her ... dying one by one ... and he could do nothing to stop it, because he had no money to save them. He'd been out of work for months, blamed for something he didn't do, blacklisted and able to find only the meanest jobs, and then he'd had to beg. And he'd had to watch his family growing weaker. If they had been stronger, not half starved, they might have resisted the fever ... but he had lost all the younger ones. It had been just him and his sixteen-year-old daughter and then she had gone too, disappeared into the night.

After that he had just wanted to die, existing on the scraps he managed to beg from strangers in the streets – and then Lucy came back, her body swollen with child, her eyes like black hollows in her pale face, too numbed with shame and terror to tell him what had happened for days. And then a name came out ... a name he knew and hated. The man who had sacked him for the thieving he hadn't done had taken his girl and raped her. He had brooded for days, half out of his mind with rage. He'd gone to the house in Newport that day hoping that he might find some weakness in the man who had hurt his girl, but what he'd seen had driven him wild. He'd stolen a weapon and he'd killed ... blindly, without discrimination, anyone who got in his way.

For a while it had eased the pain, but then Lucy's child started to come early. The child had died and he couldn't bear to think of what had happened next. And he'd gone on killing, but now he chose his victims more carefully ... and he wanted that rich bitch.

What did she think she was doing, playing at working? She had everything she could want. Why should she take a job from girls who really needed it? He had planned something special for her ... A twisted smile touched his mouth, though it didn't reach his eyes. He had forgotten how to feel anything good – but when he made that bitch pay for his wife, for his children, and his daughter, he would feel something, at least for a while.

Ben looked at the cats in their cages. As yet he hadn't seen anything he thought could hold a candle to Bella, but he was here to judge and he had to choose one of them. His gaze settled on the large Persian blue Mrs van Allen had entered. He could feel her eyes boring into his back as he hovered by the cage, knowing that she was willing him to pick her cat. It was one of two, he decided as he walked a little further along the line.

The smaller cat had a better head, but its fur was not as thick and luxuriant. He didn't really want to award the prize to either of them, but there was no choice. It had to be Mrs van Allen's cat or the smaller one. He sighed, because for some reason he was loath to give it to the president of the club, and yet in all fairness he couldn't choose the smaller cat.

He made up his mind and pinned the blue rosette to the cage of the van Allen cat, wandering back to award second prize to the smaller feline. He heard the desultory clapping and understood why the applause wasn't stronger. Mrs van Allen was an overbearing lady and perhaps not as popular as she might have been. Ben groaned inwardly as she bore down on him, a beam of delight on her face. Why was it that he couldn't like her? If he'd known as much as he knew now he would never have sold her the kittens.

'I never expected to win,' she gushed. 'How thrilling, Mr Marshall. I am so pleased you thought Merry the best cat in show. You must allow me to give you dinner this evening.'

Ben shuddered inwardly. How could the woman behave as if she hadn't a care in the world? Her husband was lying in a police morgue with his throat cut and she was carrying on with her social engagements as if nothing had happened. It was hardly surprising that people were staying out of her way; that kind of behaviour left a nasty taste in the mouth. Ben certainly didn't want to get trapped into having dinner with her.

'Forgive me, I have another engagement,' he told her. He glanced at his silver pocket watch. 'I ought to be leaving soon—'

'Oh, you can't go yet,' she said. 'You must stay until it is all finished. Everyone will want to ask questions.'

Ben smothered his sigh. 'Well, if you insist...'

'I do, Mr Marshall – and if you can't come for dinner, you must come to drinks tomorrow morning. It will be all the people from the cat club. You simply cannot refuse me. They are so looking forward to meeting you again.'

'Well, I can't promise,' Ben said, wishing himself anywhere but here. 'I'll see what I can do – but I really must go soon...'

Sarah could hear the sound of voices as she entered the house. She heard her mother's laugh and then another voice. Her heart leaped with excitement. Larch was here, waiting for her!

She put down her light jacket and purse on a chair in the hall, heading into the sitting room where they were gathered: her mother looking fresh and lovely in a peach silk afternoon gown; Brad, lounging in one of the armchairs, dressed in flannels and blazer – and Larch. He was wearing a light coloured suit, his hair touching the collar, as ever needing a cut. He turned as she entered as if sensing her, and his smile was instinctive, though it was followed by a rather tentative expression. He rose to his feet.

'Sarah, I hope you didn't mind my calling?'

'Larch, of course I didn't! You know I always love to see you.'

'I shall see about some tea,' Mrs Harland said, and she left the room.

Larch's smile deepened as she walked to meet him. He leaned forward, kissing her cheek. 'I was afraid you might still be annoyed with me?'

'I was very cross with you for a while,' Sarah said, but her voice was light, teasing, her smile soft and warm. 'I know you were trying to help me, but it upset me – but I'm over it now.' She had missed him! She hadn't really known how much until this moment. 'I am so happy to see you again.'

'Thank goodness for that,' Larch said, and looked relieved. 'I thought I might have ruined our friendship by my stupidity.'

'No, you haven't. I don't think anything could – but I would prefer it if you didn't have any more bright ideas about my career.'

'From what I hear you are doing fine yourself,' Larch said. 'You've found yourself a job on a cruise ship, I understand?'

'Yes, well, it's provisional at the moment, but I think Sam is pleased with the way things are going. He doesn't praise anyone much, but he complains furiously if something is wrong – Ellie says I shall know soon enough if Sam is not happy with my performance, and so far he just says everything is OK so I suppose it is.'

'I am sure it is.' Larch hesitated, then, 'Jenny says you should have been appearing in this year's show in London. You've been asked for, apparently.'

'You've seen Jenny? I had one postcard from her and I've sent her a few...' Sarah frowned. 'It was fun last year. Until it all went wrong...'

'It was a shame you had to be mixed up in all that stuff,' Larch said, concern in his voice. 'I think it has been good for you, coming right away to your mother, but I hope you will come back to us one day?'

'That is the idea of the cruise ship,' Sarah said. 'There is a two-week turnaround between trips, which means I shall be able to see both sides of my family.'

Larch nodded. His expression didn't give much away, but Sarah knew her answer wasn't the one he had hoped to hear. At this moment in time she wasn't ready to go back to England on a permanent basis.

'Yes, well, I suppose it might work for a while.'

'I'm going to give it a try,' Sarah told him. 'I've given my word that I shall do at least one trip there and back, and then we'll see.

Anyway, how long will you be here for, Larch? You mentioned your show but gave no details.'

'About three weeks,' he replied. 'I haven't booked a return fare yet, because I wanted to give myself some leeway. It all depends how things work out here.'

Seeing the look in his eyes, Sarah thought that his decision to leave his options open might have something to do with her. She felt a spreading warmth inside, because it was just so good to have him here and to know that they were still friends. She wasn't sure yet whether there was anything more to their relationship, but the next few weeks would be pleasant either way.

'Why don't you stay for dinner this evening?' she asked.

'I was thinking we might go out somewhere,' Larch replied. 'Dinner in the Village, perhaps? I know a nice place not far from Washington Square – and then we could go on to somewhere we could dance?'

'Yes, I should enjoy that,' Sarah said. 'I love Greenwich Village, because it has such a lovely, relaxed atmosphere, and a feel of things as they used to be years ago. I love to walk in Washington Square, explore the bookshops, restaurants, theatres, all the beautiful wide avenues and old mansions, just soak up the bohemian atmosphere. Some of the older houses are being pulled down or changed into big stores, but there is still so much I love. And I am so very pleased to see you again, Larch.'

He smiled at her. 'I know you are busy but I wondered if you might have time to sit for me, Sarah? Your father said he would like a painting of you, and I've often thought about trying a portrait.'

'Have you?' She was surprised because he had never mentioned it before. 'Well, why not? Yes, I wouldn't mind, but it would have to be in the afternoon or evening, because I rehearse every morning. Where would you do it?'

'Oh, I've been offered the use of a studio while I'm here,' Larch told her. 'It's someone I met while I was travelling last year. Annabel Lawson is an artist herself, but she is more into modelling in clay. I'll come and fetch you this evening, and I'll show you where she lives on the way to dinner. Actually, it is only around the corner – a couple of streets away.'

'I know Annabel,' Mrs Harland said as she entered the room. 'I didn't realize she was back. I think she went to London for a show or something?'

'Yes, she did,' Larch replied. 'We met there again – and we came back on the same liner. She invited me to stay but I had booked my hotel. However, I shall take her up on the invitation to use her studio.'

'It should be fun,' Sarah said. 'I shall look forward to meeting her – providing she isn't like Madeline?'

Larch pulled a face. 'Good grief no, she is nothing like Madeline Lewis-Brown. Annabel is nice. You will like her, Sarah.'

'Yes,' Mrs Harland said. 'Larch is right. Annabel is lovely, Sarah.'

'Then I shall look forward to meeting her.'

Larch shook hands with Sarah's mother. 'It was nice talking to you, Mrs Harland.'

'You must come again soon.'

'Thank you, I shall.'

Sarah walked with Larch to the door, her Cuban heels making a little clopping noise on the polished wood floor in the hall. Larch turned to her as he left, his eyes searching her face.

'You have forgiven me, truly? You know I didn't mean to hurt you?'

'Yes, of course,' Sarah said, and impulsively moved to kiss his cheek. Larch turned his head and her kiss brushed his lips, sending little sparks shooting through her. She drew back, staring at him in wonder. Larch hesitated and then kissed her again, softly but with a warmth that surprised her.

'Larch...?'

'I've been wanting to do that since you left,' he said, looking slightly rueful. 'You're not cross with me, are you?' She shook her head wordlessly, unable to answer. She had enjoyed the kiss but wasn't sure how she felt about Larch. She'd been hurt when she discovered that he'd backed the show in

86

London without telling her. Could she ever really trust him again?

'Good. We'll talk tonight, Sarah. I'm not terribly good with words, but you know I'm awfully fond of you.'

Sarah smiled but said nothing as he walked away from her. She touched her fingers to her lips, something low down in her abdomen sending little butterflies winging all over her body. Being kissed by Larch was lovely. She had liked it very much, but it had surprised her. They had been friends a long time and it was the first time he'd kissed her like that...

'Telephone for you, madam.'

Mrs van Allen walked to the desk near the window in her sitting room. Her maid had answered the phone seconds before she got there. She held the earpiece a few inches from her ear, her mouth screwed up in distaste, because it was probably that reporter again.

'I've told you I do not wish to give an interview.'

'Hi, Ma.' Jonathan's voice startled her. She almost dropped the handset, because although she had refused to give up hope she had wondered if something had happened to him. 'How are you? Feeling better now that the old devil's gone and got himself killed?'

'Jonathan! You really shouldn't say things

like that, my dear. Where are you? Why haven't you phoned me before? Do you need money?'

'I always need money,' Jonathan said, and laughed. 'But right now I'm not desperate.'

'Where are you? Are you coming for the funeral?'

'He hated my guts and I hated his,' Jonathan said. 'I won't play the hypocrite, Ma.'

'But you could come home now that he's dead. Everything is for you, Jonathan. I simply want you to come home.'

'I can't right now, Ma. I just wanted to see how you were coping. Have the police got any ideas about who killed him?'

'They seem to think he was with a woman – but they aren't sure she killed him. That whore may have knocked him unconscious but he had his throat slit, and the police don't seem to think it was her ... it was probably someone he cheated. You know he had enemies.'

'He was a selfish, arrogant pig,' her son said harshly. 'He never treated either of us decently. I'm glad he got what he deserved.'

'Jonathan!'

'Don't pretend you don't feel the same, Ma.'

'Yes, perhaps I do – but it isn't necessary to say it out loud.'

'That's why I'm not coming back yet. I can't pretend to feel something I don't.

Maybe in a month or two...'

'But people will think it strange if you aren't here—'

'Sorry, Ma. I'll call you again.'

'But don't you want money?'

'I'll tell you when.'

She looked at the phone as it went dead and frowned. It wasn't like Jonathan not to need money. He must have found somewhere to stay ... perhaps a job of some kind, though she couldn't imagine what he was doing. She wished that he would come back. He had hated his father, she knew that, but there was no reason why he shouldn't come home now.

She was frowning as she sat down at her desk and began to write envelopes for the invitations to the funeral. She might have hated her husband, but she knew that things must be done properly. It would have been better if Jonathan had come home so that he could help her, but she would manage. She had always managed to get what she wanted one way or the other, and she would get her son back one of these days.

'Thank you for coming,' Hudson said as Sarah was shown into the tiny room that his superiors saw fit to call his office. 'If you could just tell us whether this is your neckace or not...' He saw the colour drain from Sarah's face as he held it out to her. 'You do recognize it, don't you?'

'Yes, that is the diamond and pearl pendant that my father gave me last year,' Sarah said. 'I didn't wear it often because the clasp had a way of coming undone. I had planned to have a safety catch fitted.'

'Then it is probable that Maura Trelawney took your necklace – and it is probable that she was the young woman with Mr van Allen that night.'

'I should say it was almost certainly Maura who took the necklace,' Sarah replied. 'It seems likely that it came off during a struggle.'

'You are quite sure it wasn't you wearing the necklace, Miss Beaufort? You didn't go to that nightclub with Mr van Allen yourself? If you tell me what happened now it may save a lot of trouble later.'

'No, Detective Hudson, I did not,' Sarah replied meeting his eyes without flinching. 'I do realize that you have to ask. I could be lying and so could my stepbrother, stepfather and mother. It might be an elaborate cover-up to protect me – but it isn't, I promise you.'

'It happens sometimes,' Hudson said, with a shrug. 'But I think I believe you.'

'Thank you,' Sarah said. 'I hope you will give Maura the benefit of the doubt too, sir. I don't know what happened that night but I imagine she struck Mr van Allen when he tried to force her to do something she didn't want to do, because she was a good Catholic

Irish girl, if a bit naïve. However, I really can't see her using a knife to cut his throat. That would be deliberate, cold – the action of a murderer who hated him, not a frightened girl.'

'My thoughts exactly,' Hudson agreed. He couldn't help thinking that Marshall was right when he said she had a clear way of putting her thoughts into words. 'I can't let you have the pendant yet, Miss Beaufort, but thank you for coming along. I am sure your positive identification of the necklace will help with the investigation.'

Sarah hesitated for a moment, 'You haven't found her yet, then? Do you have any clues about what went on after she ran away? Could the murderer have been someone who had reason to dislike Mr van Allen?'

'This is a police investigation, miss. I am sorry but I can't tell you anything yet.' Hudson gave her a hard stare. He wasn't accustomed to sharing his thoughts with anyone at this stage of the game, especially an untrained girl.

'No, I suppose not,' Sarah replied. 'It isn't my business. I know that – but I can't help feeling involved because of Maura. She must have run away, mustn't she? But where is she hiding? She ought to come forward to tell her story. After all, if she didn't kill him someone else did – and she might have seen something.' Sarah frowned. 'Do you think that's why she is hiding – because she knows the murderer?'

'I shall consider all the angles. Thank you for coming in.'

'You want me to go away and forget about it,' Sarah said, and smiled wryly. 'I know you are right, sir. I should do exactly that, shouldn't I? Forgive me, I expect you are on top of things. Goodbye.'

'I'll let you know if she turns up,' Hudson said. His gaze narrowed. 'You are not thinking of hiring a private detective, I hope? Mr Marshall told me it was discussed, but I would rather you didn't – it might be dangerous.'

'Yes ... especially if Mr van Allen was involved with dangerous criminals – mobsters I think you call them over here. If he was the man Katie told me about, Maura wasn't the first girl he lured away to a life of depravity. I imagine you will discover some pretty murky stuff when you delve into his business affairs, sir.' She turned towards the door.

'And just what do you know about all this?' Hudson glared at her. 'I'm warning you, Miss Beaufort, this isn't one of your cosy village crimes. Get involved with these men and you'll end up on a slab!'

'Yes, that is what I thought. I certainly don't wish to become involved, Detective Hudson. I shall be very happy to leave it all to you, I promise you. I simply hope you will find Maura alive.'

'If she knows what is good for her she will come to us. I don't know where she is hiding – but if you have any idea you should tell me.'

'I don't, I really don't,' Sarah said. 'I must go now. My friend is taking me out this evening. I must go home and get ready or I shall be late.'

Hudson stared hard at the door as it closed behind her. She was a bright girl. He only hoped she wouldn't try solving this crime on her own, the way she had back home. He was well aware of van Allen's murky background. He'd suspected something from the start and it hadn't taken him long to sniff out the dirt. It was all neatly hidden behind a veneer of respectability, but with van Allen dead the screens were bound to come tumbling down. The widow would want her share of the spoils, and that's when the other *respectable* men would make their move, because van Allen wasn't alone in this murky business, and when the chips were down they would come crawling out of the woodwork to protect their investment.

As far as he could tell, the dead man had probably got what he had coming to him – but who had struck the final blow? He was of the opinion that the girl was innocent of murder. She'd knocked van Allen out and his murderer had taken advantage, but who had wielded that knife? As yet they didn't have a single clue other than the necklace.

It could have been a case of thieves falling out. Maybe one of van Allen's associates felt he wasn't getting a fair share of the profits from their criminal activities ... and yet something was bugging Hudson. He had a feeling that the answer was right under his nose and he was missing it.

Ben Marshall had made some good points concerning the Playboy Murders. He might ring him at his hotel, ask him out for a meal and talk some more. Hudson suspected he already had a clue to the van Allen mystery but he couldn't for the life of him think what it was.

It would come to him in time. The wheels of justice sometimes ground exceedingly slowly, but they turned full circle in the end.

Three

Larch left the taxi waiting as he walked Sarah to her door later that night. He hesitated, wondering whether or not he should kiss her again. They had eaten at a quiet restaurant in a pleasant area in Greenwich Village, and gone on to a trendy nightclub afterwards. She had seemed to enjoy herself, and they had danced closely for a while, but he wasn't sure that Sarah was ready to listen to a declaration of love, though he had made up his mind a while ago that he wanted her to marry him.

'Thank you so much for this evening,' Sarah said, smiling up at him. 'I really enjoyed myself.'

'Did you? I enjoyed being with you, Sarah. I've missed you terribly.'

'It was silly of me to run off the way I did...'

'No, I was the idiot. I should have asked if you would like me to back a show,' Larch said. He was hesitant, searching for the right words. 'I've done it again this year because it was such a success – you were a success, Sarah. You know I don't care about the money. I rarely touch it other than as an income, and I wouldn't have cared if the show hadn't paid its way, but it did.'

Sarah nodded. 'It was just a disappointment. I wanted to get somewhere on my own, prove to everyone that I am a professional performer.'

'But you did – you have.'

'I know you all think I should give it up, though Mummy suggested Philip could help me get something in the movies–but then she apologized because she knew it wasn't what I wanted. I have to stand on my own two feet for a while.'

'We all want you to be happy and safe,' Larch said. 'I should be devastated if anything happened to you, Sarah. You must know that?'

'Yes, of course I do. We're friends...' She looked up as Larch moved in, her breath coming faster. 'Larch...?'

He bent his head and kissed her softly on the lips. 'I'm pretty certain I'm in love with you, Sarah. I'm not good with words, and I don't want to push you. I know you like singing. I love to hear you sing – but if we got married I should want you to stay home, have a family. I know that isn't strictly fair. I shall want to go on painting and it isn't right to ask you to give up what you love, but it wouldn't work if you were away half the time.'

'Oh, Larch –' Sarah caught her breath – 'I

don't know what to say...'

'You don't know if you love me – or you're not sure if you want to give up singing?'

'I am very fond of you...'

'Not enough,' Larch said, and touched his fingers to her lips. 'Fond isn't enough to give up your singing for. I know I promised to wait when we talked about marriage last year, now I'm jumping from friend to lover and I'm rushing you. If you decide that you might love me enough to marry, I'll still be here, waiting. If it takes a year or five I'll be there when you're ready. I know you are the only girl I could bear to live with so it's you or nothing. I'm afraid that's me ... dull old Larch...'

'I don't find you in the least dull,' Sarah replied, her expression soft and gentle. 'I like you better than anyone else I know, Larch – and there isn't anyone else. I want you to know that, but ... I do need a little time to think. I'm sorry. You can't want to hear me say that, I know.'

'I would rather you took your time,' Larch replied, with a lopsided grin. 'I would hate it if we married and you were unhappy. If you decide you can't marry me I shall always be your friend, so you won't lose me.'

'You make me want to cry,' Sarah said, blinking hard. 'I ought to be able to say yes at once, but I do need a little time. Forgive me?'

'Nothing to forgive,' Larch replied. 'I shall

see you tomorrow – in the afternoon?'

'Yes, of course,' Sarah replied. 'I am excited about the portrait, Larch. Daddy did mention it once but then he forgot. I am glad he chose you.'

'So am I,' Larch replied with a smile. 'Goodnight, Sarah.'

He watched as she went in, standing for a moment to take out a cigarette, tapping the end against his silver-gilt case. His gaze was drawn across the street to a man who was standing there staring at him. Larch felt an icy trickle down his spine. For some reason he took exception to the way the man was staring, though he couldn't have explained it.

'Hey you!' he shouted. 'What do you want?'

The man took a step back, turned and ran off, rounding the corner and disappearing from sight. Larch frowned as he returned to the taxi. He didn't believe in premonitions, but for some reason he was apprehensive. His fear – because that was what it was –was not for himself but for Sarah. He had no idea why, but he sensed that the man loitering on the other side of the street had been watching her.

Rehearsals went well for Sarah the next morning, though some of the other girls weren't so lucky. She saw a couple of the chorus line in tears as they were dismissed for not coming up to scratch. One of the girls was so upset that none of her friends could comfort her and that made Sarah angry. She went back out front to where Sam was talking with Eddie, discussing one of the arrangements.

'You are a brute,' she told Sam. 'Couldn't you have been a bit kinder to Susan? Even if she didn't meet your standards there was no need to tell her she screeched like a barn owl, because it simply wasn't true.'

'If she can't take the heat she shouldn't have come,' Sam said, glaring at her. 'What I say goes around here, Sarah. You'd better accept it or—'

'If you think I'm going to keep quiet while you destroy someone's confidence, you had better think again. I want this job, but I'm not prepared to stand by and see you walk all over a young girl.'

Sam's eyes snapped with temper. 'You're good but not that good, Sarah. Watch your step or I may decide I can dispense with your services.'

'If you continue to treat girls as if they are dirt beneath your shoes I should think you will be lucky if any of them stay.' Sarah walked away but he came after her, grabbing her by the shoulder to swing her round towards him. She gave him a look guaranteed to slay a dragon and he dropped his hand from her shoulder.

'Look, I'm sorry,' Sam said, and grinned at

her. He was very good-looking, his features transformed by the smile. 'I'm always like this when I'm getting the show together. Forgive me, Sarah. I don't want to lose you. I'll give the girl a chance but with the dancers. She wasn't so bad at that, but she can't hold a tune.'

'Will you tell her,' Sarah said, determined not to let him get out of it, 'or shall I?'

'Ellie was going to give her another chance with the dancers if she wants it,' Sam replied. 'Look, I've been working you girls hard. I'm giving a bit of a party this evening. You will come, Sarah?'

'Can I bring a friend? He is only here for a short time. I couldn't come without him.'

Sam looked disappointed. 'Yeah, if you want. I hope there's nothing serious going on between you two? I don't want my leading lady running out on me at the last second.'

'I gave you my word that I would do at least one trip,' Sarah told him. 'That stands, but I'm not a doormat, Sam. If you try wiping your feet on me I shall get up and bite your ankles!'

Sam glared at her, then his head went back and he shouted with laughter. 'I always knew you had class, Sarah. Yeah, you're my leading lady, all right. I'm going to give you another spot. I might as well make the most of your talent while I have you.'

'Slave driver,' Sarah retorted, but she smiled, because even though he was a bad-tempered bear sometimes she rather liked him. 'It's a good thing you won't be coming on the cruise with us.'

'I have the next show to produce,' he said. 'Once you're ready I hand you over to Ellie and Eddie, and that's it – but know something? This time I kinda wish I was coming along.'

Sarah saw something in his eyes that made her blush and look away. The odd thing was that when he was like this she liked him. She liked him more than any other man she'd met – except Larch, of course. Larch was her best friend and always would be, but she wasn't sure yet whether she wanted to give up her singing and marry him.

Sarah was thoughtful as she left the theatre and hailed a cab to take her home. Last year she had been almost certain she wanted to marry Larch one day if he asked her, but now he had and she was dithering. She wasn't sure why. It couldn't be because she had met Sam, could it? She shook her head. He wasn't her type at all! He was a bully, too brash and thoughtless – but sometimes he could be charming.

Oh, this was ridiculous! She loved Larch, she always had. Of course she was going to marry him, but not just yet. She had given Sam her word she would do the cruise, and unless they came to blows over his treatment of some of the other girls there was no way she could break it.

Sarah decided to walk to the studio Larch was borrowing to work in while he was staying in New York. It was only two streets away, along a tree-lined avenue of graceful old houses, because this had once been the most fashionable part of the city and was still populated by some of the wealthiest families in New York.

The house was magnificent, built of a brownish stone with an imposing hardwood door and small paned windows. Sarah rang the bell, hearing it peal loudly inside even as the door was opened by a maid wearing a black dress and a spotless white apron and cap.

'Will you come in please, miss,' the girl said. She had a faint Irish accent but nowhere near as strong as Maura's had been. 'Mrs Lawson is in the studio and she said to take you through.'

'Thank you,' Sarah said, and smiled at her. 'You are Irish, aren't you?'

'My family came from Ireland, but I was born here. I'm an American, Miss Beaufort.' There was pride in her voice.

'Oh ... I was just wondering if you might know a girl called Maura Trelawney. She is Irish but she has only been here a few months.'

'Maura Trelawney...' The girl shook her head. 'Sorry, I don't think I know her.'

'No, I suppose there are a lot of Irish girls

102

in New York. It was just a thought.'

Sarah was following the girl through the house towards the back. She noticed that although it was a stylish house with a lot of European and English antiques, it had a warm, welcoming atmosphere. The studio itself was a long room looking out on to a large garden, which was at this moment a glorious blaze of summer flowers, the scent of their blooms drifting in through open windows. The whole structure was formed of glass with wooden supports, the roof domed to let in the maximum light, which made it ideal for its purpose.

At one end there was a bench, which was littered with clay models in various stages of development, and three easels were set at intervals down the length of the room. At one of them a woman and a man stood talking, their faces intent as they discussed a painting. Sarah felt a small pang of jealousy as she saw that Mrs Annabel Lawson was a very beautiful woman, the camellia tones of her skin flawless, her glossy, raven black hair drawn into a knot at the nape of her neck. She was dressed in a long skirt that revealed just her ankles and a smock, which was covered in smears of paint and clay, but still she looked fresh, cool and elegant. Only a woman sure of her own beauty and her place in the world could look like that, Sarah decided.

As Sarah hesitated, Annabel turned and

saw her. She smiled, her eyes lighting with such warmth that Sarah felt welcome even before she spoke. She came towards Sarah, her hands outstretched.

'You must be Sarah, of course. Larch has told me so much about you, my dear. I am sorry I wasn't here when he showed you the studio last evening.'

'It is lovely to meet you,' Sarah said. 'You are very generous to let us have the use of your beautiful studio.'

'Oh no, my dear,' Annabel said in her slightly husky voice. 'I am privileged to have him here for a short time. Larch knows how much I admire his work – and I must say I approve of his choice of a model. Would you mind if I sketched you in preparation for a clay model?'

'Of course not,' Sarah replied. She had a hollow feeling inside, because she knew instantly that Annabel was in love with Larch. As a widow there was no reason why she shouldn't indulge in a love affair or marry again, of course. Except that Larch had asked Sarah to marry him. 'If you really feel you would like to...'

'Show Sarah some of your work, Annabel,' Larch said. He smiled at them both with easy affection. 'Take a few minutes to accustom yourself to the room, Sarah, and then sit in the elbow chair by that plant, if you will.'

'I'll send for a glass of iced mint tea,'

Annabel said. 'You can show Sarah my work, Larch. You know how embarrassed I am over things like that...'

'Annabel is very clever with her fingers,' Larch said as she went out of the room. 'I think she has something special – but tell me what you think.'

He walked to the bench at the end of the room, and took off some cloths that covered the models. Most of them were busts of people, but some were animals, delicate, intricate and quite lovely. Sarah immediately coveted a model of a fawn sniffing at a flower.

'That is beautiful,' she said, looking at Larch, fascinated by the approval she saw in his eyes. Obviously he didn't dismiss Annabel's work as he had Madeline Lewis-Brown's paintings of pretty cottages. 'It is delicate and poignant somehow, but not over sweet.'

'I knew you would understand,' Larch said. 'You don't mind her asking you if she could model you, do you?'

'No,' Sarah said. 'I feel honoured that she should want to do it – after seeing some of these busts I am sure there must be lots of people who would be only too happy to sit.'

'I am certain there are, but Annabel only does what she likes. She doesn't work for money, and often gives her art away for charity.'

'She must be a very nice person.'

'I think she is,' Larch said. 'Don't you?'

'Yes, of course,' Sarah said, just as Annabel returned. 'I was admiring the pieces that feature animals, Mrs Lawson. They are so delicate and special.'

'Why thank you, Sarah. But please, you must call me Annabel. I know you are a good friend of Larch's and I hope we shall be friends.'

'Oh yes,' Sarah said. 'I am sure we shall.'

She was thoughtful as she took her seat by the potted camellia. Annabel was nice, a truly generous person, and she had every right to fall in love with Larch. He wasn't in love with her or he wouldn't have asked Sarah to marry him, but he did like her. It was obvious in the way he smiled at her, and the interest he took in her work.

Sarah scolded herself for feeling jealous of their friendship. She wasn't Larch's wife or even his fiancée, and even if she had been, jealousy was an unworthy emotion.

He watched as she left the house and began to walk along the avenue. He had not expected to see her here and it gave him a thrill to see that she was alone. He had begun to think she would never walk anywhere alone. It was broad daylight, but he considered snatching her right then. He knew it was a risk, but if she struggled too much he would simply kill her ... although the temptation to make her suffer as his Lucy had suffered was strong. Yet he might never have a better chance than now. He was quickening his step as the large, flashy car pulled into the side of the kerb and the passenger got out. He cursed and turned away, sensing that his chance had gone – but now she had started to walk the chance would come again, and next time he would be ready.

'Sarah,' the man hailed her, standing in front of her so that she was forced to see him. 'What are you doing in this neck of the woods?'

'Sam...' Sarah stopped walking and smiled. 'I have been sitting for a portrait. My friend is an artist – and another friend wants to model me in clay as well.'

'That sounds kinda indecent, the modelling in clay?' Sam said, with raised eyebrows. He held up his hands as her eyes took fire. 'Yeah, yeah, I know what it means. I like to joke sometimes. Can I give you a lift anywhere?'

'My stepfather's house is just round the corner,' Sarah said. 'If you leave your car there, you can walk with me. I am sure my mother would like to meet you. She is very curious about the people I work with at the theatre.'

'My driver can wait for me,' Sam said. 'I don't mind meeting your mother – as long as she doesn't change your mind about working for me.'

'Why would she do that?'

'I'm just a boy from the wrong side of the tracks who made good,' Sam drawled, his voice twanging with a heavy Bronx accent that she knew he had laid on thick just for her. 'You're a classy broad and I guess your folks might think I'm not good enough for you to know.'

'Mummy isn't a snob,' Sarah said, amused. 'Daddy is, though. You are quite right, he wouldn't approve of you at all – but he isn't here.' She laughed softly in her throat. 'You're only my boss, Sam, not my lover.'

'Yeah, shame,' he said. 'Would it do me any good if I worked on it?'

'No, I shouldn't think so,' Sarah told him with a smile. Her heart gave a little flutter, but she remembered Katie's warning. All the girls knew that Sam liked to flirt. Besides, there was Larch, her best friend and perhaps the man she would marry. 'But we could be friends, if you behave.'

Sam eyed her intently. 'You're a tease, Sarah. I'm never sure what you mean. I always behave, don't I?'

'I wouldn't know,' Sarah said, and laughed. 'I asked Larch if he would come to the party this evening. He is looking forward to meeting you. He was our angel at the show I was in at a theatre in London.'

'Hey, that sounds as though the guy has money?' Sam arched an eyebrow. 'I'm always looking for the right kind of backer for my shows. I'm thinking about a Broadway production this winter. Would he be interested in putting up some of the cash?'

'I don't know,' Sarah said. 'I know he is backing another show in London, but I'm not sure that he would be interested in anything over here.'

'My productions pay good bucks,' Sam said. 'I've never had a failure in twelve years of producing.'

'I should think the backers are queuing up to give you their money, then.'

'Yeah, but I want the right kind,' Sam remarked, an icy glint in his eyes. 'I had this guy approach me a few days back, but I wouldn't have taken his money if he were the last man with a few bucks on earth.'

'Oh...' Sarah looked at him, a little tingle at the nape of her neck. 'You don't mean Mr van Allen, do you?' She saw the wary expression creep into his eyes. 'You do mean him, don't you, Sam? You know he was murdered a few nights ago, don't you?'

'Yeah, he's the one. Got what he had coming to him if you ask me,' Sam said, and glared at her. 'I know what he was after. I've had girls disappear before after he came sniffing around.'

'I think Maura was with him the night he died,' Sarah told him. 'I think she hit him over the head with something and then ran because she was scared. Someone else killed him – and that someone may have been a man he had done business with...'

'Or some poor girl's father getting his own back,' Sam said. 'Most of the girls he lured away are never seen again. His bully boys make sure they don't get away to tell the tale, Sarah – but one or two have escaped the net.'

'Anyone you know?'

'Yeah, there was one girl in particular...' Sam glared at her. 'It isn't your business, Sarah – and if you're thinking I might have killed him in revenge the answer is no.'

'I wasn't thinking it,' Sarah told him. 'You don't strike me as being a killer, Sam. You may be a careless brute to the girls sometimes, but not a cold-blooded murderer.'

'Thanks for nothing,' he looked at her for a moment as she hesitated outside a house. 'This belong to your stepfather? I might have known you had money and breeding behind you, class always tells.'

'Yes, it does – the house, I mean, not the rest, because I'm not sure I agree with that bit,' Sarah said, giving him a straight look. 'Are you coming in or have I offended you?'

'I've got a thick skin,' Sam said, and grinned at her. 'I'll come in and meet your folks, but if they tell you not to work for me you have to promise to ignore them.'

'Oh, I will,' Sarah promised, and laughed. 'I wasn't sure for a while if I liked you, Sam – but I do. I promise I won't run out on you. At least, only if you give me good cause.'

'I wouldn't hurt you intentionally, Sarah,' he said, and as she looked into his brilliant blue eyes she believed him.

'No, I don't think you would,' she said, and her mouth felt dry. She was beginning to like him a little too much. 'Come in then. You can stay for tea. Mummy is English, and we always have tea at this hour – four not three, as the poem says.'

'Yeah, I'll try it,' Sam said, and grinned. 'I'll try anything once.'

'Sam always gives good parties,' Katie said as she stood with Sarah watching the dancing. It was one of the best hotels in Manhattan and the buffet meal had been superb. 'I've been to a couple before this, though as someone's guest not one of the cast. I like him but he only has eyes for you, Sarah. Ellie said she has never known him to look at one of the girls the way he does at you.'

'Oh...' Sarah blushed. 'No, I'm sure you are wrong, Katie. We like each other, but there's nothing more. I think Sam appreciates it when someone stands up to him. He gets pretty much of his own way most of the time. It makes him pay attention when someone talks back.'

'Well, you've got your Mr Meadows,' Katie said, her eyes moving across the room to where Larch was standing with Sam. 'Why would you want anyone else when you can have him?'

'Larch is lovely, isn't he?'

Katie rolled her eyes. 'I wouldn't say no, but he wouldn't look at me.'

'I thought you liked Eddie?'

'Yeah, he's OK,' Katie said, but there was reservation in her voice. 'He's not like Larch or Sam ... Something odd happened this morning...' she shook her head and smiled. 'I'm being silly. Eddie is great. Here comes Sam. I think he is going to ask you to dance. I'll go and find Eddie...'

Sarah looked at the show's producer as he approached, a purposeful gleam in his eyes. He was wearing immaculate evening dress and looked what he was: a successful entre-preneur but slightly dangerous. There was a touch of the bad boy about Sam. Sarah suspected there might be things in his past that wouldn't stand the light of day. She felt a flicker of something like excitement as he smiled at her.

'Larch is talking to someone,' Sam said. 'I asked if he minded me asking you for a dance and he said it was fine – will you?'

'Yes, why not?' Sarah replied. She listened to the music. 'That's a foxtrot, I think...'

'Yeah, I asked for it,' Sam said, and offered his hand. 'Shall we show them all how it's done, Miss Beaufort?'

'I should love to, Mr Garson.' She gave him her hand, eyes alight with excitement because she knew he had issued a challenge. 'If you're up to it?'

'Shall we see?'

Larch stood by the open window watching Sarah dance with her producer. She looked as if she were enjoying herself and the two of them were certainly showing the rest of the dancers the way round the floor. Sam Garson might have been a professional performer at one time, and Sarah had been given dancing lessons in London. They looked a perfect pair and he felt his own inadequacy as far as dancing was concerned. He did his best, and he knew he wasn't bad in an amateur way, but he could never perform the intricate steps of the foxtrot the way Sam did; it just wasn't in Larch to move like that.

The music was ending. Larch watched as Sarah looked up at her partner and laughed. She looked really happy, obviously pleased with herself. He knew that she loved this life, loved performing on stage. Would she be prepared to give it all up to marry him?

He remembered his proposal and frowned. He hadn't been exactly romantic. Did Sarah know how much he loved her – or did she think he was just looking for a nice girl to marry and settle down with? He hoped she understood that he wasn't being selfish when he said she would need to give up her career. It wasn't that he was ashamed of what she did, far from it! Larch wasn't a snob – but he did feel the need to keep her safe, to cherish her and look after her. He couldn't do that if she was singing on a

cruise ship at the other side of the world –
or in a London theatre come to that, he
thought.

Maybe he shouldn't have asked her. Maybe it was selfish to expect her to give it all up
for him. Some husbands were content to
follow their wives these days, especially now
that Hollywood had opened up a new world
for women who could sing and act. Sam had
been talking to him about a new production
he had in mind for Broadway, but he had
also mentioned the fact that Hollywood was
busy working on producing musical spectaculars that were sure to bring crowds
flocking to the cinemas. He had hinted that
he might be making the move in the near
future. Anyone who got in now with the
right people could probably make a fortune.
Larch had known about it for a while,
known that he could make money from
backing shows for the theatre – and there
was always a possibility of a talking, singing
movie.

It wasn't the way he wanted to live. He had
a picture in his mind of a large country
house with good grounds and perhaps a
smaller house in town so that they could go
up to London when they wished – but was it
what Sarah wanted?

Watching her this evening as she laughed
with her friends he had doubts. He had
known from the first moment they met that
Sam was in love with her – and she liked

him. Sam might not be as wealthy as Larch at the moment, but he could give her so much more in other ways, and he was on his way up. If he made his way into the movie business he could become rich and powerful, and Sarah's career could grow with his. Larch knew that he probably wouldn't make a good husband, because once he started painting he became so absorbed that he would probably forget to kiss her in the mornings. He might forget anniversaries, but he would make up for it when he remembered; he wasn't careless, just forgetful when he was working. Would Sarah find him impossible to live with? His father complained that he never got his hair cut, his mother that he left his things on the bedroom floor and forgot when she told him people were coming to dinner. Would Sarah put up with him – or would she yearn for her old life? For the life that could be hers with Sam?

Larch decided that he wouldn't push her for an answer. He had promised to wait for as long as it took. Sarah would make up her own mind and then she would tell him. He knew that if the answer was no she would be scrupulous about letting him down gently, but it would hurt just as much.

'Let me go!' Maura yelled as he entered the room. A scream had been building inside her head, because he'd left her here for hours on her own and she was going mad locked in this tiny room. 'I've told you I'll take my chances. I should have gone to the police in the first place, so I should. I didn't mean to kill him. It was self-defence. They might put me in prison, but they won't hang me.'

'Are you sure of that?' His cold eyes seemed to bore into her, making her shudder. 'If you leave me now, they will arrest you for sure and then you know what will happen.' He sliced a finger across her throat, sending a shiver down her spine.

'No...' Maura pressed her fingers to her mouth to stop the scream escaping. Over the past few days she had grown more and more desperate to get away from him. He frightened her. Sometimes he could be charming, making her feel that he truly cared what happened to her, but at others he was ... chilling. Something in his eyes made her afraid. She tried to smother the sob that rose to her lips but it came out like a whine, and he hated whining! 'Please, let me go. I shan't tell anyone you kept me here. I promise I won't mention your name.'

'It isn't me the police are looking for,' he said, his gaze narrowed, angry. 'Maybe I should let you go. I could get arrested for accessory to murder for hiding you...'

'Please, please let me go!' She flung herself at him, giving way to a storm of emotion. 'I don't want to stay here any longer.'

He thrust her back, a look of disgust in his eyes. 'Keep away from me! I don't like people who demand and I don't like whiners either. I'm not sure I can trust you.'

'But why...?' Maura stared at him, the ice beginning to trickle down her spine. She shivered. 'You're worried I might tell something ... might know something...' She gasped and reeled back as he struck her across the face. 'Why were you there outside the nightclub that night? You were there for some reason, weren't you? Did you go back there after you brought me here? What did you do?'

'Shut it!' he growled. 'Keep your mouth shut or I might decide to shut it for good.' He flung her away from him so that she fell against the bed. 'I'm going and you're staying here. I haven't made up my mind what to do with you yet.'

Maura shrank back as he went out and locked the door. Why had she ever let him bring her here? She had thought she could trust him but now she was afraid of him. He had brought her here that night and then left again, returning hours later. What had he done in the meantime? And why was he so intent on keeping her shut up here?

The only answer she had was so horrifying that it made her hug herself in fear. She knew she hadn't hit Mr van Allen very hard. The blow should have been hard enough to stun him for long enough for her to get away

– but he was dead. If she hadn't killed him who had?

Maura was terribly afraid she knew the answer.

'Did you enjoy the party?' Katie asked as Sarah came off stage after finishing her last song the next morning. She had slipped her silver dancing shoes off and was rubbing her foot. 'I saw you dancing with Sam – now tell me he doesn't fancy you rotten!'

'He is a wonderful dancer,' Sarah said. 'He told me that he started out in this business dancing in the chorus line, and when he realized he didn't have enough of a voice to make it big he changed to producing.'

'Yeah, yeah, I've heard the story,' Katie said, and grinned at her. 'Have you heard the rumours about him going off to Holly-wood after his next Broadway production?'

'No, he didn't mention that to me. Who told you?'

Katie looked down at her feet. 'I knew I shouldn't have bought these shoes; they pinch my toes. Eddie told me last night...' She looked up at Sarah. 'Eddie went off for an hour or more. I thought he had run out on me, and when he came back he was in a mood. I don't think I shall date him again.'

'I thought you liked him?'

'I do and I don't,' Katie said, pulling a face. 'Sometimes he's really great, friendly and nice to be with – but he can be moody.'

'I think most people have their off days,' Sarah said, because she had always found their piano player pleasant and helpful. 'Maybe he has something on his mind. If Sam is thinking of moving to Hollywood Eddie could be worried about his job.'

'Yeah, maybe that's it,' Katie said, and smiled. 'Anyway, there's nothing better on offer at the moment so I suppose I'll hang around with him, at least for a while.'

Sarah nodded. She was thoughtful as she hailed a cab, going straight to Annabel Lawson's house, because she had been invited to lunch. People did have moods sometimes. Larch wasn't exactly like that, but he had seemed withdrawn when he took her home after the party – and his kiss had been brief, more like the kisses he had given her in the past. She wondered if he were offended because she'd asked for time to make up her mind. She hoped not, because she knew he was the most important person in her life.

Sarah was honest enough to admit that she found her producer attractive. He made her as mad as fire sometimes, but he also made her laugh. Sam was different from anyone she had met before ... perhaps a bit dangerous in his own way, but exciting. She knew she ought to be thinking seriously about Larch's proposal, and she would – but at the moment she was having fun.

'That is enough for today, Sarah,' Larch said

119

after she had been sitting for an hour. 'I expect you feel tired after last night?'

'Oh, no, not at all,' Sarah said as she stood up in one graceful movement. 'May I look at what you've done?'

'I would rather you didn't just yet,' Larch said. 'It's just a few brush strokes at the moment, not a real face. I've been trying to get the skin tones this morning.'

'You can look at my sketches if you like,' Annabel told her. 'I work very quickly to get a likeness. It's when I start to model with clay that it takes more time. I build my model layer by layer, and that is what Larch is doing with his portrait, but it looks as if he has made an excellent start.'

Sarah glanced at the sketches Annabel had made. They were excellent, because she had caught Sarah when she was laughing and looked relaxed.

'These are good,' she said. 'May I have one when you've finished with them?'

'Yes, of course. I'll have the one you like best framed as a little thank you for sitting for me. I've decided that the bust will be sold at a charity auction for the homeless. You won't mind that, will you?'

'Not at all,' Sarah replied. 'It is a good cause and I am happy to be a part of it.'

'You must come to the dinner, you and Larch,' Annabel said. 'The tickets are expensive but the money all goes to good causes – and if you are interested I would like to take you to a home we set up for girls who have fallen from grace, if you understand my meaning?'

'Yes, I do,' Sarah said. 'As a matter of fact, Mummy and I were talking about something like that a few days ago. A friend of mine told me about girls who were abducted into a life of vice and were never seen again. I wondered what happened to them when they couldn't work anymore.'

Annabel gave her an approving look. 'You've got the idea, Sarah. Some of the girls have terrible diseases, which we can't cure. We can only give them somewhere to sleep and food, medicines. We have one girl who suffered so much that she isn't quite right in the head. Most of the time she simply sits staring at the wall, but now and then she has screaming fits and has to be restrained. The doctors have to give her drugs to calm her. Some of them say she should be in an asylum, but so far they've kept her at the home.'

'Poor girl, that is so sad,' Sarah said. 'Is there nothing that can be done for her?'

'The doctors have indicated that she might have some form of electric shock therapy, but that can be worse than the symptoms, I'm told.' Annabel shook her head. 'I am hoping that with care and rest she might come out of it herself, but no one quite knows what caused it, you see.'

'Yes, I do see,' Sarah said. 'I expect the

doctors know what's best for her.'

'Yes...' Annabel seemed undecided. 'Well, if you are interested, we could go tomorrow after you finish rehearsals.' She looked at Larch. 'Would you mind if Sarah came later tomorrow?'

'No, of course not. She mustn't think this is something she has to do every day,' Larch said. 'Oh, I invited Ben Marshall out for dinner this evening, Sarah. It would be nice if you could come too – and you, Annabel, if you would like to meet him?'

'What a pity that I have a prior engagement for this evening,' Annabel said, looking regretful. 'But you must invite him here one day. He would be welcome to lunch or dine.'

'I'll ask him this evening,' Larch said. 'I'm not sure how long he intends staying in New York. I think he has another show in Newport before he leaves for home. I don't know if he plans to return to New York afterwards.'

'I'm glad you asked Ben for this evening,' Sarah said. 'I wanted to talk to him about something.'

Larch narrowed his gaze. 'You're not getting mixed up in anything, are you?'

'No, of course not,' Sarah replied. 'I'm just interested to know if there is any news on Maura. She has been missing for several days and I'm worried about her, Larch.'

'Yes, I suppose so,' he said, and frowned. 'It does seem strange that she hasn't been back to fetch her things. I hope—' He stopped and looked at Sarah. 'That business with Esther last year...'

'Yes, it does have horrible overtones, doesn't it? And yet I am sure this is different. When Esther was murdered I knew it, but I don't feel that Maura is dead – just that she is in some kind of trouble.'

'Well, Ben may have some news this evening.'

'I do hope so,' Sarah said. 'Because the longer Maura is missing the less likely it is that she will be found – at least alive.'

'Nice place this,' Ben observed, looking round the prestigious hotel's large, elegant dining room. 'It was good of you to set this up, Larch. I was about to ring Mrs Harland and ask if I could call one evening.'

'Do you have any news about Maura?' Sarah asked.

'Nothing good,' Ben said. 'Hudson is looking for her. He has a man working on the case. He believes she may be being held by someone who thinks she knows too much. He isn't sure whether it's one of van Allen's business associates or...'

'The murderer?' Sarah asked. 'Yes, that is what I have been thinking, too. I know Maura would not have walked out on the chance to be in a show. And if she had changed her mind she would have come back for her things.'

'She could be dead already,' Larch said. 'If

she was involved with a man like that she could have seen and heard things she ought not.'

'I think she had only just met him. I wish I'd asked more about him now,' Sarah said. 'It just seemed an innocent date...'

'You can't blame yourself for that,' Ben told her. 'No one could have known this would happen.'

'No, but I can't help thinking I ought to know something I don't,' Sarah said. 'It is at the back of my mind, but it won't come.'

'Please don't get involved,' Larch said. 'This isn't like the Beecham Thorny murders – or what happened in France last year. It doesn't concern you, Sarah.'

'You are perfectly right; it doesn't,' Sarah said, and picked up the menu. 'Oh, they've got lobster as a main course. Do you think I could have that, please?'

'Of course, anything you wish,' Larch said. 'What do you fancy, Ben?'

'I think I'll stick to a steak and fries,' Ben said. 'I've been eating far too much these past few days, and Cathy will grumble if I put on too much weight – but I've been asked to a lot of lunches and breakfast meetings too. Mrs van Allen has a lot of friends and for some reason I am in demand.'

'You're a celebrity,' Sarah teased. She smiled at him. 'I was wondering if you would like to come to rehearsals one morning – but perhaps you are too busy?'

'I'm never too busy for you, Sarah,' Ben told her. 'I have an appointment for tomorrow morning, but I could come the day after, if you wish?'

'Yes, that would be lovely. I'll tell them to let you in – and perhaps we could have coffee afterwards?'

'I shall look forward to it.'

Sarah nodded and returned to the menu. She knew that Larch was waiting for her to say something, invite him to the rehearsal, but she let it pass, because she wanted the chance to speak to Ben alone. Something had occurred to her and she would rather Larch wasn't around when she mentioned it to Ben.

Larch worried about her becoming involved and she had no intention of it, but she'd begun to get those peculiar prickling sensations at the nape of her neck recently. She had the oddest feeling that someone was watching her when she left the theatre each morning, and at other times too. She had no idea why anyone would be interested in her movements, and the only thing she could think of was that it had something to do with Maura's disappearance.

Four

'It is so good of you to look at my cat, Mr Marshal,' Betty-Lou Hamilton gushed as Ben lifted the large Persian blue from its cushion and ran an experienced hand over its silky fur. 'I was telling Louise that I was worried about poor Beattie and she said that you were the right person to give me advice.'

'You've had the vet out, of course?'

'Oh, several times. He says there is nothing wrong with her – but she is off her food, Mr Marshall. She usually eats everything I give her, but she didn't touch her salmon yesterday, and she adores fresh salmon.'

'That isn't a good sign,' Ben said, and frowned. 'She hasn't started to lose weight yet, Mrs Hamilton, so I doubt there's anything much wrong with her – but keep an eye on her and have the vet again if she vomits or looks as if she is ill. Have you thought of mating her? It may just be that she is lonely for her own kind – broody.'

'Mating her? Oh, I don't know...' Mrs Hamilton looked flustered. 'I hadn't considered...'

'You could have her spayed, but my advice

would be to breed with her. Mrs van Allen has a good tom. Put them together next time Beattie comes into season and see what happens.'

'Oh, yes, well, I could –' she gave him a coy glance. 'Louise said you would put me right. Poor dear, Louise. She has had such a terrible time of it with that husband of hers. He practically drove their son away, you know. Louise hated him. Mr van Allen, not Jonathan. She dotes on him, of course – but she hasn't seen him for months. His father cut him off without a penny after they had that terrible argument. Louise has no idea why they quarrelled, but it was very bad. I shouldn't speak ill of the dead – but Mr van Allen wasn't a nice man. I've heard things, but I'm not one to gossip...'

'No, I am sure you aren't,' Ben said. 'But sometimes it is good to get things off one's chest, as the saying goes. If you know anything you should tell the police.'

'Oh, I couldn't do anything like that,' Betty-Lou said, looking upset. 'It is just that ... well, I thought I saw Jonathan the other day. He was talking to a girl as I went by in the car. He didn't see me...' She hesitated, then her manner became confiding, her voice lowered. 'I heard that Jonathan quarrelled with his father over a girl. Servants will talk, you know! Well, the girl I saw him with – she wasn't one of us, if you understand me. She looked a common sort of girl, too much make-up on her face and a very short skirt. I don't approve of these short skirts, Mr Marshall. I know that they are fashionable, but I don't think that it is quite nice for young girls to show so much of their legs – do you?'

'Well, we have to accept these fashions, I suppose,' Ben said with a smile. 'Some girls look quite pretty in them, but I prefer them not too short myself.'

Betty-Lou smiled her approval. 'I knew you would understand, a man who understands cats the way you do, Mr Marshall. I can't thank you enough for coming. I shall talk to Louise, hear what she has to say about what you suggested.'

'It may be the answer,' Ben said. 'Beattie might just start eating again of her own accord. Cats are like people, they have their fads and fancies, you know.'

Mrs Hamilton laughed as she walked to the door with her visitor. She had no intention of putting her darling little Beattie through all that nasty business of mating, but she wouldn't have dreamed of saying so to Mr Marshall's face.

'Goodbye, it was so nice of you to call,' she said, offering her hand. 'I do hope I haven't wasted your time.'

'No, it wasn't a waste of time at all,' Ben said, giving her hand a hearty shake. 'It was nice meeting you and Beattie.'

He smiled to himself as he went outside

and hailed a cab. He was about to give the address of his hotel and then changed his mind. Perhaps he would just call in and have a word with Detective Hudson before he had lunch...

'I wasn't sure whether you would be interested in coming here,' Annabel said as they got out of the car and walked up the short drive to the front of the large house. It was built of a pale grey stone and from the outside had a rather sombre, forbidding look, perhaps because of the bars at the windows. 'I don't find it difficult to interest people in giving money, but not too many want to see where their money goes.'

'Perhaps they don't like facing up to the facts,' Sarah said. 'The girls who come here have all had terrible lives – and it is because of the society we live in. If we did more to protect them they might not have ended up here.'

'I couldn't agree more,' Annabel said. 'But too often society looks on them as being responsible for their own fate. Some people I try to interest in the home insist that the girls chose their way of life and must accept the consequences.'

'Some do, I suppose,' Sarah replied. 'But others are forced into it through no fault of their own. I can feel nothing but sympathy for them.'

'Exactly.' Annabel smiled at her. 'That is

why I brought you here, Sarah. I know you don't have much time to spare, but I wondered if you would help me with a little concert I want to put on privately? The money will go towards extending the home. We have a chance to buy the house next door and I am doing everything I can to raise funds.'

'Ah, I see.' Sarah nodded. She had wondered why Annabel had suddenly raised the subject. 'Well, I am willing to give my services, but I think you are asking for more than that, aren't you?'

'Could you persuade a few more of your friends to give us a turn?'

'I'm not sure. I could ask Sam if it would be all right. If he gives permission I am sure Katie and some of the others will agree.'

'Oh, that is so kind of you,' Annabel said, looking pleased. The door was opened in response to her knock. 'Well, here we are. I'll introduce you to our matron and some of the staff – and you might like to meet one or two of the girls?'

'Yes, of course, if they want to meet me,' Sarah said. 'What about the girl who isn't quite right – shall I see her?'

'Oh, I doubt it,' Annabel said. 'She spends most of her time in her room. She isn't locked in except when she has one of her bad days, but she doesn't mix with the others very much.'

'It's so sad,' Sarah said. 'I don't know who

made her so unhappy that she had to retreat into her own world, but whoever he is I should like to take a horsewhip to him!'

'Oh, Sarah,' Annabel said with a husky laugh. 'How fierce you sound!'

'Yes, I suppose I did,' Sarah said, and smiled. 'It's just that I feel so sorry for her. I can't help wondering how and why she came to be the way she is.'

'Perhaps the doctors will discover a way to break through her pain one day,' Annabel said. 'But until then all we can do is to care for her physical needs.'

'I knew it!' Hudson said, a look of excitement in his eyes. 'It has been bugging me for days. I saw the pictures of him in her sitting room. She must have a dozen of them dotted about the room in silver frames – but none of her husband. I knew there was a clue somewhere if I could see it.'

'It struck me as odd that he didn't come home when he heard the news,' Ben said. 'At least, I haven't seen or heard of him.'

'No. He wasn't at the funeral. I attended but she was alone. Hardly anyone turned up, apart from a few of Mrs van Allen's female friends. I thought perhaps some of his business associates might crawl out of the woodwork, but as yet I haven't seen anything of them.'

'Maybe he didn't have any. Preferred to keep it in the family?'

'Why did the son quarrel with his father, that's what I would like to know. Your informant said it was over a girl?'

'She was repeating gossip, Hudson. It may mean something or nothing. I just thought you might want to know he was missing.'

'But this person thought she had seen him in New York recently?'

'Talking to a girl who wore too much make-up and a short skirt,' Ben said, and grinned. 'I should think there are only a few thousand girls who might fit that description in a city like this...'

'Yeah, too right! It isn't much but it does tell me something.' Ben raised his eyebrows. 'I've been thinking it might be a mob killing – but if van Allen worked alone I should start thinking about another angle.'

'The son killed his father – or the wife killed her husband?' Ben suggested. 'I think she might have hated him enough to kill him, but it happened in the wrong place. I can't see Mrs van Allen visiting a club like that, can you?'

'No, not her scene at all,' Hudson confirmed. 'I should say we are looking either for his son – or the father of an abducted girl.'

Ben nodded. 'Well, that narrows things down a little. And it would explain why the son hasn't come home yet – lying low until the heat cools down a bit, perhaps?'

'I think I'll pay Mrs van Allen a visit,'

Hudson said. 'Thank you for bringing this to me, Marshall. I knew I was missing something in this case.'

'Are you any closer to finding the Playboy Murderer?'

'He has been quiet for a few weeks,' Hudson said. 'Maybe it was revenge and he's finished his work. If he doesn't strike again we may never find him – and I'll be moved on to something else. There are too many crimes going on in this city for me to be stuck on this one for too long. I'm already being told to make progress or file it.'

'You don't want to give up on him, do you?'

'I want to nail the bastard before he kills again,' Hudson replied grimly. 'I don't know why he started this, but I have a gut feeling he isn't finished yet.'

'Well, I wish you luck with both cases,' Ben told him. 'Tomorrow afternoon I'm leaving for Newport. I'm not sure if I shall see you again.'

The two men shook hands. 'It was good to meet you, Marshall.'

'Same here,' Ben replied. 'I hope you solve both your cases before the killers strike again.'

'You don't think van Allen's killer will do another? That doesn't fit the MO we were discussing.'

'I'm not sure,' Ben said. 'But Maura Trelawney went missing that night and I can't help feeling that she may be in danger. If she happened to be in the wrong place at the wrong time...'

'He might decide to kill her?' Hudson frowned. 'So why hasn't he done it already? Or has he and we just haven't found the body?'

'I have no idea,' Ben said. 'Maybe he doesn't really want to kill her – but he might if he gets frightened that she could bring him down.'

'I'll put some men on to it,' Hudson said. 'I hadn't really thought about that angle. If my officers ask around that area they might find someone who saw something unusual that night. I don't see what else I can do. This is a big city and she could be any-where.'

'It was just a thought,' Ben said. 'I may be completely wrong, but if you could find her she might give you your killer.'

'Yeah, she might.' Hudson looked thought-ful. 'It's worth a try. I'll put some men on it today.'

'You don't need to walk me home,' Sarah said when she prepared to leave Annabel's later that afternoon. 'Unless you would like to, of course?' She smiled at Larch. 'It is just around the corner, as you know, but you can stay for dinner this evening if you like.'

'I was hoping we might go out later on our own,' Larch said. 'We haven't had much time alone since I got here, Sarah.'

'No, we haven't,' Sarah replied. 'Yes, walk back with me, Larch. To be honest I was thinking I might call a cab, but if you come with me I shan't.'

'Any reason why you wanted a taxi?' Larch frowned as he remembered the night he had stood outside Sarah's home and thought someone was watching her.

'Oh no, not really...' Sarah hesitated and then decided it was silly not to tell him. 'I think someone may be following me, Larch. I've noticed him a few times now. Mostly when I leave the theatre at lunchtimes. I'm not sure he is hanging about for my sake, but I think he followed me from Annabel's once...'

'Why didn't you tell me before?'

'I wasn't sure. Besides, I didn't want you to worry. It may be nothing, but –' she shivered – 'I can't explain it, but I feel it has something to do with Maura. At least, I think it is Maura...' She shook her head. 'I could be imagining it. I don't have any idea what is going on, Larch.'

Larch was silent for a moment, then, 'No, I think you are right, Sarah. I saw someone – the night I kissed you outside your house that first time. He was standing across the road, staring. When I called out and asked him what he wanted he ran off.'

'You didn't tell me!'

'I thought it was an isolated incident. I

135

didn't know it had happened more than once.' Larch frowned. 'I think we should tell the police, Sarah.'

'Tell them what? He hasn't said or done anything. He's just there, watching ... waiting maybe.'

'Why is he watching you? That's the question,' Larch said. 'You've only been here a few months, Sarah. Why should anyone be following you? You can't think of anyone you've upset?'

'We spent a lot of time at the ranch, and I've only moved in Mummy's circles, and the theatre,' Sarah said. 'Everyone is very friendly. Besides, that man doesn't belong with Mummy's crowd. He looks as if he might be a down-and-out...'

'Maybe he picked you at random,' Larch suggested. 'But what does he want from you? Money?'

'Perhaps.' Sarah felt icy cold. 'I don't know. I would rather not think about it.'

'Should I talk to the police?'

'Let me talk to Ben first.'

'Is that why you asked him to rehearsals tomorrow?'

'Yes. Please don't be cross, Larch. I didn't want to tell you – but I think it has something to do with Maura. I sense that he wants something and I don't see what else it could be.'

'You think he snatched her.' Larch frowned. 'Do you suppose he wants money for her return?'

'Oh, Larch, if only that were true! I know Mummy would pay to get her back safely. She might have complained about Maura being lazy, but she feels worried about her, I know she does. Do you think it might be that?'

'I don't know,' Larch said. 'If it is money he wants why doesn't he ask for it? Send a ransom note or telephone?'

'Perhaps he can't write,' Sarah said. 'I don't know ... but I wish I did...'

Larch looked at her hard. 'Stay away from him, Sarah! Promise me you will never approach him. He might grab you too. If your parents would pay for Maura think what they would pay for you – what I'd pay to get you back.'

He sounded so serious, so unlike himself that Sarah gave him a quick hug. 'I promise I won't do anything silly, Larch. Believe me, I don't want to be more involved in this than I have to be. I shall see what Ben says, but I think the best person to speak to about this would be Detective Hudson.'

'Thank goodness you are being sensible, Sarah,' Larch said, obviously relieved. 'I don't think we should wait until tomorrow. I'll give Ben a ring now and ask him to come round this evening.'

'I'm glad you decided to call me in,' Ben said. 'I said my goodbyes to Hudson last night, because I'm leaving for Newport tomorrow afternoon, but I'm going to ring him this evening, ask him if he can recommend someone to keep an eye on you, Sarah.'

'Must you?' She sighed as she saw the look in both Larch's and Ben's eyes. 'Well, I suppose if you think it necessary, I can't stop you. It may scare him off, of course.'

'That would be a good thing!' Larch said. 'Just because he hasn't done anything yet, doesn't mean he isn't dangerous, Sarah.'

'I know.' Sarah smiled at him. 'Well, better safe than sorry – isn't that what Gran would say?'

'In this instance Mrs Beaufort would be right,' Ben said. 'I'll tell Hudson that I need someone who will be as invisible as possible, because I agree that this man may be able to tell us something. It might be as well to bring him in for questioning. But that's up to Hudson, of course.'

'Why should he just hang around watching Sarah?' Larch objected. 'I disagree with both of you on this one. If he wanted money he would approach Mrs Harland or her husband, surely? I think this has more to do with Sarah herself, but I can't tell you why. I just feel she may be in danger.'

Sarah gave him a teasing look. 'You don't believe in premonitions, Larch.'

'Call it a hunch – isn't that what they say in all the best private eye novels?'

'Have you been reading some?' Sarah's eyes sparkled with mischief. 'You're not going to set up as one, are you?'

'Sarah!' Larch threw her an awful look. 'Sometimes you deserve—' He shook his head, because the idea of spanking her was surprisingly pleasing but not a subject for open conversation. 'All I am asking is that you take this seriously. I know I didn't always trust your premonitions, or Mrs Darby's visions, but this time I'm worried.'

'Please don't be, Larch,' Sarah said, because she could see that he really was concerned for her. 'I shall accept whatever kind of protection Ben and Detective Hudson see fit to provide for me – and I promise to think twice before I do anything. I won't get into cars with strange men or ... you know what I mean.'

Ben looked at Larch thoughtfully. 'If you don't think this has anything to do with Maura, what could it be about? Sarah, your stepfather – does he have enemies?'

'Philip is an absolute sweetie,' Sarah replied. 'He may have made enemies in business – I daresay most people do – but he isn't one of those ruthless men who walk roughshod over everyone.'

'I'm just wondering why someone should follow you,' Ben said. 'I know you are pretty and he may just be an admirer.'

'No,' Larch said. 'I'd stake my last shilling on it. He has a look about him and I felt something ... menace.'

Sarah felt cold all over. It was strange to hear Larch saying something like that, because normally it was she who got those feelings and he who denied them.

'Well, whatever he wants, I shall try to keep out of his way,' she said. 'If I don't take a cab I'll make sure that someone walks with me.'

'Yes, do that,' Larch said, and smiled. 'So now that all this is out in the open, may I come to rehearsals in the morning too?'

'Yes, of course. I am sure Sam won't mind,' Sarah said. 'But be careful, Larch. I know he is looking for backers for his latest show – and he might be moving to Hollywood in the future.'

'Yes, he told me,' Larch said. 'I considered backing him, Sarah, but it would take a lot of commitment – perhaps more than I am willing to invest at the moment. Money is one thing but I think this might need time as well.'

'Oh, well, you must do whatever you think right for you,' Sarah said. She was surprised to feel disappointed, but she didn't know exactly why. Did she want Larch to take more of an interest in her world – or was she disappointed that Sam would still need to look for a backer for his show?

He had decided to follow the other one for a change. The girl he was after never seemed to be alone, but he knew she had gone somewhere in a car with the woman from the big brownstone house. He couldn't follow, because he had very little money left. He had sold most of what he'd taken from his previous victims and some of it was impossible to sell, because the silver had crests, and in one of the shops where he'd tried to sell it, the sales manager had looked at him suspiciously. He'd snatched it up and run, knowing that he'd made a mistake. The silver was useless. It could be traced. He needed things that were of small value and could be easily disposed of. People like him didn't own expensive stuff and the honest pawnbrokers were suspicious; the dishonest ones would give him cents for it for melting down.

He needed to get money, and he needed an outlet for the frustration building inside him. When he wasn't watching the girl ... Sarah ... he thought about her name and about seeing her on her knees crying, begging for mercy. Despite all the difficulty he hadn't given up on that idea yet, but he needed something more in the meantime. When he wasn't watching Sarah, he spent his time searching for Lucy. He would never rest until he found her. Someone had her hidden away somewhere and one day he would find her – and then he would kill for the last time.

He watched as the woman came out of her

house. She hesitated by her car and then walked on by. She was going to walk and she was carrying a smart leather bag. It was sure to contain money, and that would be better than silver or jewellery. He didn't want much, just enough to get by while he continued the search for his little Lucy.

He began to follow the woman. There were too many people about to try snatching the bag now. He would wait for the right moment. He was a patient man, and perhaps this was his lucky day.

'That was great, sweetheart,' Sam said, as Sarah finished her fourth song. 'OK, we shan't need you anymore for a couple of days. We have a dress rehearsal on Monday. Take some time off. Another week and you'll be on your way to the ship.'

'Is it as soon as that?' Sarah felt a tingle of excitement. She'd known they didn't have long for rehearsals, but she hadn't realized it was that close. 'Thanks, Sam. I shan't be late on Monday.'

'Make sure you aren't,' Sam said, watching as she disappeared backstage. He turned to the two men sitting next to him. 'She's good. I don't think she realizes how good. I've got her ready for this show in a few days. I think she could do Broadway in a few months – or maybe a musical spectacular for the movies. I've been talking with a director and he told me they are looking for fresh talent. Some of the silent movie stars will never make it in the talkies – but Sarah could. She has a presence, and her voice is nearly there. If she wanted it, I could arrange for lessons. She could go a long way if she wanted to work for it.'

Larch frowned. 'Have you discussed this with Sarah?'

'Not yet. I'm waiting until the time is right. Maybe when she comes back from this trip.'

'I see,' Larch said. 'I think I should be honest with you, Mr Garson. I have asked Sarah to marry me – and I am hoping she will say yes.'

'She hasn't given you her answer yet?'

'No, not yet. I told her to take all the time she needs. I want her to be happy with her choice.'

'Does marrying you mean she has to give all this up?'

'Yes, it probably does,' Larch told him. He cleared his throat self-consciously. 'I dare say you think that makes me a selfish prig?'

'What I think doesn't matter,' Sam said, and shrugged. 'It is what Sarah thinks – but if it is any consolation, if she was mine I'd probably feel that I wanted to keep her all to myself. I wouldn't though, because she loves this business.'

'Yes, I know—' Larch broke off as Sarah came down some steps at the side of the stage. Ben had wandered off when Sam started to speak to Larch and she was talking to him, laughing at something he said. 'It's just that I want to protect her ... keep her safe...'

'Is she in some danger?' Sam's gaze narrowed. 'What's going on?'

'Sarah is being followed. I'm worried about her.'

'Damn!' Sam looked at her. 'She knew the girl who disappeared, didn't she? Is it something to do with her?'

'We don't know for sure. We're arranging to have her shadowed by the police or a private eye.'

'She won't like that much.'

'She doesn't but it can't be helped. It may be best if the police take him in for questioning—' Larch broke off as Sarah came up to them. 'You were very good. I should think you'll be a sensation on that cruise liner. You're much better than the singer we had coming over.'

Sarah looked pleased. 'Was I really? Thank you. Sam just told me we only have one more week of rehearsals.'

'Don't think you're getting out of it on the ship,' Sam told her with a grin. 'Ellie and Eddie will be with you, and they'll work you hard.'

'Not as hard as you, slaver driver!' Sarah teased. She looked at Larch. 'Ben says he will be coming back after that show in Newport. Detective Hudson asked him to return.

Apparently, they've had a bit of a break-through in one of the cases Ben has been helping him with, and he wants him to stay for a few days longer.'

'Who is this Detective Hudson?' Sam asked. 'You're not in trouble with the cops, sweetheart?'

Sarah laughed, her eyes bright. 'No, you haven't hired yourself a criminal, Sam. Mr Marshall used to be Scotland Yard and he has been helping the police here – because of Maura Trelawney.'

'Yeah, right,' Sam said, and glanced at Larch. 'Maybe they've found her?'

'No, I don't think it is that or Ben would have told me,' Sarah said. 'It may be to do with another case, but I couldn't say even if I knew – it is police business. Nothing to do with us.'

She turned towards the stage and saw that Eddie was standing there watching them. She had a feeling that he had been listening to their conversation – listening as if he needed to know what they were saying. He saw that she had noticed him, grinned and went back to the piano, running his fingers over the keys.

'Eddie is reminding me we haven't finished,' Sam said. 'Some of the other girls need more rehearsal than you, Sarah. Make yourself scarce and take your pals with you.'

'I think he wants us out of the way,' Sarah said as Ben came up to them. She saw that

145

he was looking thoughtful. 'Something on your mind?'

'Not sure,' he said. 'I know we arranged to have lunch, Sarah – but I have an errand to run. Someone I need to see before I leave.'

'Of course. We'll see you when you come back, I hope?'

'Oh yes, certainly,' Ben said. 'If I have news I'll telephone you before that. I must dash...'

Sarah watched as he walked quickly from the theatre. 'I wonder what made Ben go off like that?'

'He has one of his hunches,' Sarah said. 'No doubt he will tell us as soon as he is sure of his facts...'

'Oh, Mr Marshall!' Louise van Allen looked at the gilt clock on her mantelpiece. 'I wasn't expecting you to call this morning. I have several important guests coming for lunch. I would ask you to stay, but it isn't cat show business this time.'

'I couldn't stay if you did. I just called in on my way back to the hotel. I wanted to ask if you would let me have a chance of a kitten if you breed your tom with Mrs Hamilton's cat.'

'Oh...' She looked startled. 'I'm not sure that it will happen. Betty-Lou hasn't actually made up her mind to it, and I don't think she will.'

'Oh, well, not to worry. It was just a

thought.' Ben turned to look at a silver frame on the mantle. 'This is a nice frame – is it a picture of your son, Mrs van Allen?'

'Taken some years ago when he was seventeen,' she said. 'Jonathan doesn't care to have his picture taken and the others were all done when he was at college. I should like a more recent one of course – but why do you ask?'

'No reason,' Ben said. 'I've not had the pleasure of meeting him as yet.'

'Jonathan is travelling,' Louise replied. 'He sends a postcard now and then. I dare say he will come home when he is ready.'

'Yes, I am sure he will,' Ben said. 'I am sorry to have troubled you. I must go now.'

'You will excuse me if I do not come to the door with you.'

Ben felt the temperature drop several degrees. He'd aroused her ire by asking questions about her son. Did she know he was here in New York? Had she any idea that he was playing a piano for a living?

Ben was thoughtful as he went outside and hailed a cab. He hadn't been one hundred per cent sure at the theatre but he was now. The pictures might have been taken when Jonathan van Allen was seventeen and at college, but he hadn't changed all that much. Ben was pretty certain that Mrs van Allen's son and the piano player known as Eddie Reeder, who had accompanied Sarah as she sang her songs, were one and

147

the same.

Why was he living in New York under an assumed name – and why hadn't he gone to his father's funeral?

Ben had a feeling that that young man was mixed up in this business somehow, but at the moment he wasn't sure how.

'You're certain it was the van Allen boy?' Hudson asked as they met for a quick drink. 'You couldn't be mistaken?'

'I'm pretty certain,' Ben said. 'What will you do – pick him up and question him?'

'If I did that I better have good reason,' Hudson said. 'Mrs van Allen would have her lawyers come down on me like a ton of cement if I arrested her son for nothing. She is an important lady. Her husband might have been a first-class shit but she is respected in this city. As far as we know, her son hasn't done anything wrong.'

'Supposing he walked in when his father was struggling with the girl and decided to finish his quarrel with him permanently after she ran off?'

'It begs the question as to why he was there – and what he did with the girl. Did he go after her and kidnap her?'

'She had been to the theatre that morning. She knew him, probably liked him, fancied him...'

'After he slit the old man's throat?' Hudson frowned. 'Doesn't sound right to me, though I agree he may have something to do with it.'

'Well, I'll leave it with you,' Ben said. 'You know where he is if you want to pick him up.'

'Sure, thanks,' Hudson said. 'Don't think I don't appreciate your help. I'll set a man on his tail, see what happens. About that other business – I told you we had a clue, didn't I? Well, the jeweller came in this morning. He wasn't sure when he rang but when I showed him a print of the crest that made his mind up. It is silver from the first Playboy Murder victim's house.'

'Did he give a good description?'

'He said he could identify the man in a line-up,' Hudson said, with a snarl of satisfaction. 'He's about five-ten, medium build, thin brown hair and grey eyes – longish nose.'

'All you have to do now is find him.'

'Yeah, easy as taking candy from a baby.' Hudson grinned. 'But you must admit it is a breakthrough. We had nothing; now we have something.'

His telephone rang. He picked it up, listening for a moment and putting out his hand urgently as Ben turned to leave. Ben hesitated, thinking he ought to leave, but it was clear Hudson wanted him to wait.

'Go on,' he growled into the phone. 'Is she alive? ... Barely, but she's been rushed to hospital? OK, get someone over there. I

want a guard outside her door twenty-four /
seven.'

'You've found the girl?' Ben asked as Hudson replaced the receiver.

'What ... no, sorry.' Hudson frowned. 'The Playboy Murderer struck again, but this time he made a mistake. His victim is still alive and he was seen.'

'The Playboy Murderer?' Ben's eyebrows shot up as Hudson nodded. 'How do you know it was him?'

'It's a guess but a good one,' Hudson replied. 'He followed her to a house – secluded grounds – and then he tried to snatch her purse. She wouldn't let go and he pulled a gun on her. He shot her three times, left her for dead. But this time he was unlucky. Someone saw him and went for him, wrestled the gun from him. It's the same make as the bastard used for all the killings – and it was stolen from the house in Newport. It has some initials engraved on the barrel. I don't think there's much doubt that it was the same gun.'

'They didn't get him?'

'No, worse luck, but he isn't invincible, Marshall. For a while he had us running after our arses. His luck has begun to go sour. It's only a matter of time now.'

'It was a woman he attacked?' Ben frowned. 'He usually goes for men, doesn't he?'

'Mostly men, though some of his first victims were women, at the house in Newport. He went on the rampage there, shot anyone who came near him – but the survivors were all too drunk or drugged to remember much. After that he seemed to pick his victims more carefully. They've all been the sons of wealthy men, the playboy type. Mrs Lawson certainly wasn't his usual mark. She is an artist, wealthy, respectable – and she does a lot of work for the homeless. It was in the grounds of a home for them that he attempted to rob her.' Hudson scratched the shadow of beard on his chin. 'I have an odd feeling about this, Marshall. Why didn't he just kill her and take the damned purse – that's his usual MO. Why try to snatch it, give her a chance to fight back?'

'Maybe he didn't want to kill her,' Ben said. 'He might just have needed some money. You said he had been quiet for a bit – and he couldn't sell the silver. And there's another thing – it may be the same gun but a different man. The killer you're after might have got rid of the gun.'

'Why would he do that?'

'It's just a maybe. He probably just needs money.'

'Yeah, I think you've got it,' Hudson said. 'She wasn't supposed to die. He just wanted money. There's someone else he wants to kill ... but he's made a mistake. He's lost his weapon.'

'Which means he'll have to use other

methods next time – or steal another gun.'

'Yeah.' Hudson smiled. 'The bastard is losing his touch. I'll have him soon.' He scratched the itch at the side of his nose. 'He's made one mistake. I guess he'll lie low for a while. He has to work out what to do next – and that gives me some time to work on the van Allen case...'

Five

Sarah came downstairs wearing one of her prettiest frocks that evening. She was smiling at the prospect of an evening alone with Larch, but the look on her mother's face made her heart catch.

'What is it, Mummy? I heard the telephone – have they found Maura?'

'No, darling. It wasn't about Maura. Larch rang. He said he would be late. He has to go to the hospital. The police rang him this afternoon after you left him. Annabel Lawson is fighting for her life. She was attacked in the grounds of the Larkspur Home for Girls. A man tried to snatch her purse and when she wouldn't let go he shot her three times.'

'Oh no!' Sarah sat down on the nearest chair. She felt a little faint and the sickness roiled in her stomach. 'That is absolutely awful. Poor Annabel. She is such a generous person and she supports that home with her own money as well as the money she collects from other wealthy people.'

'Yes, it is horrible,' Mrs Harland said, a look of dismay in her eyes. 'You were with her only the other day. You went to that place – it could have been you, Sarah.'

'I should have let him take my purse,' Sarah said, and gave her mother a hug, because she could see how upset she was over it. 'It isn't worth fighting back over money. I don't know how much Annabel was carrying, but whatever it was it couldn't have been worth her life.'

Mrs Harland gave a little sniff. 'Larch says Annabel doesn't have a close family. He says he hopes to see her if the police will allow visitors. Apparently, they have a guard on her room all the time.'

Sarah frowned. 'I wonder why. I know she was almost killed but ... I suppose they are hoping she may come round and be able to tell them something. Do you think they always have a police guard when someone is robbed and shot? I mean, it does happen...'

'I don't know, Sarah. I really don't care to know these things. What on earth possessed Annabel to walk there? If she had taken her car her driver might have deterred him from trying – whoever he is.'

'I know she likes to walk sometimes. She says that she likes to get on a bus or a train sometimes, because it keeps her in touch with the way other people live. She is a remarkable person, Mummy. I should like to visit her soon if Larch thinks it would be all right.'

'Well, I am sure he will either come later

this evening – or he will telephone,' Mrs Harland said. 'And you look so nice, my love. What a pity your evening is spoiled.'

'It doesn't matter. I can go out with Larch another time,' Sarah said. 'I just wish it hadn't happened. Annabel doesn't deserve this, Mummy.'

'Who does, my dear?' Mrs Harland shook her head. 'We can't do anything, I suppose. Perhaps you should just come and sit down. We might have a cup of tea if you like?'

'Yes.' Sarah sighed. 'I wonder...' She shook her head. It was foolish to speculate, but she couldn't help wondering if the attack on Annabel had something to do with the man who had been following her for the past few days. However, as she hadn't told her mother anything about that, she had better keep her thoughts to herself.

Sarah flicked through the pile of fashion magazines on the occasional table next to her. Her teacup still contained most of the tea she had accepted from her mother. It had gone cold long ago and Larch still hadn't phoned. She supposed he must still be at the hospital, sitting with Annabel or waiting for news.

She wished that she had a telephone number for Ben but she knew he had gone off that afternoon on his visit to Newport. It was the last of the cat shows he had been asked to judge. After that he would be looking to book his return passage to England.

Sarah wished she understood what was going on here. She wanted to talk to someone and Ben was the best person to listen to her thoughts. Larch would be horrified if he thought the man who had been following her was the one who had attempted to rob and then shot Annabel Lawson. She couldn't even think of speaking to Detective Hudson. He would simply stare at her as if she were mad and she could never explain that she had begun to have those odd feelings that came to her when she was involved in something like this: he wouldn't believe her. Why should he? Sarah couldn't explain it to herself.

It wasn't like what had happened at Beecham Thorny or in France. The clues had all come to her easily then. She'd been told things and she had worked it out in her mind, but this time there was no gossipy postmistress and no bad tempered Nancy to alert her to what was wrong. All she had was her intuition and she couldn't expect a police officer to listen to that!

She jumped as the phone suddenly shrilled. Her mother answered and then held out the receiver. Sarah jumped up to take it from her.

'Larch?'

'Sarah, I am sorry about this evening. Annabel has been in surgery for hours. I felt

I had to wait. I couldn't desert her, even though she doesn't actually know I'm here.'

'Of course you couldn't, Larch. You must not worry about me, really. I don't mind. I couldn't go out and just ignore what has happened. What did the doctors say?'

'Two of the shots were superficial, but the third narrowly missed her vital organs. They think she will survive but she is going to be in hospital for a while – and she may need a nurse when she goes home. I'm not sure how long it will be before she is back to normal, if ever.'

'I am so sorry,' Sarah said. 'Look, you must do whatever you can for her. I know you have your show coming up – but don't bother about me. You should spend all your spare time visiting Annabel, and my portrait can wait until she is recovering.'

'I was certain you would say that,' Larch said. 'This isn't what I'd planned – you know that, Sarah.'

'Yes, of course I do,' Sarah told him. 'We have all the time in the world, Larch. Help Annabel through this and then we'll have some time together.'

'Promise me you won't take any risks? No walking out by yourself. It might have been you, Sarah. You went to that place with Annabel. If this lunatic had been there…'

'Have you heard anything more about what happened?'

'No, just the bare details. The police want

to interview me – check my movements, I suppose.'

'You were with me.'

'Yes, well, they may want to speak to you too – but I think it is just routine. Hudson was apologetic, said it was necessary but nothing to worry about.'

'Is Detective Hudson on this case, too?'

'He came to the hospital. I visited for a few minutes when they brought her back from surgery, but a police officer was there all the time.'

'Yes, that is a little odd, don't you think? They surely don't do that for every victim of a robbery gone wrong – do they?'

'I hadn't thought about that,' Larch said. 'Now you mention it, the precautions are a bit heavy ... but they must have a reason.'

'Yes, they will have a reason,' Sarah said. She put a hand up to her neck, massaging the tingle. 'Telephone me when you have time.'

'I'll come round when I can – but the show begins Tuesday evening. You are coming to that – you and your family?'

'Yes, we are coming,' Sarah said. 'You know I wouldn't miss it for the world, Larch. I want to see all the pictures you've painted since last summer.'

'They are mostly landscapes, Norfolk and some Cornish. I went down there for a few weeks in the spring. I think seascapes suit my style – and they are the most popular.'

'Yes, I remember that they sold well last year,' Sarah said. 'If – *when* – Annabel recovers, you will give her my love?'

'Yes, of course.'

'Would I be able to visit tomorrow?'

'I am not sure. Ring the hospital in the morning and ask. I think they are keeping visitors to a minimum. Annabel doesn't have family but she has lots of friends.'

'Yes, I am sure she does,' Sarah said. 'She does a lot of good work – especially for that home.'

'Yes. Look, I need to do a few things tonight. I'll call you tomorrow.'

'Yes, thank you. Take care, Larch.'

'You too.'

Sarah stared at the receiver before putting it back. She felt so helpless. There was nothing she could do for Annabel – and no one she could tell about the thoughts swirling in her head. Even the escape of rehearsals wasn't open to her, because Sam had given her two days off. He'd believed she would spend it with Larch, which she would have if this hadn't happened.

Sarah went upstairs to her room feeling restless. She wanted to do something ... useful. Maybe she could visit the home and see if they needed help. With Annabel likely to be out of action for a long time, there might be something she could help to sort out – though in just over a week she would be at sea. At least she could try, she thought –

though she wouldn't mention it to her mother, because she would forbid her to go near the place after what had happened to Annabel...

Sarah telephoned the hospital the next morning. She was kept waiting a few moments while the receptionist fetched a nurse, and then she explained again who she was and asked if it would be possible to visit.

'I'm sorry, Miss Beaufort,' the nurse said. 'We have instructions to allow only one visitor. Mrs Lawson's fiancé is with her now and he is the only one authorised to visit for the moment.'

Sarah bit her lip. It was a natural mistake for the nurse to make, because obviously Larch had shown great concern for his friend. 'I see – well, when she is feeling better please give her my best wishes and tell her I shall visit when I can.'

'Yes, of course. I think she is awake now but still very poorly. I'll give her your message later.'

Sarah replaced the receiver and went upstairs to fetch her jacket. She picked up her handbag and then opened it, taking out some notes and slipping them into her coat pocket. No point in tempting fate by carrying an expensive bag. She decided that she would take a taxi to the home, but she would stop on the way and buy some cakes and sweets for the nurses and patients. They

160

would all be upset and it was the only practical thing she could do.

Ben wandered along the rows of cages. His mind was hardly on the task. Normally, he would have been keenly interested, because there were a lot of good cats here – one or two whose owners he envied. He had his eye on a beautiful Persian blue. It was a tom and would be a perfect mate for Bella, though he doubted the owner could be persuaded to part with his prize cat. Maybe there were some kittens in the offing though...

He frowned as he stood by one of the cats. Something was nagging at him but he couldn't think what it was for the life of him. He knew it had to do with what was going on in New York, but he wasn't sure if it was the van Allen case or the Playboy Murders that were bothering him.

Maybe he should have telephoned Sarah, told her that Hudson suspected that Annabel Lawson's attacker was the Playboy Murderer. It wasn't his case and he had hesitated to break a confidence, but if anything happened to Sarah he would blame himself. Not that she would go near the place. She had more sense than that, of course she did! After what had happened, she would give the wretched place a wide berth!

Besides, he didn't necessarily agree with Hudson on this; it didn't follow that it was the same man just because they thought it was the gun that had been used in the earlier murders. It could easily have been ditched and found by someone else, or simply sold on, which was often the case in the criminal world.

His frown eased. He walked back to the cage containing the cat he had liked best from the beginning and pinned the blue ribbon to it. He could have done that ten minutes ago, but it might have seemed rude not to give the others their due consideration. Not that it would please anyone but the owner anyway. He smiled inwardly. Having been on the judging side, he'd seen things from a different point of view. Cathy was always telling him that he shouldn't suspect the worse every time Bella lost first place to another cat, and perhaps she was right.

Thinking of his wife, he realized that he had been away from her long enough. Postcards and a greetings telegram weren't enough. He would have to get his passage booked, otherwise he might find himself on the end of a divorce suit when he got back...

Maura paced about the small room. She was going mad caged up in here. She couldn't stand it much longer. She looked at the jug Eddie had brought her the previous night. It had been full of water but now it was empty. She had drained the coffee jug he'd brought her and eaten the toast and cookies he'd left for her and she was still hungry and thirsty.

When was he coming back? He had been gone longer than usual and she was afraid he had abandoned her for good.

She went to the door, tugging at it furiously. It wouldn't budge. She banged on it, screaming his name again and again. Damn him! Why didn't he come? Was he going to leave her here to die of thirst and hunger? She looked at the window. It was locked by means of a nail through the frame. He'd done that the first night he brought her here – for her protection, he'd said then, but now she knew it was to keep her a prisoner.

She had asked him over and over again to let her go, but he wouldn't. He just kept saying that the police would put her in prison. Maura sobbed in frustration as she went back to the bed. Even prison would be better than being left to starve to death. She would rather he killed her!

She had to get out of here! Next time he came she would attack him with something – the empty water jug. She didn't care if he hit her, she would hit him back and scratch and bite ... anything to get out of this place. She hadn't washed properly for days and she could smell the stink of her own urine in the bucket he'd given her.

'Damn you, Eddie Reeder,' she muttered. 'I don't care what you do. If I had a knife sharp enough I would kill you.'

He was careful not to give her things like that, because he knew she was getting desperate. Why was he keeping her here? Why didn't he just let her go and take her chances?

He had to have a guilty secret he was afraid she knew. He was afraid that the police would believe she was innocent – and that he had killed that horrible man! Maura shuddered. Why had she ever gone out with that rotten man? She ought to have known that he wouldn't do the things he'd promised, but a part of her had wanted to believe he was a movie producer. She had wanted to believe he was going to make her a star.

She should have known he wanted only one thing. Even that might have been better than this ... She tensed as she heard someone coming. At last! He was coming back. He hadn't decided to let her starve just yet. She picked up the jug, her nerves coiled like a spring as she stood just inside the door.

He opened it and came in. He was carrying a basket of fresh fruit and a brown paper bag containing some buns that smelled so good that her mouth watered.

'Put that jug down,' Eddie said, eyeing her coldly. 'Don't even think about trying to escape, Maura. Your picture is all over the city. You wouldn't get far before the police arrested you.'

'I don't care. I don't care if I go to prison...' She advanced on him with the jug in her hand. 'Let me out of here or I'll—'

He moved towards her so swiftly that she

wasn't prepared. He caught her arm and twisted it so that she cried out in pain and dropped the jug. It broke in two at her feet. Eddie jerked her arm higher so that she screamed.

'I warned you not to try anything. I'm not him – you can't blind me with your promises of sex ... I'm not interested in girls like you.'

'I didn't promise him sex,' Maura cried. 'I'm not that kind of a girl.' Her accent was strong, muffled by tears. 'Sure, I wish I'd never met him, so I do – or you.'

'I'm not like him. I don't ruin young women the way he did. I don't want to hurt you, Maura.' His voice was soft, persuasive. 'You just have to trust me for a little longer and then you'll be free. I promise you, you'll be free.'

'How long?' she demanded. 'How much longer are you going to keep me here?'

'A week or so. I can't leave before that,' Eddie said. 'When I'm ready I'll leave New York and I'll take you with me. I'll get you a berth on a ship for England. You would like that, wouldn't you?'

She looked at him suspiciously. 'You don't mean that ... you're just trying to keep me sweet.'

Eddie grinned. 'You don't smell very sweet. If you promise to be a good girl I'll let you have a bath – and tomorrow I'll be here with you. Sam gave me the day off. I'll cook us a meal. Be nice, Maura. I promise I'll look after you.'

She looked at him through tear-laden eyes. 'I can really have a bath – and you'll let me go to England?'

'I promise,' he said. 'I haven't been sure what to do. I can't tell you about it, but I never meant to hurt you. If you promise to be good I'll help you get away. Give me your word now, Maura.'

'I had a job promised me – a new life...' She looked at him resentfully.

'And you will have. I need money and I've got some coming to me. When we get to England, I'll buy you a lot of new things, and I'll give you some money to make up for all this – you just have to trust me, Maura.'

'All right,' she said, because there was nothing more she could say. 'I'll do whatever you tell me.'

'Good girl,' he said, and smiled, reaching out to touch her cheek. 'You know, you're quite pretty. You'll look better when you've had a bath. I've brought you something to wear.'

'You bought me some clothes?'

'Borrowed them from the theatre,' Eddie said. 'Your friend has been worried about you, Maura. If you wanted to write her a note I could give it to her – or at least put it where she will find it.'

'You would do that?'

'Why not? It would save Sarah being so worried, and you are all right, aren't you? I haven't hurt you. I've fed you and you're safe.'

'Yes...' Maura bit her lip. When he was like this she believed he was trying to help her, but when he left her for hours on her own the fears came back. Could she really trust him? Had that blow to the head killed Mr van Allen – if that was his name. She didn't know if she could trust her own memory, because sometimes her mind went hazy when she needed something to eat or drink. 'I should like a bath, Eddie. I promise I'll be good.'

'I'll be watching you,' he said. 'If you try to leave I shall stop you – and you might not like what happens then.'

'Why don't you want me to leave?' she asked.

'Because I should be in trouble for helping you,' Eddie said. 'You're the one who killed him, Maura – but if the police get you and you talk I shall go to prison too.'

'I wouldn't,' she breathed. 'I promise I wouldn't.'

'You won't get the opportunity. You want to go to England, and that's where you're going. Just trust me and everything will be all right.'

'It was so kind of you to come and to bring all these things,' Matron said. 'The news was so shocking that we are all still stunned. This place relies on money from Mrs Lawson. I

167

have no idea what will happen to it if—'
Miss Whitelaw shuddered. 'We mustn't
think about that, because she is going to be
all right. In the meantime, I know the girls
will love these treats you've brought for
them. Especially Lucy. Mrs Lawson is the
only one who ever gets through to her, you
know. She loves those chocolate toffees.'

'Oh ... is that the girl who is a little bit
confused sometimes?'

'Most of the time, actually,' Matron said.
'She was in her room last time you came but
today she is much better. Would you like to
meet her? You could give her the toffees.'

'Oh yes, I should,' Sarah said. 'Annabel
told me about her and I haven't been able to
put her out of my mind. Where is she?'

'That's her – sitting out on that bench. It's
her favourite place and the garden is quite
secure at the back.' Matron frowned. 'We
shall have to be more careful now though,
because that madman might come back. I
can't help wondering why he chose to attack
Mrs Lawson. She is one of the nicest people
I know.'

'She certainly didn't deserve what happened,' Sarah said. 'Perhaps it was simply that
she refused to give up her purse.'

'We found it after he fled, you know. There
were four hundred dollars inside. She always
gives us four hundred dollars at the end of
the month. It's what we use for everyday
expenses.'

'That explains why she didn't want to let go,' Sarah said. 'But it wasn't worth her life.'

'No, it certainly wasn't,' Matron agreed. 'I know we need every penny we can get, but we need Annabel more.'

'I was wondering whether there was anything I could do for you while she is ill? I shall be leaving New York in a week's time, but before that I could arrange something.'

'We need funds all the time. If you lived here I would suggest a fundraising party of some kind.'

'We could give a concert before I leave,' Sarah said impulsively. 'Annabel wanted us to do it at her house, but Sam might let me have the theatre. We could have some refreshments and charge something for the tickets – and my mother might step in for a while. I know she helps out with various charity affairs. She might help you if I ask her.'

'That would be so kind,' Matron said. 'Why don't you go out and talk to Lucy now? She is quite harmless. Even when she is in one of her black moods she never tries to hurt anyone other than herself.'

Sarah nodded. She left Matron's private sitting room through the French windows, walking up to the girl sitting alone on the bench. Lucy seemed absorbed in watching some birds on the lawn. They were feeding on breadcrumbs and the girl's face reflected pleasure as she watched them.

'Hello, Lucy,' Sarah said. 'Are you watching the birds?'

Lucy turned to look at her. She was a pretty girl with fair hair, but one side of her face was scarred. It looked as if something hot had touched her skin, burning deeply into the flesh. She had obviously healed long since, but it was still yellowed and puckered, marring what ought to have been a beautiful face.

'I like birds,' Lucy said, her tone flat and without emotion. 'Who are you? I haven't seen you before.'

'I'm a friend of Annabel's. Mrs Lawson. You remember her?'

'Of course I do. I'm not mad, you know. I can't remember things and sometimes my head hurts so much that I want to die – but I'm not mad.'

'Did someone say you were?'

'They think I am here because sometimes I say things...'

'What kind of things?'

'Oh ... things,' Lucy said vaguely. 'I don't know. I don't know what happens when my head hurts. I can't remember – but I'm not mad.'

'No, I don't think you are,' Sarah replied. She placed the bag of toffees on the seat beside Lucy. 'May I sit with you for a while?'

'If you want...' Lucy turned her head to look at the birds again. She appeared to have lost interest in Sarah.

Sarah watched the birds with her. It was fascinating to see the way they chattered and fought over the food left out for them.

'He did it on purpose, you know.'

'Did he?' Sarah wasn't sure what she meant. And then something told her Lucy was referring to her face. 'I wouldn't do what he told me so he held a hot flatiron to my cheek. It hurt so much that I begged him to stop but he just kept it there until I fainted – and then he went out and left me. I ran away, but the pain was so bad that I got ill.'

'Who did that to you, Lucy?' Sarah felt the horror curl inside her. 'Who did such a terrible thing?'

'He said I had to tell who gave me the child, because he didn't believe me when I said it was the other one,' Lucy said in that same flat tone. 'He wanted to kill him, but I wouldn't tell ... I never told ... even when he did it...'

'You were very brave. But who did it to you?'

Lucy looked at her for a moment. 'You believe me, don't you?'

'Yes, I do. He deserves to be punished for what he did to you.'

'That is what my father said, but I would not tell him the name of my lover,' Lucy said. 'I never told him. I shan't tell you...'

'Are you saying that your father did that to you because you had an illegitimate child?'

'I never told,' Lucy said, her eyes becoming glazed. 'I never told anyone –except her...' She picked up the packet of toffees and unwrapped one, popping it into her mouth. 'I like these. When is Annabel coming?'

'When she can,' Sarah said. 'She isn't very well...'

'He hurt her, didn't he?' Lucy's hand trembled. 'I saw him from my window. He hurt her...'

'You saw it happen?' Sarah asked. 'You have to tell someone, Lucy! What did he look like?'

'No!' Lucy got to her feet, her eyes suddenly scared. 'I never told ... I won't tell. He would come back for me ... he would hurt me—' She suddenly took off and ran across the lawn, disappearing into the house.

Sarah got to her feet and followed more slowly, walking into the house and the little reception area. Lucy had disappeared. She had been frightened because she had seen what happened from her window. Lucy had suffered too much herself. It had upset her to see her friend gunned down in such a wicked way. She couldn't have meant what she had seemed to say. It wasn't possible...

'Lucy has gone to her room,' Matron said, coming out of her office to join Sarah in the reception hall. 'Don't look so upset, Miss Beaufort. It happens all the time. She seems perfectly well and then she starts to say things ... her mind goes and she makes all kinds of accusations about people.'

'Does she say her father did that to her face?'

'Her father is dead, Miss Beaufort. He was killed in a riot at a factory. It closed down and a lot of men were thrown out of work. Lucy Barrett's father was one of the those who were killed in the fighting that broke out when they closed the gates. She turned up here months later with a fresh wound to her face. It couldn't have been her father.'

'Oh, I see.' Sarah frowned. 'She seemed to be saying it was him, but if he was dead before it happened...'

'She was in service with Mrs van Allen,' Matron said. 'She became pregnant and lost her job. No one knows quite where she went after that, but she lost the child – at least we think that is what happened. And then she was found on the streets, wandering, her mind gone, her face burned so badly that there was little the doctors could do. It is a shame because she was a pretty girl.'

'She still is apart from the scar,' Sarah said. 'I wonder why she thinks it was her father who hurt her?'

'She doesn't know anything really. She seems to be talking sense, but she isn't – at least, that is what the doctors say.'

'And it is certain that her father was killed in the riot?'

'His name is on a pauper's grave somewhere. He was buried by the city administrators because there was no one to pay for the burial.'

'I see. It was a terrible thing to do, whoever did it.'

'Yes, it was. I imagine it tipped her over the edge.'

'Yes.' Sarah smiled at her. 'Would you mind if I rang for a cab from here? I don't want to chance picking one up on the street.'

'No, of course not. Thank you for offering to help. We shall be pleased if Mrs Harland would consider helping out, even on a temporary basis.'

'I'll ask her what she can do,' Sarah promised. 'And I shall talk to Sam – see if we can arrange a little concert before I leave. If not we could always do it when I return.'

'How kind,' Matron said. 'Do come and see us again. I know Lucy is a little difficult, but she doesn't get visitors.'

'I shall visit her again,' Sarah promised.

She was thoughtful as she rang for her taxi and she was still wrapped in thought as she was driven back to her stepfather's house. Matron was certain that Lucy's father had been killed in those riots, but Sarah had seen the expression on Lucy's face when just for a few minutes she had allowed herself to remember. She'd asked if Sarah believed her and despite everything Matron had said afterwards Sarah could not help thinking that Lucy had known exactly what she said...

* ★ ★

'A charity concert?' Sam looked at her through narrowed eyes. 'You're not serious? That takes weeks to arrange.'

'It needn't,' Sarah told him. 'Annabel intended to hold it at her home. It was meant to be a small affair and she was giving a dinner. We could put on a show and provide some refreshments backstage, couldn't we? It would only be like an end of show party – before we join the cruise?'

'That gives us six days. How do you advertise an event like that in six days?'

'We telephone Annabel's friends,' Sarah said. 'Mummy knows them all, because they are her friends too. They won't expect too much, because they know it is for charity.'

Sam glared at her. 'If I have anything to do with it, it will be a professional production.'

'But we could all do the things we are going to do on the ship,' Sarah said. 'It will be like a last dress rehearsal only in front of friends. Please, Sam. Even if it only raises a few hundred dollars it will be welcome. Annabel wasn't expecting too much.'

'Are you twisting my arm, Sarah?'

'Yes, if you will let me.' She got up to pour some more coffee. It was Sunday and she had invited him to lunch at her stepfather's home, and now they were sitting on the back porch enjoying the sunshine. 'I know it is a lot to ask, but we could do it – couldn't we?'

'You know that the theatre owners might

175

have something to say? We only have the use of the theatre during the mornings.'

'Couldn't we have it for one performance? I thought they didn't have a show on this Friday night? Didn't someone say it was changing over to a new revue on Saturday?'

'The reason there is no show is because the new production wants to put up its own set.'

'Couldn't they do it after we leave? We could hold the show at seven and be out of the theatre by ten ... or eleven...'

'That would mean getting the set changers to work through the night to be ready for the Saturday matinee.'

'I suppose it is asking too much,' Sarah said with a sigh. 'I thought you might be able to swing it, but if you can't...'

'You, Miss Sarah Beaufort, are a witch,' Sam muttered. 'What chance do I have when you look at me like that?'

'You mean you will do it?'

'Yeah, I'll have a word. I just hope your friends come through with the money – and you'll have to speak to the cast yourself. I don't ask favours.'

'I already have,' Sarah told him, with a naughty smile. 'Katie was the first to agree and then the others said they would go along with it if you said yes.'

'It will make things tight for the props,' Sam said. 'You'll need your costumes and I'd planned to ship them off on Friday, but they can be packed after the show.' He glared at her. 'Do you know how much you're asking, Sarah?'

'Yes, Mr Garson,' she said, and laughed up at him. 'It's really good of you—' She gasped as he reached out and grabbed her, kissing her hard on the mouth. 'Oh ... Sam...!'

'Don't look like that,' he muttered. 'I'm not about to ravish you in your mother's back garden. I'm not saying I wouldn't enjoy ravishing you anywhere, but I know better than to try. You're a marriage or nothing kind of girl, Sarah. I am aware of that, but you owed me something.'

'Yes, perhaps I did,' Sarah said. 'I am grateful for what you're doing, Sam. These girls really need help.'

'Yeah, I know,' Sam replied. 'You haven't heard anything about that girl who worked for your mother yet?'

'No.' Sarah shivered, an odd expression coming into her eyes. 'I am afraid she may be suffering somewhere...'

'What makes you look like that – was it the girl you spoke to at the home yesterday?'

'Yes...' Sarah frowned. 'Matron says her father is dead. Lucy says her father burned her face with a flatiron because she wouldn't tell him who gave her the child, but Matron says her father was dead before her face was burned. He was supposed to have died in some riots at a factory that closed down.'

'I remember hearing about that,' Sam said.

'It happened about a year – no, more like eighteen months ago. I know four or five men were killed at the time and at least fifty injured. It was bad...'

'Why did it close down?'

'The new owner of the property tore it down to build a fancy nightclub. A lot of people thought he had no right, but he had influence and he got his way. At least, that was the intention but it may not have come down yet. I think the whole area is derelict.'

'I see.' Sarah frowned. 'If so many men were injured or killed could there have been a mix-up over names?'

'It happens,' Sam said wryly. 'What's going on in that beautiful head of yours, sweetheart?'

'I'm not sure yet,' Sarah replied, 'but I think Lucy may be right. I know her mind is confused and she has her bad times, but I think she knows who hurt her. She didn't mean to tell me. She didn't realize she had, but it slipped out in a muddled way. I think her father did do that to her, Sam – and I think he is alive somewhere in the city.'

'Why do I think that is a bad thing?'

'I don't know, but I feel that way too,' Sarah said. 'If everyone thinks he is dead, he is at liberty to come and go as he pleases. He could do whatever he liked and no one would know it was him. They wouldn't look for him and so they wouldn't find him...'

'That makes sense in a mad kinda way,'

Sam agreed. 'But I don't know where it is leading to – do you?'

'No, not really,' Sarah agreed, and laughed. 'Oh, don't let's talk about it! We have far more interesting things to talk about, don't we?'

'We sure do,' Sam agreed, his gaze centring on her face.

Something in the way he looked at her made Sarah feel that he didn't mean just the show or the charity event she had persuaded him to put on at such short notice.

Lucas Barrett nursed the jug of rot-gut whisky he had bought in the speakeasy. It tasted worse than anything he'd ever drunk in his life but it warmed his guts. He knew that he had made a terrible mistake when he went after that woman. He hadn't planned it enough and it had almost brought him down. In his heart he didn't care what they did to him when he was done – but he had to find Lucy first. He had to find his little girl and beg her to forgive him.

He lifted the jug of illicit whisky to his lips and drank deeply. He could feel the rough spirit warming away the ache inside him, robbing him of the power to remember. He didn't like to remember what he'd done that night. He loved his Lucy. He hadn't meant to hurt her that way. God forgive him! He'd been out of his mind with bitterness and the drink.

He had always been too fond of the drink, even when his wife and children were alive, but they had kept him straight. He hadn't slipped much in those days. It was after he lost his job, after his wife and babies died of the fever that he had turned to the drink.

Lucy would never have given in to the devil that made her pregnant if he hadn't forced her to find a job – a job with the wife of the man who had thrown him out of work. He'd thought it justice then. He'd hated the very name, but Lucy had disappeared one night, and found herself a job because she was sick of living the way they did. And it was because of that job – that man! – that she had got into trouble. He had suspected it from the start. He'd gone on at her, threatening her with what would happen if she didn't tell him. If Lucy hadn't refused to tell him who the father of her child was he wouldn't have hurt her. She had made him angry and he'd been drinking. It was his fault she had run off that night...

Tears of self-pity slipped down his face as he admitted the truth to himself. He clutched the jug to his chest as the self-pity and remorse seeped over him. He wasn't a bad man. He would never have done all those things if they hadn't driven him to it ... those idle rich bastards who didn't care about anyone else. They had driven him down and down until he had rebelled. He hadn't gone to that house to murder anyone the day he started to kill people. He had thought it still belonged to van Allen. He hadn't known that it had been sold a few weeks earlier. He had meant to ask humbly for a job, but when he'd seen the way those people squandered money ... seen the way they behaved ... he had lost his head. He'd found the gun and ammunition just lying there in one of the rooms he'd gone into and he'd picked it up. After that he hardly remembered what he'd done, but he knew it had made him feel good. He knew that he'd done it again and again – but now he'd lost the gun and he had no money to buy another.

He wasn't sure what he wanted now, but for tonight he was going to drink himself into a state of forgetfulness...

Six

Sarah was surprised at the enthusiasm her mother showed in contacting Annabel's friends, because she had thought her mother might not feel that the home for fallen women was something she wanted to support. However, the attack on Annabel had aroused Mrs Harland's fighting spirit. She threw herself into the task, and soon discovered that everyone felt much the same.

'We are all angry at what happened,' Mrs Harland explained. 'I think you will find that your party will turn out very well, Sarah. I've contracted my caterer, because you can't expect people to eat sausages and cheese rolls at this sort of thing. Besides, it is a lot of work.'

'But we want to make as much money as possible, Mummy.'

'Of course you do, my darling. You can take this as my little contribution – and we shall all be there to support you. Philip and Brad have rallied a few of their friends too so I am sure it will be a success.'

Sarah flew to hug her. 'You are a darling, Mummy! I thought you might not like the idea of my having anything to do with that home.'

'Well, I can't forbid you, and, actually I do think it a good cause. You're old enough to be sensible, Sarah. All I ask is that you take care.' Mrs Harland shuddered. 'After what happened to Annabel...'

'I shall be careful,' Sarah promised. She didn't add that her shadow seemed to have gone missing the last couple of days, because her mother didn't know anything about it. 'I telephoned the hospital and they said Annabel is conscious now. She asked if I would go in so I may be late home this afternoon.'

'Thank you for telling me, Sarah. If you hadn't I might have started to worry.'

'Please try not to, Mummy,' Sarah said. 'I am very aware of the dangers and I do try not to take risks. I never go out with strangers the way some of the girls do, and when I do go it is always with a party of friends.'

'As I said, you are old enough to be sensible, but if anything happened to you while you were here your father would never forgive me.'

'No, he wouldn't,' Sarah agreed, and laughed. 'He would keep me wrapped in cotton wool if he could, I expect.'

She smiled as she left her mother and went out to the waiting taxicab. Only three more days of rehearsals and they would put on their charity show. It would be a good test for the success of their show before they left to join the ship. She was excited about it, and she was looking forward to seeing Larch at the exhibition of his work later that evening. She had hardly seen him for days, because he was spending all his spare time at Annabel's bedside.

Sarah couldn't grudge the time Larch was devoting to his friend, because Annabel had hovered between life and death for a while. He was naturally worried about her. However, she did miss him, and she couldn't help wishing that they had managed to have more time together while he was in New York.

'You mustn't neglect your work for my sake,' Annabel whispered, as she lay propped up against the pillows. She was in a small, private room, surrounded by vases of beautiful flowers, a large bowl of fruit on the chest beside her bed. She looked pale but still beautiful. 'Please go now, Larch. I know you must have so much to do before this evening.'

'I have meetings,' Larch admitted. 'I don't like deserting you, but I must if I am to keep my word to the gallery owner.'

'Yes, of course.' Her hand lay limply in his as she gave him what was a ghost of her former smile. 'Sarah is coming to see me this afternoon.'

'I knew she wanted to,' he said. 'She is working hard for this charity event they are putting on, on Friday night. It was short notice, but I understand that everyone has been brilliant. All your friends are either attending or buying tickets anyway.'

'Sarah is a nice girl,' Annabel said. She coughed gingerly because it hurt. 'I think I need to rest, Larch.'

'I'll leave you to sleep,' he said. 'I shall come tomorrow.'

Annabel's eyes were closing as he went out. He saw the doctor who had been caring for her approaching along the corridor and went to meet him.

'She seems very tired still,' he said. 'Is she really out of the woods, Doctor?'

'The crisis is over, if that is what you mean,' the doctor replied. 'But she was damaged internally, Mr Meadows. She may never truly be out of the woods, as you term it. She will need rest and care. Quite a lot of care, actually. I think she may be an invalid for some months, perhaps for the rest of her life. Her lungs were damaged as well as other things. I don't think she should live alone for a while. It's just as well she has you.'

'What do you mean?'

'Well, you are her fiancé, aren't you?'

'Just a very good friend actually,' Larch said, and frowned. 'Annabel has her maid, cook and a chauffeur, but ... I need to think

185

about this. Thank you for telling me, Doctor. Something will need to be arranged.'

Larch was thoughtful as he left the hospital and began to walk to the gallery, which was a matter of five streets away. He had originally planned to leave New York soon after his exhibition closed. He had hoped that Sarah might have agreed to be his wife in the meantime and that he might be planning his wedding for the autumn or Christmas at the latest – but Sarah hadn't given him an answer and Annabel needed him.

He was a free agent. He could come and go as he wished, because although his parents were always very pleased to see him, they never interfered in his life. If he told them he was staying in New York for a while they would accept it – and he could work in Annabel's studio. Perhaps when she was able to leave hospital he could take her away somewhere, help her over this difficult period in her life.

Larch believed that Sarah would understand. If Annabel had had family, someone who really cared what happened to her, he would have wished her well and left her to them. However, she needed a friend to stand by her. Larch had known what it was like to lie in a hospital bed and feel utterly alone. His war experiences were still lodged somewhere at the back of his mind. It was a while since he'd had one of his nightmare attacks when he felt himself back on the battlefields of Flanders. The last time had been when he carried Ronnie Miller from the woods on that freezing day two winters ago. But the memories would never leave him. He doubted that any of the men who had fought in the trenches of the Great War would ever truly forget.

He hadn't deserted his comrades under fire, and he wouldn't desert Annabel now. Besides, Sarah was having too much fun to feel hurt because he was spending time with a friend. He wasn't even sure that she wanted to marry him.

Sarah stopped to buy a box of special sweets, a couple of fashion magazines and some cologne that might come in handy if Annabel felt a headache coming on. Hospitals were stuffy and often too warm in Sarah's experience, and it was nice to have cologne for your handkerchief.

When she entered the room where Annabel lay propped up against a pile of snowy pillows, she saw that her friend was awake, though looking very pale and fragile.

'Annabel, how are you feeling?'

'Sarah...' a small smile lit Annabel's eyes. 'It is so good of you to visit.'

'I wanted to come the first day, but they said only one visitor and Larch was here all the time.'

'He has been wonderful,' Annabel said. 'A really good friend. I couldn't have asked for more even if—' She broke off and shook her head. 'Are these all for me?' She glanced at the little pile of presents that Sarah placed on the cabinet beside her. 'You are so sweet to me. I have been overwhelmed with gifts ... all these lovely flowers. They had to take some away because the perfume was making my head ache.'

'This cologne may help,' Sarah said. 'Gran always uses it when she has one, and I do too sometimes. Is there anything I can do for you, Annabel? Do you need anything from home?'

'My maid has been in several times,' Annabel said. 'It is kind of you to enquire, but you are already doing more than I could have asked, Sarah. This charity show will be such a help to us.'

'I hope it will be a success. Mummy has phoned simply everyone. Even Philip and Brad have got involved – and that is something. Brad isn't into these things as a rule. Everyone is so angry about what happened to you.'

'Yes, I know...' Annabel frowned. 'The doctors let me talk to the police for the first time this morning – but I couldn't help them much. I remember that someone tried to take my purse and I wouldn't let go – and then he pulled a gun from under his coat and shot me. I don't remember what he looked like ... but there was a strong smell.'

'What kind of a smell?'

'Oh ... not a very nice one. Perhaps he hadn't washed for a while, something like that...'

'He might have been a tramp, perhaps,' Sarah suggested.

'Do tramps carry guns?' Annabel sighed. 'In the course of my charity work I've dealt with poor people, men as well as women, but I've never been attacked before. Poverty doesn't make someone a thief or a murderer, Sarah. It takes something more.'

'Yes, I am sure you are right, and I am certain you don't want to talk about it to me. Let me tell you about the show we are putting on instead. Sam has been absolutely marvellous. We couldn't have done it without him.'

'He is your producer?'

'Director, producer, bully and defender,' Sarah said, and laughed. 'He runs the whole thing. I don't know how he does it but he manages to get the best out of us all.'

'That sounds as if you like him rather a lot?'

'Yes, I do like Sam,' Sarah agreed. 'When we first met I wasn't sure if I could work with him, but I've got to know him better and I understand why he says the things he does.'

'And do you intend to go on with your work – or will you get married soon?'

'Oh, I don't know,' Sarah said, and blushed. 'I have this cruise first and, well, I'm not sure yet...'

'Perhaps I shouldn't have asked,' Annabel said. 'Forgive me?'

'Of course,' Sarah smiled. 'I just haven't thought about it much.' And that wasn't true at all! She had thought about it a lot, but the more she thought the more confused she became. She would be seeing Larch that evening and she hoped he wouldn't ask her again, because she still didn't feel able to answer.

'So there you are,' Ben said as he joined Detective Hudson for a drink on his return from Newport. 'I am fairly certain he is the van Allen heir. He looks older, naturally, and I think he has darkened his hair, but I would say it is van Allen. If it is, why doesn't he go home and claim his inheritance? Unless his father cut him out of his will?'

Hudson grimaced. 'After you told me of your suspicions, I asked the lawyers about that and it seems the estate is divided between Mrs van Allen and her son. It was made twenty years ago and hasn't been touched since.'

'Fortunate for the son,' Ben said, and frowned. 'You say you are watching him? Has your officer seen anything suspicious yet?'

'Nothing. We'll keep a watch for the moment. He seems to go to the theatre each morning, spends most of his day there.

Sometimes he goes for coffee or lunch with one of the girls, and at night he goes home and stays there. He seems to be a normal, decent, clean-living man. We can't arrest him for that, Marshall.'

'No, of course not. Well, we may have had it all wrong. If he is in the clear you might have to think about the father of one of the girls he led astray. Do you have any clues in that direction?'

'We're working on it,' Hudson said. 'And I've got an officer watching Miss Beaufort, but as yet we haven't seen anyone following her.'

'Good,' Ben said, and smiled. 'She is leaving New York on Sunday so if you can keep her safe until then she will be in the clear.'

'I wish all my cases were as easy.'

'No more news on the Playboy Murderer?'

'Not yet, but again, we're working on it. The wheels of justice are exceedingly slow at times.'

'You don't have to tell me that, I had cases that stayed on the books for years when I was at the Yard – some of them never did get cleared up to my satisfaction.'

'I'm a terrier when I get hold of something. I never let go, even if it takes a long time.'

'Well, I'll leave you to it and wish you good luck,' Ben said. 'I thought I would just check again on my return from Newport. I took a look at the house where the first of those murders took place while I was there. Not that there is much to see, because it is boarded up and has a "for sale" sign in the grounds, but I can't see anyone wanting to buy it after what happened there.'

'Oh, you never know,' Hudson said. 'Some people like that kind of thing. Have a good trip home, Marshall.'

Ben was thoughtful as he left. Hudson seemed convinced the van Allen heir was in the clear, but if it had been him he would have brought him in for a chat anyway. However, it wasn't his investigation, and he'd interfered enough already. It would be best just to forget about it now. After all, Sarah would soon be at sea and away from whoever had been following her for a while, and he doubted that Maura would be found. She was either dead or deliberately hiding – and that wasn't his case either!

'I love this picture,' Sarah exclaimed, as she stood before a large landscape of the Cornish coast that evening. 'The way you've painted it – on a winter's day, captured the wildness ... the loneliness of a windswept beach. It is beautiful.' Sarah didn't know why the picture seemed to touch her soul, but it did ... made her feel that she wanted to reach out to the man who had painted it, because there was so much of him in it. If they had been alone she might have put her arms around him, but in a room full of people it was impossible. 'It is Daddy's birthday soon. I think I should like to buy it for him – if no one else has claimed it already?'

'Several people have shown an interest,' Larch said with a smile, 'but I'll tell them to put your name on it, Sarah – and you don't have to buy it. You like it, so it is yours.'

'Larch...' the protest died on her lips. 'You are too generous. Thank you. I love it and I know Daddy will treasure it.'

'I painted it when I was missing you,' Larch told her, with a lopsided smile. 'So in a way it was always meant for you.'

'Oh...' Sarah held her breath but he didn't say anything more. 'I visited Annabel this morning,' she said, changing the subject. 'She seemed very tired but happy you had been visiting her regularly, Larch.'

'I've been meaning to talk to you about that,' Larch said. 'I think she is going to need a lot of care. I know she can afford nurses, but she needs a friend, someone she can talk to...' He hesitated, then, 'I intended to go back to England after the show but if Annabel needs me I may stay on for a while.'

'Yes, I think you should,' Sarah said. 'You know that I am leaving New York for the ship soon, but when I come back I should be happy to help.'

'You won't mind that I ... well, I haven't been around for you since Annabel was hurt? You do understand, Sarah? It isn't that

I don't want to see you, but I feel that I must give Annabel my undivided attention for the moment. She has no one else.'

'Yes, of course I understand,' Sarah said. She banished the little voice that said Annabel had lots of other friends, because she didn't have anyone else like Larch. Larch was special. He would be there for Annabel as long as she needed him. It would be selfish and mean of Sarah to resent that, and she wouldn't, because if she had given Larch her promise in the first place they would have been engaged. Annabel had obviously assumed that he was her special friend, and to make a fuss at a time like this would be unthinkable. 'Please don't worry about me, Larch. I am so busy with the show that I couldn't have spent much time with you anyway.'

'I thought that might be the case,' he said. 'So we'll just leave things on hold until we see how it goes?'

'Yes, of course,' Sarah replied, because there was nothing else she could say. She felt a little hurt, though she knew she really ought not to, because Larch was just being Larch – and he wouldn't be her very best friend if he were any other way.

'There really isn't any reason for me to stay around any longer,' Ben told Sarah when he came to dinner that evening. 'I've spoken to Hudson, told him my thoughts and there's nothing more I can do here. So I've booked a passage leaving on Saturday on the Princess State Line, I think it is called the *Star Fish* or something like that...' His eyebrows lifted as he saw the expression in Sarah's eyes. 'What did I say?'

'That's the ship we're on,' Sarah told him. 'What a coincidence! I didn't know there were any berths left. I did enquire because—' Sarah shook her head. 'I was told it was fully booked.'

'Yes, it was,' Ben agreed. 'A cancellation had just come in, and I was able to book at something less than the full price, which means I get a first-class cabin for the price of an inside one. I thought it was a bit of luck, but I had no idea you would be travelling on it too.'

'Oh, that is lovely. Did you hear that, Mummy? Ben is travelling back to England on the same ship as me.'

'Well, that will be pleasant,' Mrs Harland said, as she brought in the coffee. 'Larch told me it was fully booked a week ago...'

'Larch told you that?' Sarah frowned. 'Was he thinking of making the trip? He didn't say anything to me.'

'Well, I am not sure what happened, but he did mention it to me,' her mother said. 'Sugar and cream, Mr Marshall?'

'Yes, please.'

'Larch has decided to stay on longer because of Annabel,' Sarah said, feeling disappointed. 'It would have been lovely if he had been with us too.'

'It is very kind of Larch to stay for Annabel's sake,' Mrs Harland said. 'I popped in this afternoon, Sarah. Her doctor has told her that she is going to need a lot of rest. He has recommended a stay at the sea somewhere. She is thinking of going away once she is feeling stronger. I'm not sure if she means somewhere in this country or Europe. I suppose a cruise might be a good way of recuperating. Not to England, because it might not be warm enough, but the Bahamas or the Caribbean, something like that I imagine.'

'That would be a trip of some weeks, perhaps months...'

'Yes, I imagine it would,' Mrs Harland agreed. 'Especially if she decided to stay there for a while before returning. She might as well. After all, she has no reason to return in a hurry. I know she is involved with charity work, but someone can stand in for her.'

'Yes, I suppose so.'

Sarah was thoughtful as she sipped her coffee. Larch had warned her that he intended to be around for Annabel for as long as she needed a friend. Did that include a cruise to the Caribbean as well?

He had said they would put things on hold for a while, but she'd thought he meant a few weeks. It was going to be less than a couple of months before she returned to New York. She had expected that Larch would be ready to talk about the future by then.

It was her own fault for dithering! She should have given him her answer that first night, because she knew she was going to say yes eventually – wasn't she?

Ben was talking to her mother about the charity concert. Sarah considered whether she should tell Ben about her visit to the home for fallen women, and her ideas about Lucy Barrett's father being alive. But there was nothing he could do, and the other ideas she'd had seemed foolish when she'd thought them through a bit more. So there wasn't any point in saying anything to anyone. After all, it was very unlikely that Lucy Barrett's father and the Playboy Murderer could be the same man. She didn't know why it had even occurred to her that he might be...

'You have to be ready tonight,' Eddie told Maura when he entered her room that Friday morning. 'I've thought of a way to smuggle you out of the city, but you will need to trust me.'

'What do you mean?' She looked at him suspiciously. 'What are you going to do to me?'

'Nothing that will hurt you,' he told her. 'I'm going to smuggle you out in one of the baskets they will need for the show onboard ship. But if you make a sound you'll give it all away and then you'll be in trouble.'

'So ... what does that mean?' Maura held her breath, because she was afraid of what he was going to say next. 'You won't hurt me, will you?'

'Why should I hurt you?' Eddie said, a flash of annoyance in his voice. 'If I wanted you dead I could have killed you ages ago.' He gave her an angry look. 'If you're not prepared to trust me you can leave now – go on, take your chance on the streets and see if the cops believe one word you say.'

Maura looked at the door. Would he let her go if she made a dash for it or would he turn nasty? Faced with the offer of freedom she was suddenly doubtful. Maybe she had killed that man when she hit him.

'I didn't mean to make you angry. I'm scared.' She sat on the edge of the bed. 'Sure, and I don't know what to do...'

'Then you will just have to trust me, won't you?'

'Yes,' she agreed in a small voice. 'I do trust you. Please, Eddie, don't be angry with me.'

'I'm going to take you into the theatre when no one is around,' Eddie told her. 'I shall give you something to make you drowsy and then I'll put you in the prop basket. You'll be taken onboard with the rest of the stuff, and once we're under way I'll come and let you out and take you to my cabin. When we get to England you can just walk off with the rest of the girls.'

Maura stared at him. He made it all sound so simple and the questions were buzzing in her head, but she stopped herself asking them. If he took her to the theatre she would be out of this place and then maybe she could get help. If Sarah was there she would ask her, because she knew Sarah would be her friend whatever happened.

Eddie was walking towards the door. Maura had a sudden icy feeling down her spine, a terrible fear overwhelming her.

'Where are you going? You will come back for me?'

'I have things to do before we leave,' Eddie said. 'I've told you to trust me, Maura. I'll be back for you later.'

She sank down on the edge of the bed as he went out and locked the door behind him. Where did he go when he left her? He must have another place somewhere else. She was shaking, icy cold. She pulled one of the bedcovers around her shoulders. She didn't know why she hadn't tried to run when he told her, but somehow she had come to rely on him. He said the police were looking for her and she had to trust him because she didn't know what else to do.

'Jonathan, where are you?' Louise van Allen spoke into the telephone. 'Someone told me they had seen you recently. If you are in New York why don't you come home?'

'I have no intention of coming back ever.'

'But why? I don't understand. You know he is dead now. He can't punish you or threaten to beat you the way he did when you were a child.'

'I wasn't afraid of him, Mother. I hadn't been for a while.'

'Then why not come home? I'm your mother and I want you here. Surely you can visit for a while just to please me ... after all I've done for you?'

'Shut up and listen. I want money. A million dollars in cash and I want it by tonight.'

'That's impossible, Jonathan. You know I can't find a huge amount of money like that so quickly. I would have to sell assets—'

'He had a load of cash stashed away. Don't pretend you didn't know, because I wouldn't believe you.'

'I don't care to be spoken to that way, Jonathan.'

'Then don't mess with me, Ma. I'm leaving America soon and I don't intend to return, at least not for a long time. I want that cash and I want it tonight.'

'I could give you what is here. I don't know how much it amounts to –' Louise frowned at her reflection in the mirror. 'I don't understand what this is all about, Jonathan. What have you done? Why can't you come home and live here with me?'

'Maybe I know things you wouldn't like anyone else to know, Ma,' he said. 'And maybe I would rather live with a rattlesnake. Have that money ready for me tonight when I come or you will be sorry.'

'Jonathan! How could you speak to your mother like that?'

Louise stared at the receiver as the line went dead. Her son had never spoken to her like that before in his life and she didn't understand it. What had happened to the little boy she had adored? Why had he turned against her?

She frowned as she looked at his photographs. What could Jonathan possibly know that she wouldn't like? She felt an icy trickle down her spine as she thought about things she wouldn't want him to know ... but he couldn't know what she had done. No one could know about that! Jonathan was just being silly. She would give him the money when he came, but he couldn't possibly mean that he was going away for ever.

Her eyes had the dead stare of a reptile as she looked back at her image in the gilt-framed mirror without seeing herself. He couldn't leave her alone after all she had done to protect him. She would talk to him this evening, make him see sense. He was her son and she wanted him home where he belonged.

★ ★ ★

'Sarah, there's a telephone call for you,' Mrs Harland said as her daughter came downstairs that morning. The usual rehearsals had been cancelled in favour of a last-minute dress rehearsal later that afternoon. 'She said she was from Larkspur House...'

Sarah took the receiver and held it to her ear. 'Sarah Beaufort speaking.'

'This is Matron – from Larkspur House. If you have a free moment today, Miss Beaufort, I wanted to speak to you. Or to be more precise, Lucy has been asking for you.'

'Oh...' Sarah hesitated, because she had a full day ahead of her. 'I could pop round for a few minutes this morning. I don't have long because we have the show this evening.'

'I know how busy you are and I wouldn't ask, but Lucy keeps asking for the lady who brought her the sweets. I don't suppose it is anything important, but it's the first time she has shown any interest in anyone so I thought if you could manage to visit before you go?'

'Yes, of course I will,' Sarah said. 'Is there anything I can bring for her – not just sweets? I wondered how she goes on for clothes and things? I have a couple of simple dresses she might like.'

'She hasn't taken much interest in her appearance up to now,' Matron said. 'But she might like to have them. You never know with someone like Lucy. She could come out of that state of confusion at any time.'

'I'll sort a few things for her and get a cab. About half an hour all right?'

'Yes, of course. It really is very kind of you, Miss Beaufort.'

'I am going away tomorrow, but when I come back I'll visit her again.'

'It's lovely of you to take an interest in the girl. She has no one else.'

Sarah was thoughtful as she went upstairs to sort out a few pretty clothes for Lucy. What could the girl have to say to her that was so important?'

Lucas woke up feeling as if he had been run over by a traction engine. His body ached all over and he felt sick. It was his own fault for going to that speakeasy. He should have known better than to indulge in that rot-gut whisky he'd bought. He stared around the filthy room. It was stacked with empty crates that had been left to moulder away, becoming bedding for the rats that frequented the derelict warehouse.

He shuddered as the pain started to gnaw at his guts. How could he bring his little girl to a place like this, even if he found her? He had to have money, enough money to pay for a couple of decent rooms and food in the cupboard – and then he would find his Lucy. He would beg her forgiveness on his knees. If she came back to him he would never do another bad thing in his life.

Tears ran down his cheeks, making little

white streaks through the ingrained dirt. It was so long since he'd felt clean. Too long, he realized, because the stench of poverty clung to him. He had to go somewhere and get cleaned up, and he needed food. He hadn't eaten for several days. Before he could do any of those things he needed money.

He tried to remember the plans he'd made a few days ago. There was a girl he had been following, a rich girl. He'd meant to kidnap her for money. He had wanted to hurt her and her family, to make them feel the way he'd felt when his wife and children had died of the fever. His thoughts were hazy. He seemed to remember that he'd done terrible things, but there was a fog in his mind and he couldn't remember.

There was a woman ... he had followed her and ... the memory hit him and he remembered that she had fought back, refusing to give up her purse. He had shot her – he could remember the way the blood had spurted all over him. It was what he could smell on his clothes; the stench of dried-in blood rather than poverty.

He needed fresh clothes, money and food. He tried to remember something. This area was rundown, derelict houses and commercial property that was due to be torn down soon. It had been bought a few months back by ... a man he had good cause to hate. The project had been put on hold for some reason. But he'd seen someone coming and going from one of the other properties. It had puzzled him, because he'd thought they were all empty. The man didn't look as if he would be sleeping rough in a place like this ... maybe the house was still furnished. He might be able to break in and steal something he could sell. He didn't want much, just enough to tide him over until he could find work again.

He had decided that Lucy would never come back to him if she knew what he'd done. He had to get himself cleaned up and then find a job, but first he needed a few dollars in his pocket so that he could make himself look respectable.

He knew the house wasn't far from here. He just had to remember which one it was ... but his head was spinning and his stomach ached. He bent over, retching as the bile rushed up his throat and spilled over in a foul torrent on the floor. He leaned against the wall feeling faint. It was difficult to think straight. When the world stopped spinning he would move, but already he was forgetting what he meant to do...

'Lucy is in her room, Miss Beaufort,' Matron said when Sarah arrived. 'I'm not sure if she will talk to you. She was fine when I rang you, but she is standing by the window staring down and she won't speak to me. I may have got you here for nothing.'

'It doesn't matter,' Sarah told her. 'I've brought the clothes anyway. Lucy is very welcome to them, because I have more than enough.'

'Your clothes are so smart...' Matron looked doubtful.

'I've only brought simple frocks,' Sarah said. 'I am sure she wouldn't feel uncomfortable in them. She is a pretty girl.'

'Yes, she is – or was,' Matron agreed. 'It was probably her pretty face that got her into so much trouble.'

'Yes, I dare say. Apart from the scar she is still pretty.'

'Yes, but who can ignore it? Lucy certainly can't.'

'No, I don't suppose she can. I just think it's a shame if she has to live shut away for the rest of her life.'

'Well, that is the way things happen.' Matron sighed. 'If you would like to go up. It's the second door at the top of the landing. Just go straight in. She won't answer if you knock.'

'Thank you for telling me,' Sarah said, but thought that she would knock anyway, because Lucy had as much right to her privacy as anyone else. She found the right door, knocked and waited, and then opened the door and looked in. Lucy was still at the window, her body rigid as she stared down at the front drive. 'Hello, Lucy, it's me – Sarah. Can you see something interesting?'

For a moment Lucy remained staring out of the window and then she turned to look at Sarah. 'I saw him kill her, you know. I told you, didn't I?'

'Yes, you did, Lucy – but she isn't dead. She was badly hurt but not killed. Have you remembered something more you wanted to tell me?'

'Did you bring me some more sweets? She always brought me sweets...' Lucy frowned, looked upset. 'Will she come again? She was nice to me.' Her eyes focused on Sarah. 'You're nice too...'

'Yes, I brought you some sweets – and some frocks, too. I think they will fit you.'

'Are they your frocks?'

'Yes, they are mine. I think you will like them.'

'Yes, thank you.' Lucy glanced down at the shapeless blue gown the home had given her. 'I hate this – it's worse than the uniform I wore for her.'

'Was she your employer, Lucy?'

'Mrs van Allen,' Lucy said. 'She said I was an evil girl. She sent me away without a reference. It is hard to find another job without a reference.'

'That was not kind of her, Lucy. If you wanted a job I could help you find one.'

'I do not think anyone would want me now.' Lucy put a hand to her face. 'My father did this to me because I would not tell him the name of the man who fathered my child.'

'Was it someone you loved, Lucy – or did he force you?'

Lucy stared at her for a moment and then she smiled. 'I loved him – and he said he loved me, but then –' a shudder ran through her – 'the other one ... raped me. He called me a slut for going with his son and he raped me. When she found out that I was having a child she was so angry...'

'Whose child was it? Mr Van Allen's or his son's?'

'It was Jonathan's,' Lucy said. 'He was lovely to me. He said he loved me, but after his father raped me he went away – and then she sent me off without a reference. I had to go home, but my father wouldn't let me rest. He was on at me all the time, asking who the father was and I wouldn't tell him. And then...' Lucy gave a little sob, putting her hand to her face. 'It hurt so much and I ran away ... the baby was dead so what did it matter?' Her eyes held a tearful appeal. 'Why did he have to do that to my face?'

'I don't know, Lucy. It was a terrible thing for anyone to do.'

'He wanted to make sure that no other man would look at me, but I wouldn't have gone with anyone else. I loved Jonathan or I wouldn't have gone with him.'

'It was a cruel thing to do,' Sarah said. 'But you could still have a life, Lucy. You don't have to stay here for ever.'

'People would stare. They would laugh and

point their fingers at me.'

'Only foolish people would do that,' Sarah said. 'I wouldn't laugh at you and nor would my mother. She would give you a job in her house.'

'No,' Lucy swung away from her and her shoulders heaved. She was crying silently. 'I don't want pity.'

'My mother would expect the work to be done well,' Sarah said. 'It wouldn't be pity, Lucy. She is always looking for a girl she can rely on.'

Lucy was silent. Sarah stared at her, wondering whether she had sent her back to one of her fits, and then the girl turned to look at her.

'Perhaps one day,' she said. 'It was him, you know – he hurt her. Annabel ... she told me to call her Annabel.'

'And I'm Sarah. Who do you mean, Lucy? Who hurt Annabel?'

'My father. I saw him try to take her bag and I saw him fire the gun. I know it was him.'

'Your father was the one who shot Annabel? Are you sure, Lucy?' Sarah felt chilled. She did not know why but she had somehow expected this, though she couldn't have said why. 'It was seeing him that made you remember the things that happened to you, wasn't it?'

A tear trickled from the corner of Lucy's eye. 'I didn't want to remember, because it hurts – but when I saw his face it came back. I wanted to tell you before but I couldn't bear it. If he finds me here ... I won't go with him. I would rather die!'

'Oh, Lucy, I am so sorry,' Sarah said. She put a hand out but Lucy stepped back, shaking her head. 'Thank you for telling me your story. There is no question of your father forcing you to go with him. When I tell the police what you've told me they will arrest him. He should be in prison ... you do understand that, don't you?'

'Yes.' Lucy's voice held a sob. 'I hate him.'

'I think I should if I were you,' Sarah agreed. 'I have to go now, Lucy. I am leaving these things for you here on the bed. Inside you will find my mother's address and a little money. If ever you need help you can go to her.'

'Thank you. Shall I see you again? Will you visit me?'

'When I return from England. I am going away for a few weeks, but I'll come and see you when I get back.'

Lucy nodded. She turned away, looking out of the window again. Sarah suspected she was crying silently. She wanted to put her arms about the girl and comfort her, but Lucy wasn't ready for that yet.

As she left the home, Sarah made a mental note to speak to Ben as soon as possible. Detective Hudson might find it impossible to believe what she had to tell him and she wanted to get Ben on her side first – but she had to go straight to the theatre, because otherwise she was going to be late for their last rehearsal.

Sarah made it on time – just! Sam was already in a terrible mood and he glared at her as she slipped into her place on stage.

'I am glad you could make it, Miss Beaufort.'

'I'm sorry if I kept you waiting.' She glanced at the art deco platinum watch on her wrist. 'I don't think I'm late—'

'Where the hell is Eddie?' he demanded. 'Ellie says he hasn't been seen all morning, and Katie is late. We'll start without them – Eddie can do his solo when he gets here, if he ever does. The rest of you will be accompanied by the band; you're used to it now so don't look for Eddie to cue you in.'

Sarah went through her songs, but got no more than a curt nod from Sam. She found Ellie waiting for her when she got off stage.

'You don't know where Katie is, Sarah?'

'Sorry, I have no idea,' Sarah said. 'It isn't like her to be late. She hasn't mentioned any friends – except Eddie, of course. I know she has been out with him a couple of times, just coffee and a drink. He isn't around either—' she broke off as she saw him come in. 'Eddie, have you seen Katie this morning?'

'No, sorry. Isn't she here?'

'She's late. Sam is on the warpath.'

'Are you talking about Katie?' One of the chorus girls came up to them. 'She said she wanted to talk to you, Eddie. She was going to see if you were at home – at least, that's what she said.'

'Katie doesn't know where I live.' Eddie frowned. 'And I haven't seen her since last night.'

'Well, I saw her this morning,' Jan told him. 'She said she needed to talk to you, and she said she was going to call a cab, go over to your home.'

'If Katie said it she meant it,' Sarah put in. 'She must have found out where you live somehow.'

'Silly bitch,' Eddie said. 'That area is too damned rough for a girl on her own. Tell Sam I'll be back later. I had better go and look for her.'

'You can't go,' Ellie told him. 'Sam is yelling for you now. You'd better get out there or he'll have your head.'

Eddie swore and went through the curtains on to the stage. Sarah listened to him playing: it wasn't his usual polished performance. She knew he was on edge over something. Surely it couldn't just be because Katie had taken a cab to his home? He wasn't there anyway so she wouldn't have stayed long when there was no answer. Surely she would come straight back, because she couldn't afford to miss the final rehearsals...

Seven

Maura heard the sound of breaking glass downstairs. She had been lying on the bed trying to sleep, but her nerves were in tatters. Sometimes she thought she was living through a nightmare and that the past couple of weeks were just something she had dreamed, but the shadow of what she had done hung over her, hovering at the back of her mind like an evil demon.

She had killed a man. Eddie said the police would arrest her if she left this house without him, and a part of her believed him. She wondered what it would feel like to be hanged, or to be strapped into an electric chair. She was frightened of dying. She didn't want to die.

She heard another cracking sound downstairs, this time like wood being wrenched away from a doorframe or a window. A tingle of terror ran down her spine. She knew they were in a rough area by the docks. Most of these buildings were due to come down soon. Eddie had told her that when he'd brought her here that night. He had a black Ford car and he'd parked it in a derelict shed. She'd asked him why he lived in a place like this and he'd told her it suited him for the moment. She had thought it odd even then, but she had still trusted him, still believed that he was trying to help her. He was just Eddie, the man who played the piano at the theatre. She'd had no reason to think he would lock her in this room and keep her a prisoner.

Something had been knocked over downstairs. Maura swallowed hard. Someone was breaking in! What could they be after in a place like this? The furniture was old. Eddie said the people who had lived here had abandoned it when they left. Surely there was nothing worth stealing? She got up as she heard the sounds of someone moving about downstairs. Whoever they were, they were searching for something, because she could hear noises – like things being thrown about, glass and china broken. It sounded as if the thief was ransacking the place, angry perhaps because there was nothing worth stealing.

Maura was terrified. What was going on? They hadn't started to knock the place down, had they? She could be buried alive. Suppose the heavy machinery was about to move in and demolish the place? Her fear made her run to the door. She tugged at the handle, screaming as she found it locked as always.

'Help me ... help me!' she screamed. 'I'm

locked in here. Don't kill me. Let me out, let me out!'

She heard the sound of someone coming up the stairs and she stopped screaming, holding her breath. He was outside the door, because the footsteps belonged to a man. Maura held her breath. Had the key been left in the door? She moved back as she heard the sound of it turning in the lock and then the door swung back. A man was standing there. A scream of terror rose in her throat as she saw him, because he was a fearful sight. His hair was long and unkempt, his clothes filthy and covered in dark brown splotches – and the smell of him made bile rise in her throat.

'Stay away from me!' she cried. 'Don't touch me!'

'Lucy ... Lucy, it's only me...' he said in a slurred voice. His eyes had a strange glazed look, as if he didn't really know what he was doing. 'There's no need to be frightened. I shan't hurt you. I've come to take you home.'

Maura gave a scream and rushed at him, pushing at him hard. He was taken by surprise and stumbled, falling against the wall as she went on past him and out of the door.

'Lucy, don't go!' he cried. 'I'm going to make it up to you ... don't leave me again ... I'm sorry ... so sorry.' A loud sobbing noise broke from him, mucus bubbling from his mouth and nose as he sank to his knees.

'Please come back to me...'

Maura ran down the stairs. She saw the door, wrenched back on its hinges, and she rushed through the open space, her terror propelling her into the back alleys. She had to get away, from the awful wreck of a man back there and this place. Everywhere she looked the property was derelict, rotting wood and metal, piles of debris and broken glass lying on the ground. In her haste, she stumbled and fell, cutting her hands as she put them out to steady herself. The cuts stung, blood trickling down through her fingers as she ran.

All she wanted was to escape from this terrible place and the man – the awful man who smelled so bad that he had made her want to vomit. She was so blinded with terror that she didn't hear the cab coming round the corner and ran straight into its path. The driver didn't stand a chance of stopping. She was caught across the bonnet and thrown several feet, landing face down in a puddle of rusty water.

'Oh my Gawd!' the driver said as he got out and looked at her. 'The silly broad didn't look where she was going. You saw what happened, miss. It wasn't my fault.'

'No, it wasn't,' Katie said, as she hopped out of the back seat of the cab and went over to where the girl lay. Something made the back of her neck start to tingle as she looked at the dress the girl was wearing. She stared as the cab driver turned the girl over. 'Oh no ... it's her. It's Maura!'

'You know her?' the cab driver said, looking sick. 'Is she the person you were coming to see?'

'No, it wasn't her,' Katie said. 'But yes, I do know her. I think we had better call for an ambulance and the police. I'll tell them what happened. It wasn't your fault, but the police have been looking for her for a couple of weeks or more.'

'Well, we found her for them,' the driver said, 'but I sure as hell wish we hadn't...'

Katie felt for a pulse. She looked up at him. 'I don't think she's dead, but we have to get that ambulance here fast, because she's bleeding and I don't like the look of her face at all...'

'Ben, I know it sounds wild, but the man Lucy saw shoot Annabel – I think he is the one who was following me. He was obviously after money and perhaps he thought she was an easier target, because she was carrying an expensive handbag.'

'Yes, perhaps,' Ben said, and looked thoughtful. 'And you say Lucy is sure he is her father – even though Lucas Barrett was supposed to have died in that riot at the factory?'

'She was quite lucid when she told me what she saw – and she mentioned the van Allen family. She had an affair with Jonathan van Allen, but then his father raped her – and Mrs van Allen turned her off without a reference. I think she was badly treated by all of them, but she was in love with Jonathan. So maybe when he went off she felt betrayed – and that could have been the worst thing of all.'

'And then her baby died and her father held a hot flatiron to her cheek,' Ben said. 'She's had a rotten time of it, poor girl. It isn't much of a surprise that she had a mental breakdown, is it?'

'No, it isn't, but I think when she saw what happened to Annabel it brought it all back to her. She did try to tell me the first time, but she couldn't cope with it then – but now she seems perfectly normal to me. She is still distressed, but I believe she knows what she is saying.'

'And you want me to talk to Hudson about this?'

'Lucy will never feel safe until her father is behind bars,' Sarah said. She hesitated, then, 'There's one more thing, Ben...'

'Yes, go on, tell me what you're thinking, Sarah. I know you've had something on your mind.'

'It sounds so ridiculous. Detective Hudson will think I'm mad...'

'Never mind him for the moment, tell me what is bothering you.'

'I don't have any proof. I don't know why I think it – but the man who followed me, and the man who attacked Annabel ... could be the man Detective Hudson has been trying to find for months.'

Ben frowned, his eyes narrowed. 'You're talking about the Playboy Murderer, as the press call him, aren't you?'

'Yes. It sounds ridiculous, doesn't it?'

'It is a bit of a leap, Sarah.' Ben was doubtful. 'Tell me how you got there. I'm not with you this time.' He was remembering something Hudson had told him. He had dismissed it at the time, but now he realized that it all made sense.

'Then maybe I'm wrong,' Sarah said. 'But the police haven't been able to trace him – well, they weren't looking for a dead man. Think about what happened to him. He lost his job and he was caught up in a riot. He must have been injured, perhaps lay unconscious for a while, but he didn't die. He discovers that someone else has been buried in his place. He can't go to the police because he was concerned in the riots – he may have been in trouble with the police because of what happened at the factory. How can he find work when he doesn't have an identity? Then his daughter has a baby but won't tell him the father's name. He suspects it was something to do with the man she worked for ... and that house in Newport, well, it had belonged to the van Allen family until a few weeks before the murders. He must have hated the name. He probably didn't know the house had been sold...' She hesitated. 'And there's what he did to his daughter...'

'That would play on his mind – it would mine if I had done such a thing,' Ben said. 'I can see that you've made a case, Sarah. I'm not sure Hudson will see it, but I can put it to him if you like.'

'Perhaps it is enough that Lucy can identify him as the man who attacked Annabel,' Sarah said. 'It might be as well not to muddy the water too much. He doesn't trust me the way you do, and he might think it was all too far fetched.'

'Yes, he might,' Ben agreed. He was caught between a rock and a hard place, because he couldn't tell her what Hudson had told him about the gun. It was police business and he had been told in confidence. 'I hadn't made that connection myself, and it is a big leap. But you could well be right.' He frowned. 'I'm not sure Hudson would take kindly to your theory of it being Lucy's father, though.'

'Then just tell him what Lucy told me. If the rest of it fits I'm sure they will work it out,' Sarah said. She smiled at him. 'It was good of you to come and have tea with me, Ben. I'm glad to get this lot off my mind, I can tell you.'

'Yes, I imagine you are. You need a clear head for the show this evening.'

'Katie hasn't turned up for the rehearsals,'

Sarah said. 'One of the girls said she had gone somewhere – to Eddie's house – but he seemed to think she didn't know where he lived.'

Ben hesitated. He wondered if he ought to tell her that he thought Eddie might be Jonathan van Allen, but he didn't want her to start worrying about her friend. She was still upset over Maura. Katie would probably turn up when she was ready. He was thoughtful as he left her. Sarah was heading back to the theatre for last-minute costume changes, and he wanted a last word with Hudson. It might help the New York police in their search if they knew who they were looking for in the matter of Annabel's attacker – but he didn't think it necessary to tell Hudson about the rest of Sarah's theory. Hudson had his own and he could make the connection himself if he wished.

Jonathan looked at the door hanging off its hinges, a little nerve beginning to twitch at the corner of his eye. What the hell had happened here? He went inside, glancing round at the damage. He didn't care about the destruction, because he hadn't left much of value lying around, just a few dollars and some clothes. In a few hours he would be out of here. And once he got his money he would be on his way. He just hoped that whoever had broken in here had left without discovering the girl in the bedroom upstairs.

'Maura,' he called, taking the stairs two at a time. His heart was hammering in his chest, his mouth dry. He wished he'd never gotten himself into this mess, but once he had the girl he couldn't let her go ... just in case she'd seen something. She might have put two and two together – or the police might if she told them her story. It had seemed best to keep her here until he could get her out of the country; he had no intention of hurting her, though the stupid girl had made him angry a few times. The door to her room was open. He went in, looking round as he saw that it had been turned over like the room downstairs. There was no sign of Maura or anyone else. Whoever had broken in had taken what he needed and gone. 'Damn! Damn him!'

He had no idea whether the intruder had Maura or if she'd simply run off in a panic. He sat down on the edge of the bed, trying to think. It couldn't have been Katie who broke in – it needed a man's strength to break that door down. He had no idea how Katie had discovered where he was living for the moment. He hadn't told anyone. He'd known about the house because his father had bragged about the people he'd turned out of their homes.

'It's progress, Jonathan. They were living in slums. I came along and bought the property and they moved on – they'll thank me for it one day.'

'That's all you care about, isn't it?' Jonathan had been so angry when he saw the way his father bragged, the gloating expression in his eyes. 'It's just another million dollars or so to you. Those people could be living on the streets because you turned them out of their homes.'

'If they had any guts they would find somewhere better. If they want to lay down and die in the streets that's their problem.'

Jonathan had hated his father at that moment, and with good reason. He knew that Lucy had run away because of what his father did to her – his mother had told him.

'He raped her, Jonathan. She told me what he'd done before she left.'

Jonathan had vowed he would never go home while his father lived, but at that time he hadn't known the rest of it. He hadn't known that his mother had turned Lucy off because she was carrying a child. She'd put his Lucy out on the streets without a reference. It would have been impossible for her to find a job in her condition, and she had no one to turn to, because Jonathan had run off after the row with his father. It had turned him sick to his stomach when he knew what his father had done to Lucy. He had wanted to kill him, but instead he'd run away. It was only afterwards that he'd thought of Lucy. When he'd returned to look for her it was too late. One of the other servants had told him what *she* had done. He'd gone away without speaking to her that time – the woman who called himself his mother. He couldn't bear to look at her because he might not have been able to keep his hands from her scrawny throat.

He couldn't think about Lucy now. He had searched for her for months without success. He had to think about Maura. If she was running free in the streets it wouldn't be long before the police picked her up. Damn her! He couldn't trust her not to talk about where she'd been. She would drag him into it and that could spoil all his plans.

He couldn't afford to return to the theatre that night. He would have to find somewhere to stay safe until he could go to his mother's house. He hoped she had the money ready for him. He needed it to get out of the mess he'd got himself into more than ever now. If she refused to give it to him he would tell her what he knew ... that he'd seen her leaving through the back door of the nightclub when he'd returned to see just what damage Maura had done and he'd found his father lying in a pool of blood with his throat slashed.

Jonathan didn't know who had killed his father. It wasn't him, and it wasn't Maura – but it could just have been his mother. He had been protecting her in a way, because she was his link to the money he knew his father had stashed away.

* * *

'Where the hell is Eddie?' Sam was saying as Sarah went backstage. She could sense that something was going on, and she felt a surge of relief as she saw that Katie was standing there with Ellie. But Sam was clearly in a temper. 'First you turn up hours late and tell me you've found that other stupid girl – what did you call her? Maura? And now Eddie has gone missing again...'

'Katie!' Sarah said. 'Did Sam just say that you've found Maura? Is she all right? Where was she?'

'She's in hospital at the moment,' Katie said. 'She ran out in front of the cab I was in and we hit her. The driver slammed on his brakes, but it was too late. Fortunately, we were going slowly, because I was looking for street names and he didn't hit her hard enough to kill her. She is unconscious and badly bruised, but the hospital says she doesn't have any fatal injuries.'

'Thank God for that,' Sarah said. 'Have you been at the hospital with her all day?'

'Most of it. I didn't want to leave before they said she was going to be OK.'

'But where has she been? Did she say anything at all?'

'Nothing,' Katie said, and frowned. 'It was a real deadbeat area, Sarah. All the buildings are scheduled to come down soon. I was shocked, because I never thought Eddie would shack up in a place like that – it's known to be an area where down-and-outs hang out. I mean, I must have got it wrong.' She looked bewildered. 'I found a piece of paper in his coat pocket with an address by the docks and I thought ... but he couldn't live there. The cab driver told me the residents were cleared months ago...'

'What I want to know is how Maura came to be there,' Sarah said, frowning. 'What was she wearing?'

'That's the odd part – it was a costume, not a proper dress. I recognized the skirt as being one that was in the costume department here. Ellie took me there to pick something for one of my songs, and I noticed that skirt because of the colour. It was a pretty green but not suitable for me. I looked for it again when I went back, but it had gone.'

'Don't tell me she sneaked in here and stole a skirt!' Sam looked daggers at them. 'I'm glad your friend has been found, Sarah, but we have a show to get on the road and no piano player to do his solo.'

'Ellie plays a bit,' Sarah said. 'I am sure she would step in if you asked her nicely, Sam.'

He glared at her. 'Yeah, I know. She ain't as good as Eddie, but I suppose she'll do – but where the hell is he? This damn show was jinxed from the start.'

'I don't see why,' Sarah said. 'Stop fussing, Sam. Katie is here and Ellie can step in if Eddie doesn't show up. I dare say we'll manage.'

'Manage isn't good enough,' Sam said,

and then grinned at her. 'At least we've got Katie back in one piece, even though I ought to sack her for missing rehearsals.'

'He's only joking,' Sarah said, as she saw the look of alarm in the girl's eyes. 'Even Sam wouldn't sack you for taking a friend to hospital.'

'I'll have something to say about her being there in the first place,' Sam growled. 'And if Eddie ever turns up I'll hang him out to dry for messing us up this way.'

'His bark is worse than his bite,' Sarah said, and smiled at Katie. 'Thank you for what you did for Maura. I shall go to the hospital after the show and see how she is...'

Sarah turned away. She just had time to telephone her mother before she needed to start getting changed. Katie must have told people that Maura was the girl the police were looking for, but it might be as well to make sure that Detective Hudson knew about it, and Mrs Harland was the one to make that call, because Sarah wasn't sure where Ben was at the moment and there was no time to lose.

'Thank you for ringing me,' Hudson said. 'I had received a rather muddled call about a missing girl being taken to the hospital, but you've been helpful. I shall go over now and see if she is able to give us any clues about her whereabouts these past weeks.'

'Sarah thought you should be told personally. She is busy herself just at the moment, but she said it was important that you knew where she was found – and that one of the cast might possibly live in the area. A Mr Eddie Reeder? I say possibly because the whole area is under a demolition order, so that may not be correct. However, it was because one of the cast had taken a taxi to go and see him that Maura was found. Unfortunately, she ran out without looking and was knocked over.'

'Eddie Reeder...' Hudson frowned. 'That name rings a bell ... well, thank you for taking the trouble to tell me. Where can I find Miss Beaufort if I need her?'

'She will be on stage at the Belmont Theater this evening. They are giving a charity show – for Larkspur Home for Girls.'

'Oh ... yeah, that's the place where Mrs Lawson was shot.' Hudson nodded to himself. 'I may swing over that way later.'

'The tickets are twenty dollars. It is all for a good cause.'

Hudson stared balefully at the receiver as he replaced it. Now he was being dunned for twenty dollars for a charity show he'd had no intention of seeing – but what the heck, he might take an hour off to look in. First of all he wanted to see this missing girl. If she had been hiding out in that derelict area he would have something to say to his officers. It ought to have been searched, and if it had been, he would want to know why they hadn't found her.

Damn it! He'd remembered something Ben Marshall had told him. He suspected that Eddie Reeder and Jonathan van Allen were one and the same. If he were right ... it raised all sorts of questions. He was certainly going to have to talk to that young man, and the sooner the better.

'Larch, I am so glad you could come,' Sarah said. He had turned up at her dressing room door a few minutes before curtain up with a huge basket of flowers. 'I wasn't sure you would make it.'

'Annabel insisted I should,' Larch said. 'Good luck for this evening – oh, I shouldn't have said that, should I? What is it – break a leg?' He grimaced. 'That sounds so awful!'

'I'm not superstitious,' Sarah said with a smile. 'But I know a lot of the cast are. Those flowers are lovely, Larch – but I haven't told you the good news. Maura has been found. She is in hospital, and she was unconscious when Katie was there, but at least she is alive.'

'I thought she must be dead,' Larch said, looking serious. 'That's good news – but how did they find her?'

'She ran out in front of a taxicab and got knocked down,' Sarah said. 'Katie happened to be in the cab ... it's a long story, Larch.' She heard the knock and the call of five minutes at her door. 'That means they are

229

nearly ready for me. I have to go. Will you stay for the party?'

'Yes, of course. I'll see you later.'

Sarah nodded, feeling pleased that he had brought her flowers. She had wondered if he would feel it necessary to stay with Annabel that evening. She got up, leaving her dressing room and walking through the narrow passageways that led to the stairs and backstage. She couldn't think of anything else for the moment. They had a show to put on!

Sarah stood with the rest of the cast, listening to the clapping and cheering from out front. This audience was certainly pleased with the performance they had seen, and even though they had come prepared to be entertained and give their money to charity, she felt that it had gone well. They took their last call and then the lights went up and everyone stood up.

The curtains remained shut for a while as the backstage people rushed about clearing props and setting up trestle tables to hold the food. People were mingling out front, making the best of the cramped conditions between the aisles, generally having a good time and laughing. When the curtains were drawn back to reveal three tables set with snowy white clothes and a professional buffet there was some cheering.

Sarah looked for her mother, who was

making her way towards the stage. She went to meet her, kissing her cheek as she congratulated her on providing a splendid buffet.

'You were so good, Sarah,' Mrs Harland said. 'I knew you could sing, my darling, but I was surprised at how professional you are.'

'Thank you, Mummy. I think everyone did very well.' She glanced round at the richly dressed men and women mingling with the cast as they chatted and helped themselves to the food. 'People seem to be enjoying themselves, don't they?'

'Yes, I am sure they are,' Mrs Harland said, and smiled. 'Detective Hudson is here. I rather twisted his arm over the ticket, but he paid – even though I suspect he wants to talk to you about Maura.'

'Yes...' Sarah frowned. She noticed that Ben, Larch and Detective Hudson seemed to be talking seriously together. However, before she could join them Sam came up to her. 'Mummy was saying how well it has all gone. I hope you are pleased, Sam?'

'Yeah, it went OK,' he said, and grinned at her. 'Maybe I'll give you all a bonus.'

'Promises, promises,' Sarah teased. 'A kind word would be good, Mr Garson.'

'You were wonderful, the others were good – how's that?'

'Getting there,' Sarah said. 'I thought Katie was brilliant, and Ellie did well for a last-minute ask.'

'Ellie was a concert pianist once,' Sam said, surprising her now. 'She gave it up when her husband died. I persuaded her to come along and help with productions, but she wouldn't play – until this evening. I think she thought she might have lost her touch, but she did pretty good.'

'Will she take over on the ship if Eddie doesn't turn up?'

'Maybe. I'm trying to find someone to take his place. Ellie has her job and I don't want to lose her; besides, she doesn't want to perform. She did it tonight as a favour. I know a few guys who may be able to step into Eddie's shoes.'

Sarah nodded. Sam was resourceful and she suspected quite powerful in his own sphere. He would find what he wanted, though there wasn't much time.

'I think I had better talk to Detective Hudson,' Sarah said. 'He keeps giving me looks...'

She smiled at Sam, leaving him to talk to her mother.

'Ah, Miss Beaufort,' Hudson said, as she approached. 'I've been speaking to Marshall about you. He tells me you have come up with some ideas for me.'

'It is just what I've been told,' Sarah said. 'I don't know if Lucy will talk to you, but she seemed perfectly sensible to me. She knows her own father and she said he was the one who attacked Annabel Lawson.'

232

'I'll get around to her in a few days. I went to see Miss Trelawney at the hospital on my way here, but she is still unconscious. What is this about one of the cast being involved?'

'We don't really know that part,' Sarah said with a frown. 'Eddie hasn't been seen since early this afternoon. He came in for rehearsals and then disappeared. Katie hadn't turned up. We didn't know why then, but one of the other girls thought she might have gone to his home this morning – but Eddie said she didn't know where he lived. Katie was the girl in the cab that knocked Maura down. We none of us know why Maura was in that derelict area –' Sarah paused significantly. 'Of course, if Eddie had a place she could hide...' Sarah smiled apologetically. 'I know it is all conjecture, but it is odd that Eddie hasn't turned up for the show, isn't it?'

'You think he's done a bunk because Maura was found and she might have something to say?' Hudson looked at her hard. 'That could mean he was hiding her for reasons of his own, I suppose.'

'Well, yes, but I don't see where he fits in,' Sarah said, and then caught Ben's eye. 'You know something I don't...?'

'Sorry, Sarah. I mentioned my suspicions to Hudson, but it wasn't my case so I didn't tell you – but I think Eddie Reeder is Jonathan van Allen.'

'Lucy's lover and the son of the man

233

Maura went out to dinner with and hit over the head – the man who subsequently had his throat slit.' Sarah felt angry. 'And you thought it wasn't necessary to tell me we might have a murderer in our midst? Katie went out with him a few times!'

Ben looked uncomfortable, but Hudson stepped in. 'Hold on, young lady. He may be Lucy's lover and he may be van Allen's son, but that doesn't mean he killed his father.'

'He must have been there at the nightclub that night if he was hiding Maura,' Sarah said. 'And he may have had good reason to hate his father. If he knew he had raped Lucy— But you are right, it doesn't necessarily mean he is a killer. If he were, Maura probably wouldn't be alive to tell the tale.' She gave Hudson a straight, no-nonsense look. 'He has to be involved in this somewhere. Even if he didn't kill his father, there is something he is hiding from you.'

'Yes, I'll give you that one,' Hudson said. 'I had hoped the girl might tell us something, but as I said, she hasn't recovered consciousness yet. I shall visit Mrs van Allen in the morning and ask if she knows where we can find her son.'

'I think you should go tonight,' Sarah said. 'I have an awful feeling that the morning might be too late.' She saw the look of disbelief in Hudson's eyes. 'I know you think I am a foolish English girl who thinks herself the bee's knees, but this is important. I don't

234

know why but I feel it is important that you should go there tonight.'

Louise van Allen looked at the French gilt clock on her mantelpiece and frowned. It was past ten o'clock. She had expected her son long before this and she was beginning to think he wouldn't come. She frowned, because she had everything ready and she really had gone to a lot of trouble on his behalf.

'Hi, Ma.' Jonathan's voice made her jump as he slid into the room unannounced. 'Sorry I'm late. I've had a bit of bother getting here.'

'Jonathan!' She stood up and turned to look at him. 'I didn't hear the bell...'

'I didn't come through the front door. I used to live here, remember? Besides, I would rather no one but you and me knows about this visit.'

She looked at him coldly. 'Are you in some trouble?'

'Maybe – but I could ask the same of you, Ma.'

'What do you mean?'

'I saw you the night *he* was killed. You left the nightclub by the back door seconds before I got there.'

'Nonsense!' She gave him a haughty stare. 'You must be mistaken. Why should I want to go to a place like that?'

'Exactly. I can think of only one reason. He

was lying there in a pool of blood when I went up – and I saw you leaving. Don't try to lie to me, because I saw you, Ma. You had a veil over your face, but I know the hat. I know the way you walk, hold yourself. It was you.'

'Well, if it was, I didn't kill him,' Louise said, and sat down heavily. 'I thought it might have been you. When Betty-Lou told me she had seen you talking to a girl near that theatre I decided to take a look myself, and I knew you were here in New York. You refused to come home for the funeral – and that made me think that perhaps you had killed him.'

'Why would I do that, Ma?'

'Because of the way he treated you.'

'He didn't treat you much better. You had good reason to hate him.'

'He raped that girl, the one you said you were in love with...' Louise curled her mouth in distaste. 'She was such a common thing, but it seems your taste runs to common girls. You have more of your father in you than I thought.'

'Lucy was sweet, innocent and lovely,' Jonathan replied. 'I was going to marry her.'

'Over my dead body!'

'Don't tempt me, Ma. If I could find her I would still marry her.'

'If you want to know where she is I can tell you – but it won't do you much good.'

'What do you mean?'

'I visited the place because Annabel Lawson asked me to give money to the cause.'

'Who the hell is Annabel Lawson?'

'Everyone knows her. She is always writing letters begging for money.'

'So get to the point – what about Lucy?'

'Someone burned half her face – and she is mad. They say she sits and stares at the wall all day.' Louise twisted her mouth. 'They have no idea who she is – of course I didn't tell them I knew her.'

Jonathan moved towards her. He grabbed her, his fingers digging into her arms. He shook her as she gave a cry of protest. 'Don't think I don't know what you did to her, Ma. She told you she was having a baby, my baby, and you couldn't wait to get rid of her. You turned her off and you knew she had nowhere to go. You sent her out there to starve on the streets.'

'The baby died,' Louise said. 'If you really want to see her, she is at Larkspur House – a home for fallen girls...' She saw the murderous expression in his eyes. 'What? If you had asked I would have told you. I didn't imagine you would still be interested in a girl like that...'

'You knew I loved her! You kept it from me on purpose!'

'She isn't suitable, Jonathan. Why don't you put all this nonsense behind you and come home?'

'I told you, I would rather live with a

rattlesnake!' Jonathan glared at her. 'Did you get my money?'

'I have eight hundred thousand. It was all the cash I could find at such short notice, but if you come home and let the lawyers sort things out you will find there's five or six million dollars coming to you, some of it in property – but we can sort that out between us.'

'I'm leaving New York tonight – at least I was.' Jonathan flung himself into a chair. 'How do I know I can trust you? You might be lying to me about Lucy being at that place.'

'If you don't believe me go and ask them.'

'It isn't just that,' Jonathan said. 'Someone cut Father's throat. I know it wasn't me, and you say you didn't do it – so who the hell was it?'

'I have no idea,' Louise said. 'I do not appreciate your language, Jonathan, or your suspicion.'

'You thought it might be me.'

'That is rather different.'

'You were just as likely to kill him as anyone else. You hated him as much as I did.'

'We had an understanding. He didn't interfere in my life and I left him to wallow in his own filth. I was prepared to wait for a natural death – I doubt whether he would have lived as long as I shall. His habits were taking a toll on his health. You should learn from that if you don't want it to happen to you.'

'God, I could kill you with my bare hands!' Jonathan was on his feet glaring at her. 'For what you did to Lucy and me – Father too. I'm not surprised he looked elsewhere for his pleasures. He couldn't have found much in bed with you!'

'How dare you!' Louise slapped him across the face.

'Because you are a cold-blooded bitch!' Jonathan threw himself at her, his hands reaching for her throat, but Louise picked up an ornament from an occasional table next to her and struck him a glancing blow to the side of the head, sending him crashing to the floor. Neither of them heard the door-bell ring.

Jonathan lay on the floor, shaking his head. He looked up at her.

'I was right, you are dangerous, Ma. If you ask me, you were the one who found Father still reeling from the blow Maura gave him – and you were the one who slit his throat.'

'How dare you? I've told you I did no such thing!'

'Then why the hell were you at the night-club that night? You never go there—' He broke off as he became aware that someone was standing in the open doorway, looking at him. 'Who the blazes are you?'

'Name is Hudson, Detective Hudson, and these are my colleagues: Mr Marshall, a police colleague from England, and Detective Rosenburg – and you, I believe, are Mr Jonathan van Allen. I wanted a word with you, sir. And it seems as though perhaps you neglected to tell me something, ma'am – like why you were at that nightclub the night your husband was murdered?'

'Mr Marshall, what must you think of us?' Louise had gone white. She seemed to stagger as if something had hit her, sitting down on the sofa with a little plop. 'I didn't think it necessary to inform the authorities; I know nothing about the murder, as I have already told my son. I went to that place to discover something I wished to know and I discovered my husband lying there...'

Ben wisely said nothing.

'And you didn't think you should report it?' Hudson's eyes were stormy.

'I thought—' She looked at her son, who was rubbing the side of his head. 'I didn't hit you that hard, Jonathan. You shouldn't have attacked me...'

'What did you think, Mrs van Allen?' Hudson brought her back to the subject in hand. 'I should have thought you might wish to summon help?' The irony in his voice made her blush, something he guessed she hadn't done in a long while.

'He was obviously dead.' She threw a bitter glance at her son. 'I didn't report it, because I thought my son might have done it. I didn't want Jonathan to be arrested for

240

murder. I hated my husband, but I would never have done anything as vulgar as murder him. He mixed with rogues and villains, Mr Hudson. You should be looking for someone with a criminal background.'

'Thank you for your advice, ma'am, but at the moment I think I have two prime suspects right here. Give me one good reason why I shouldn't arrest you both?'

'If I'd wanted to kill him I could have done it ages ago,' Jonathan said. 'I knew where he was, and we met on a couple of occasions. I asked him for money and he gave it to me. Not as much as I wanted, but enough to get by on. We argued over money and other things, but I never touched him. I despised him, but I'm not a murderer. If you want the truth, I haven't got the guts for it. Had I had been less of a coward I might have thrashed him when I found out what he did to Lucy, but I ran off and left the only person I care about to *her* tender care.' He gave his mother a look of hatred. 'I wish I *had* been the one to slit his damned throat, but I wasn't. And the reason I didn't come to you was because I thought *she* did it. I don't care for her much either, but I needed money and she's the only way I can get it fast. I wanted to leave, go to Europe and forget it all, but now...' He shook his head. 'She says Lucy is alive but mad ... and if she is it's partly my fault.'

'You don't deserve a penny after the way

you've spoken to me tonight!'

'Hard luck,' Jonathan grunted. 'It's too late for me to clear off now so I might as well stick around and take my share, but don't think I'm coming back here to live. I'll tell the lawyers to sell everything and when I get my share I'm off. I've always wanted to live in Paris and that's where I'm headed.'

'You can't do that,' Louise shrieked. 'You ungrateful boy! I've done everything for you. I won't let you sell this house!'

'Watch me! He left half of everything to me, and that includes this house.'

'At the moment neither of you is going to sell anything, and neither of you is going anywhere,' Hudson said, before they could come to blows again. 'I'm taking you in for further questioning, Mr van Allen – and you will give me your word not to leave town, Mrs van Allen. I'm not satisfied with either of your stories yet. I shall be bringing a team in to search this house – and if I discover that either of you are lying to me, you will wish you had never been born.'

'You might as well know that I kept that girl locked up,' Jonathan said with another glare at his mother. 'Maura Trelawney. She was in a panic when I met her. He tried to force himself on her and she hit him. I took her somewhere she could hide and then I went back to see what damage she'd done – but I saw my mother leaving by the back door of the nightclub and when I found him lying there I thought she had done it. I still think she might have.'

'You can repeat all this down at the precinct,' Hudson said. 'Once you've given a signed statement I'll consider whether you spend the rest of the night in custody.'

'What happened to Maura?' Jonathan said. 'I was going to smuggle her to England on the ship, in a basket of props, as it happens, but someone broke into the house. Whoever it was let her out and she ran off. I suppose she came straight to you?'

'As a matter of fact she is lying in a hospital bed,' Hudson said. 'A girl from the show was in the cab that hit her. She recognized her and we've gone from there.'

Jonathan nodded. 'I hope she will be OK. I know she was scared I meant to kill her, but I thought she might mention me and I was trying to keep out of it. I should have told you that bitch killed him –' he nodded towards his mother – 'and saved us all a lot of time.'

'Jonathan!' Louise van Allen stared at her son. 'I can't understand why you've turned against me like this. I've always done my best for you.'

'Have you, Ma?' His eyes were as cold as hers. 'And I always thought you were clever. If my Lucy has lost her mind it's your fault and I'll pay you back for it – just see if I don't.'

'I think you had better come with me,' Hudson said. 'You can continue this discussion when I've finished with the pair of you...'

Eight

'They are a nice pair of characters,' Ben remarked when he was sitting with Hudson in the bar of his hotel in the early hours of the following morning. 'I'm grateful to you for taking me along. I wouldn't have missed that little performance for the world.'

'I think they just about deserve each other,' Hudson agreed with a grim smile. 'I asked you along because I wanted you to identify Eddie Reeder, but as it turned out they did a good hatchet job on each other.'

'Do you think either of them did it?'

'They both had good cause,' Hudson said. 'Unfortunately, I don't believe either of them are guilty of using the knife on van Allen. They are both guilty of other things – conspiracy to alter the course of justice and, in his case, kidnapping. If Miss Trelawney will press charges we can put him away for a few years.'

'She probably won't want to,' Ben said. 'I suppose he started out with good intentions, but messed up because he wasn't sure what was going on. I hate people who think their money places them above the law. I thought she was as cold as ice when I met her the first time, but I saw the real Mrs van Allen last night. Her son called her a rattlesnake and I think he isn't far wrong.'

'Yeah, you're right about that, Marshall. In fact, you were right about Jonathan van Allen all the way through. He was involved up to his ears in this business.'

'But if he didn't kill his father – and she didn't kill her husband – you still have a case to solve.'

'It may well be that he was killed by one of his business associates. It was my first thought when this started, but it got mixed up with the Trelawney girl. At least that bit of it is cleared up now.'

'You don't think Maura finished him off herself?'

'Nah – do you?'

'No, I don't,' Ben said. He glanced at his watch. 'Well, I'm for my bed. I think this really is the last time we shall meet, Hudson.'

'I'm grateful for all your help. We made a good team in the end.'

'With a little help from Sarah. We might have got there sooner if I'd told her about Eddie Reeder.'

'She was mad about that,' Hudson said, and grinned. 'I must have a little chat with her one day. I still have some loose ends to clear up – like the Playboy Murderer and Lucy Barrett's father.'

'You don't think he could be the one, do you?' Ben asked, because he was remembering Sarah's theory, and embroidering on it. 'I'm talking about the van Allen murder now. He must have known that his daughter was working for the family. He could have put two and two together...'

Hudson stared at him hard. 'Damn it! Didn't I say I should be looking for the father of one of the girls van Allen led astray? Lucy Barrett wasn't stupid enough to give him what he wanted so he raped her. His wife turned her off and she ran away ... back to her father.'

'Because she knew he wasn't dead even if everyone else thought he was?'

'Yeah...' Hudson warmed to his theory. 'He would have found it hard to get work. She lost the baby, probably because she didn't get the right food or medical treatment. He demanded to know who the father was and—'

'Lucy ran away from her father after he held a hot iron to her face.'

'Yeah, it all fits,' Hudson said. 'But why wait all that time to slit van Allen's throat? Why didn't he do it sooner?'

'Who understands the mind of a murderer?' Ben asked. 'Maybe if we knew a bit more we might be able to stop them before they commit their crimes.'

'Some hope,' Hudson said gloomily. 'So I'm looking for Lucas Barrett on two counts now. Not that it helps. I haven't a clue where to find him.'

'What do you know about his life before he was presumed dead? Where did he live or work? He might have been hiding out there – if it meant something to him for any reason?'

Hudson looked thoughtful. 'The place where that girl Maura was found – there used to be a factory there. Barrett worked there before he was sacked. Mr van Allen owns that whole area. He bought up most of it after the riots, but the factory was always his. It was all supposed to come down before this, but the project was delayed.'

'Barrett might hang around there sometimes. It would be familiar, a part of his life he can't forget.'

'Yeah.' Hudson grinned. 'We just might have got one step ahead this time. At least we have some place to start...'

Lucy looked at the frocks Sarah had given her. She had hung them up in her wardrobe, but she had been thinking about the pretty green one. She knew it would suit her, and she could still look nice if she didn't look at one side of her face. She reached out to touch the dress. The material was soft and silky to the touch, much nicer than anything she'd ever owned in her life.

Sarah was generous, kind. Mrs Lawson was nice too, and she hadn't deserved to be shot like that – it was wrong of her father to do something so wicked. Lucy had been frightened for a while, because she was afraid he had come here looking for her. Why else should he come here? The thought had terrified her, making her sick to her stomach, but since Sarah's visit she had begun to think about things.

No one believed her when she told them it was her father who burned her face. They all thought he was dead, but Lucy knew better. After the mistake he had been too frightened to go to the police. He had hit one of the cops during the rioting and he was frightened they would arrest him, so he'd let everyone think he was dead. Without papers he'd found it hard to get work, even harder than before. Lucy had been too ill with a pregnancy that was going wrong, and her baby had been born dead too soon. He'd lost his temper over that and threatened her with the iron if she didn't tell him who the father of her child was. She hadn't believed he would really do it, but he had ... the agony of it had lived with her, at the back of her consciousness. She had pushed it all to a far corner of her mind, not wanting to remember. And when she tried to tell people things they didn't believe her.

Sarah believed her. Sarah had given her the frocks and some money. Lucy had enough to pay for her fare on the subway if she wanted to go to the police and tell them what she knew. She had thought they might come here, but they hadn't – which meant they didn't believe her.

If someone didn't stop her father, he would go on killing people. Lucy didn't know where he'd got the gun he'd used to shoot Annabel, but she knew there was a deep bitterness inside him. It was that bitterness that made him hurt people. He had to be stopped. Someone had to make him go to the police and give himself up. She was the only one who knew where he might be. Perhaps if he saw her, saw what he'd done to her, it would make him understand that he couldn't go on hurting people.

She reached out and took down the green dress, slipping it over her head. Sarah was right; it did fit her very well. She felt good wearing it, confident. Her face was ugly, but she couldn't change that and it didn't matter. She would find her father, make him see that what he had done was wrong. She could remember when he hadn't been a bad man, though he had always been violent when he was drunk.

She didn't really care what he did to her now. Her life was over, because living in this place was worse than death. She didn't know what would happen when she found her father, but if she lived through it she wasn't going to come back here ever. She would go away somewhere ... perhaps she would ask Sarah's mother for help. First, she had to find her father and make him go to the police.

She felt a bit nervous, because he could be so violent, but she knew it was something she had to do…

'Your show was a big success,' Mrs Harland said when Sarah came downstairs that morning. She sighed as she saw that her daughter had brought down a suitcase. 'I shall miss you, Sarah. You are coming back? Promise me?'

'I've already promised Sam. I shan't jump ship at the other end.'

'Sarah!' Mrs Harland laughed, because her daughter came out with the oddest expressions. 'It was nice of Larch to come last night, wasn't it?'

'Yes, it was,' Sarah said. 'I brought the flowers home. I thought you would like them.'

'I suppose you can't take them on the ship. Are you seeing Larch today? I thought he might be driving you to the ship.'

'I've arranged to go with Ben,' Sarah said. 'He's coming for lunch – if that is all right, Mummy?'

'Yes, of course it is, my darling,' her mother said, and came forward to give her a hug. 'I rang the hospital this morning. They told me that Maura is improving. She came round in the early hours. Apparently, she was a bit hysterical so they gave her a sedative, but she will be fine with rest and care. I shall visit in a few days. She will need somewhere to stay for a while when she comes out of hospital.'

'Mummy, you are a darling!' Sarah hugged her tight. 'You were always grumbling about her, but you've been really worried about her, haven't you?'

'Well, you know how it is,' Mrs Harland said. 'I couldn't bear to think of her at some horrid man's mercy, but I think she was lucky.'

'Ben will tell us what happened when he comes,' Sarah said. 'I had better get on with the rest of my packing.'

'Yes, you do that,' Mrs Harland agreed. 'I know you are concerned for Lucy, but you needn't be, Sarah. I shall visit and see if there is anything I can do to help.'

'I'll be back before you know it,' Sarah told her. 'I must get on, because Sam said he might call this morning.'

'I shan't be here. Annabel rang me from the hospital. I told her I would pop in and tell her how things went last night. I shall be back for lunch.'

Sarah smiled and ran upstairs. Larch hadn't said anything about coming to see her off, but of course he was still anxious about Annabel. Sam had insisted on seeing her this morning. She wasn't quite sure why.

Lucy looked around her as she got out of the cab. She had been too nervous to take the subway, because there were so many people, and they stared at her face. Instead she had done something she'd never done before in her life and hailed a cab. She had worried all the way here that she wouldn't have enough money for the fare, but she still had some dollars left in her pocket. Sarah had given her far more than she had ever had in her life. It was too much for Lucy to comprehend, and her hand clutched the purse nervously.

It looked so different from the last time she'd been here. There had still been people living in some of the houses then; now they were empty, their windows broken or boarded up. Rubbish had collected in the gutters, adding to the forlorn air that hung over the derelict buildings. She saw that someone had pasted bright posters to some walls, and children had chalked squares in the middle of the road to play games.

Lucy walked up the road. She had lived with her father in one of these houses for a few months after the factory closed; that was before the people were made to leave their homes. She hesitated outside her old house but changed her mind. Something told her that her father wouldn't be there; he hadn't spent much time there even when it was their home. He said it brought back memories – memories of her mother and brothers, all of them dead of a fever. Lucy sometimes wished that she had died of the fever too.

And yet she'd found happiness for a while at the van Allen house.

She had fallen in love with Jonathan almost from the first, but she had tried to resist him, tried to be a good girl. He had been so sweet to her, his kisses so tender that in the end she'd lain with him in her bed up in the attics of the house. He had promised that he would marry her as soon as he got enough money. He was going to get it from his mother, because he said she was easier to persuade than his father.

Lucy had laughed when he said it, because he made it seem funny, but she knew it wasn't funny – her lover had feet of clay. He had lied to her and then he'd run away when she told him what his father had done to her.

Lucy could see the horror in his eyes even now. He couldn't bear to listen and he'd left her standing there ... he hadn't even waited to hear the bit about his baby. He wouldn't have cared if he had. Lucy knew he had just used her, as his father had used her. They were both the same; it was just that Jonathan was younger and had a lovely smile – but his smile was false. He hadn't loved her at all, and he certainly wouldn't love her if he saw what had happened to her face.

She wouldn't try to find him. She would speak to her father and then she would go to the address Sarah had given her. Sarah's mother might give her some money or a job;

she didn't much mind which because it didn't matter what happened to her now. She just had to make sure her father didn't hurt anyone else.

'I ought to keep you locked in,' Hudson told Jonathan the next morning. 'Don't plan on going anywhere. I haven't finished with you yet. Miss Trelawney hasn't pressed charges so far, but she may do – and if she doesn't I still may. So stay in the city, and let me know where you are.'

Jonathan stared at him sullenly, and then he shrugged. 'I wasn't planning on going far. I'll stay at the Renaldo Hotel for the moment. I intend to see my lawyers this afternoon, see how soon they can start things moving. I want my money and the old bitch is going to have to move out into somewhere smaller.'

'That is your business,' Hudson said. 'Just make sure you're around when I come looking.'

Jonathan nodded. He resented the way the police officer spoke to him, and he had no intention of telling him where he was going first thing that morning. The old bitch had told him that Lucy was at Larkspur Home for Girls so that was where he was heading right now. He wanted to see Lucy. He didn't believe she was mad, and if she were – well, maybe there was a doctor somewhere who could put her right. She was the only one he cared about – the only one who could make him forget all the things he hated.

'Are you all ready for the trip?' Sam asked when he arrived at eleven thirty that morning. His eyes went over Sarah hungrily. Over the time they had worked together he had discovered that she was more than just a pretty woman, and he knew she was the one for him. He knew that he had a rival, but the English guy didn't seem bothered, or he was a fool, taking her for granted. 'I think you'll have fun and the experience will be good for your career.'

'Yes, I am sure I shall,' Sarah said, and smiled. 'Come and sit in the front room, Sam. Mummy has gone visiting. She won't be back until lunch. We can have coffee and talk.'

'That sounds kinda nice,' Sam said appreciatively. 'Did she go out on purpose or was it just luck?'

'I think it was luck,' Sarah said. 'Mummy likes Larch a lot – and so do I.'

'Is that telling me to keep my big mouth shut?' Sam sat down in a wing chair and leaned back, a smile in his eyes. 'Or do I get a chance to make my pitch?'

'You get a chance to say what you want,' Sarah assured him. 'We are friends, Sam. I think we like each other a lot, don't we?'

'It is more than liking on my part,' Sam told her. 'I know you have a lot you want to do, Sarah – but I don't see why you should not do it with me around. I have this show to produce for a Broadway theatre, and then I'm headed to Hollywood. I've been offered a job with one of the big studios. They are going to be making musical spectaculars and they need someone with my experience. I've convinced them I'm the man for the job. I think I could convince them that you are star material.' He grinned at her. 'I see fire in your eyes. Maybe I put that wrong; I just have to introduce you. It wouldn't take much to convince anyone that you have what they need. In five years you could be a household name, have your picture in every fashion magazine going, all the newspapers...'

'It sounds exciting,' Sarah said, her head spinning with the pictures he was painting. 'But what about love, a home and family?'

'You could have those too – with me. The fame bit is only the bait.' Sam grinned. 'You could have either or both, but I prefer you have it with me.'

'I see...' Sarah looked at him consideringly. 'Are you telling me you are in love with me?'

'Sure – what else? You know me, babe. I ain't big on words – not that kind, anyway. I can shoot my big mouth off when I want someone to jump through a hoop, but you make me shake in my boots.'

'You could have fooled me at the theatre last night.'

'Yeah, I was out of order. I get like that at times. I ain't a saint, sweetheart, but you know that already.'

'Yes, I do,' Sarah replied, and laughed softly. 'I have to admit that I like you a lot, Sam.'

'But you're not sure?'

'I have another friend I like. You know about Larch, Sam. I had thought I should like to marry him one day, but...' Sarah stood up. 'I'll see about that coffee.'

Sam was up in an instant. He grabbed her wrist, swung her round to face him and kissed her on the lips. Sarah didn't struggle as his arms enveloped her. As the kiss deepened, she melted into his body, responding to him because it was nice and she liked being kissed this way.

'I love you, Sarah. I know singing means a lot to you,' Sam growled huskily. 'I don't want to take you away from it – I just want to share your life, to have you in my bed when I wake up in the morning.'

'Sam.' Sarah felt breathless, slightly giddy. 'I'm not sure. I do feel something. I like it when you kiss me, but I need more time.'

'Sure you do,' Sam said, and stroked her cheek with the tips of his fingers. 'I'm not trying to rush you, sweetheart. I want you, but I know you have other needs. Will you have an answer by the time you get back?'

'Yes, I think so,' Sarah said. 'I wasn't sure whether you were serious, Sam. I thought you might just be flirting with me. Now I know you mean it, I shall give your proposal serious thought.'

'That's my sweet baby,' Sam said. 'I'll give that coffee a miss if you don't mind. I have someone to see. Be good and dream about me, Sarah.'

'Yes,' she said, touching her fingers to her lips as he went out. She was torn between her love for Larch and this new feeling Sam had aroused in her heart. It was difficult to choose who she liked best. Besides, Larch had made it clear that Annabel had first call on his time for the moment.

'What do you mean, she has gone?' Jonathan demanded. He stared at Matron, feeling as if he wanted to wipe that stupid look off her face. 'I thought she was in need of special care – that her mind wasn't right?'

'Well, yes, she does wander a bit sometimes. I wouldn't call her mad, though; that is far too strong a word. And she has been so much better recently. I think it was because of Miss Beaufort. They got on so well together. Lucy took the things Miss Beaufort gave her and she left early this morning. Her bed had been slept in, but no one saw her go so it must have been early.'

'Do you let people just walk out of here?'

'Oh yes, of course. The girls are free to come and go as they please. It isn't an asylum, just a home for girls who need somewhere to stay until they feel able to leave. As I said, Lucy was much better recently. We couldn't have stopped her if she'd said she wanted to leave, but she just went without telling anyone.'

'Where could she go? She doesn't have anyone. Her family is all dead.'

'Lucy seems to think her father is alive,' Matron said. 'We didn't believe her at first, but Miss Beaufort believes she knows what she is saying – perhaps she has gone to find him.'

'Would she do that if he was the one who burned her face?'

'I really do not know, Mr van Allen. I am very sorry, but I can't tell you anything more. If you had come here yesterday she was here then.'

'I didn't know where she was until last night.'

Jonathan's fists balled at his sides. He felt like hitting her. He wanted to hit out at something or someone. His frustration roiled inside him, because if that bitch had told him sooner he could have come for Lucy – taken her away. Now he had to start searching all over again.

He didn't have to do it alone! He had money now and he could use it to hire agents to look for her. He would visit his mother, pick up the cash she had been going to give him before they had a row and the cops arrived – and then he would move into a hotel. Once he had a chance to talk to the lawyers he would be rich. No more begging from his father or his mother.

He would find Lucy and they would go away, perhaps to Paris. He didn't give a damn what the cops thought. As soon as things were sorted out he would leave and never come back! But first he wanted what was owed him – the illegal cash his father had stowed away. He would bet his last breath that there was more than eight hundred thousand, and he would make the bitch pay up if it was the last thing he did...

Lucy saw the man sitting on an empty crate in the yard. When she'd come here as a child this place had been a hive of activity, men hurrying here and there with planks of wood, hammers in their hands, nails between their teeth. Her father had been a craftsman then, a carpenter and builder of quality furniture, but that was before things started to go wrong. Looking at him now, she shuddered, feeling cold all over. He looked like a down-and-out, his clothes filthy, hanging off him as though they were too large for his thin frame. She realized that he had lost a lot of weight. He had always been a big man with broad shoulders and strong. He looked as if he had become emaciated, his shoulders sloping, and as he turned unseeing eyes in her direction, she saw that his face was gaunt, colourless.

It was him, though. She would have known him anywhere, just as she had known him when she looked down and saw him trying to wrest Annabel's purse from her hands. Annabel should have let him take it, but she'd hung on determinedly and he'd pulled a gun from under his coat and shot her.

Lucy wondered if he still had the gun. She felt a shiver of fear as she considered whether or not he would use it on her – but it didn't matter. She didn't have much to live for anyway. Maybe he would be pleased to see her.

She took a deep breath and walked up to him. He didn't seem to notice right away. She could smell the stink of unwashed clothes and the strong drink on his breath. At his feet was a jug, the kind that held illegal spirits; she had seen them before and guessed that he had been drinking the foul stuff they sold in the speakeasies.

'Father...'

His head jerked up and he turned to look at her. For a moment he just stared as if he couldn't believe he was seeing her. He stood up, his hand shaking as he reached out, took hold of her chin and turned her face so that he could see the scars. A look of horror came into his eyes and he dropped his hand as if he had been stung.

'Yes, you did that with the flatiron. Are you pleased with yourself?'

'Lucy...' the word came out in a sob,

mucus spitting out of his mouth and running from his nose. He was crying, sobbing like a child as he stared at her. 'I didn't mean to hurt you ... I never meant to do this...' He turned away from her violently and vomited on the ground. The vile smell of it hit her stomach, making her feel like retching too. 'I'm sorry...' he wiped the bile away on the sleeve of his filthy coat.

'Crying won't change things,' Lucy said. Her tone was harsh, cold, but she didn't care. He didn't deserve her pity. 'It stopped hurting a long time ago.'

He turned his head to look at her, and the last vestige of colour left his face as he saw how angry she was. 'Lucy ... forgive me...'

'You've done worse things,' Lucy said. 'I saw what you did to her – Mrs Lawson. She wouldn't give you her purse and you shot her. I watched you from the window and I knew it was you.'

'You saw me...?' His eyes were dark, glazed, hurt like a child that has been beaten. 'You hate me. I wanted to find you, to make it up to you, Lucy. I wanted to get a job, be the kind of father you needed.'

'You!' Her voice was like the lash of a whip. 'Have you seen what you look like – what you smell like? Who would ever give you a job now? You don't deserve it. You deserve to be in prison. You have to give yourself up. You have to pay for what you've done.'

'Pay for what I've done?' He stared at her dully. He saw the bodies falling, blood spurting from the wounds he'd inflicted, eyes staring up at him ... dead eyes that came back to haunt him in the nights when he couldn't sleep. 'I killed them ... they will kill me ... I deserve it...' He raised his head to look at her, his expression so strange that she felt icy cold. 'You should have seen them with their fancy clothes and their big house ... the cars they had and all the food wasted ... thrown around ... enough to feed a family for a week or more.' Suddenly, his eyes blazed. 'Of course I killed them! They deserved it for living that way.'

'You killed them? What do you mean?' Lucy stared at him in horror. Sarah had told her Annabel was still alive so that meant he had killed others. She felt the sickness churn inside her as she stepped back, shocked, her mind reeling from the horror. 'You're evil ... evil...'

'Lucy, no!' he cried. 'It was because of what they did ... your mother, she died...' He stumbled towards her, hands outstretched. Lucy screamed, her foot catching against some coiled wire in the rubbish behind her, trapping the heel of her shoe. She fell and hit her head, the blackness closing about her just as three cars came screeching up to the derelict factory. 'Lucy, don't leave me ... don't be dead. I didn't mean to hurt you...'

Lucas knelt down in the dirt beside her.

He reached out, stroking her white face, his own streaked with lines where the tears ran down and washed away the layers of filth ingrained in his skin. He was still there, sobbing, unaware of anything but his daughter, when the uniformed officers walked up to him. He didn't notice them until they went for him, and then he fought.

He fought wildly as they grabbed his arms, trying to get back to her, to Lucy, his precious daughter. They didn't understand that he had been looking for her so long. It was more than his tortured mind could take, and he was screaming and cursing as they dragged him away to a police van and threw him inside, slamming the door shut. He couldn't see anything as one of the officers bent over the unconscious girl.

'It must be the girl,' he said. 'Hudson was right. As soon as he heard she'd gone missing, he said she would be here.' He felt for a pulse. 'It's all right. She isn't dead, just unconscious. Looks like we got to him just in time.'

'He didn't look as if he were trying to kill her to me,' one of the others said.

'Well, she didn't get this way all by herself,' the first officer said. 'In my book she's only alive because we got here before he could finish his work.'

'What do you want?' Louise van Allen turned to look at her son. She was sitting at an elegant antique French writing desk and she closed her blotter on the letter she had been writing as he came up to her. Her expression was sour, unforgiving. 'I thought you didn't want to live here?'

'I have no intention of stopping,' he said. 'I came for the money I left here last night.'

'You can't expect me to give you that now – after what you said to me? You practically accused me of murdering your father when the police were here. You will get nothing more from me, Jonathan. If the lawyers decide to agree to your wishes over this house I shall fight you through the courts. By the time they have finished you'll get less than I offered you last night.'

'Bitch!' He glared at her. 'You *will* give me the money. It wasn't all of it. I know Father, he never paid more taxes than he need. He had a load of cash hidden here somewhere – and I want my share of it.'

Louise smiled coldly. 'Find it,' she invited. 'It took me years to discover his hiding places. Your father was devious, Jonathan – not clever, just devious. He thought I was stupid, that I would put up with his dirty little habits, but I bided my time. I watched what he did, where he went – and then—' She turned away to look at herself in the mirror. 'I loved you. I would have given you everything, but you are no better than he was. You like your little sluts, too. Well, I haven't put up with your father all those years to lose everything now. I would have shared it with you, but I won't let you take it away from me, Jonathan.'

'You can delay things for a while, but you can't stop me getting my hands on the cash.' He moved towards her menacingly. 'I'm not afraid of you, Ma. I cared for you once but you made a mistake when you turned Lucy off like that.'

'The little slut deserved it!'

'Did she?' Jonathan's eyes narrowed. 'I loved her. If you had ever cared about me, you would have helped her for my sake – but you chose to put her out without a hope. If she is dead, I'll pay you back in full.'

'No, Jonathan, I don't think you will,' Louise said. She slipped her hand into the pocket of her gown and brought out a small pearl-handled pistol. 'This was your father's, you know. He kept it in one of his secret places. I took it because I thought it might come in useful after your behaviour last night. You threatened me. No one does that, my dear. Not even your father.' Her eyes narrowed to icy slits. 'He wanted a divorce. After all these years, he thought he could get rid of me just like that...'

Jonathan stared at her in horror. She smiled as she saw his eyes widen. He had suddenly understood what she was saying. 'Yes, of course it was me, but you didn't expect me to admit it, did you – especially when those fools were here last night? I wouldn't have told you either, but you don't matter anymore. I have decided you are expendable. You turned against me the way he did – and I don't love you. I don't love you, Jonathan...' Her finger pressed down on the trigger. The shot surprised him. His eyes stared at her in disbelief as he felt the pain. He hadn't believed she would do it. She bent over him as he sank to the floor, the blood gushing from the wound in his chest. She pushed the small gun into his hand, closed his fingers over it and began to scream. 'Help me ... someone help me!'

The sound of running feet heralded the arrival of her maid. Louise waved her hands about as if she were hysterical. 'He tried to kill me, Mary. I wrestled with him and the gun went off...' she cried. 'He shot himself. He's bleeding. We need a doctor! My son needs a doctor or he'll die...'

The maid looked horrified and went to the phone, picking up the receiver and giving the emergency number to the operator. From the corner of her eye she saw her mistress bending over her son, apparently in acute distress. Mary had never seen her mistress in a state before, but then she'd never seen anything like this. She asked for the emergency doctor, and then, as an afterthought, the police.

'Why did you call the police?' Louise asked as she got to her feet. Her eyes flashed with annoyance. 'We don't need them yet.'

Mary shivered. She took a step back, suddenly afraid of the woman she had worked for for most of her life. 'I thought I should,' she mumbled, and then turned and ran from the room. She didn't know what had gone on in that room before she heard the screams, but she was staying out of the way until the police arrived, because she didn't like the look of Mrs van Allen. And she wasn't at all sure she believed her story...

'They were accusing each other,' Ben said as he sipped his coffee after lunch. 'I wouldn't tell anyone else, Sarah, but I thought you should know – and I know you'll keep it to yourself.'

'Yes, I shall,' Sarah replied. 'I only met her once at one of Mother's friends' houses. Mummy isn't particularly close to Mrs van Allen and I didn't like her very much. Not that I would ever have thought her capable of murder, but people do some odd things out of jealousy or greed, don't they?'

'Yes, they certainly do,' Ben agreed. 'We don't know that either of them had anything to do with van Allen's murder – though my money would be on her rather than him. Hudson didn't think either of them were guilty, but I have a feeling she may just have done it.'

'Yes, I think so too,' Sarah said. 'From what I saw of Jonathan he could be charming. Katie said he had moods, but if he was hiding Maura and thinking his mother had killed his father that isn't surprising, is it?'

'No, perhaps not...' Ben looked up as the door of the small sitting room opened and Mrs Harland came in.

'Detective Hudson is on the phone, Mr Marshall. He wants to speak to you please.'

'Really?' Ben got up and followed her into the hall, leaving the door slightly ajar. 'Hudson ... what can I do for you?'

'We've got Lucas Barrett in custody.'

'What? That's good news, isn't it? Has he confessed to shooting Mrs Lawson?'

'He has done a lot more than that,' Hudson said. 'He says he is the Playboy Murderer. I'm not sure if I believe him, but it sounds right – the gun that came from that house is the one that he used to shoot Mrs Lawson. I didn't think it could be that simple, even though I had the evidence all the time – but it looks that way. He's maudlin dunk and confessing to everything I ask. He says he killed them all, even van Allen, but I think he would confess to killing the President at the moment.'

'Why is that?'

'His daughter was with him when we found him. He keeps saying she fell, but he may have pushed her. They took her to the hospital but she was conscious by the time she got there and she walked out before a doctor could see her. Maybe she didn't want them to put her back in that home.'

'Yes, perhaps that was it,' Ben said. 'So you've wrapped it all up then?'

'Yes. I just have one more problem...'

'What is that? If he has confessed to all of it you should be able to wrap up these cases.'

'I can – but I just got a call. Jonathan van Allen is fighting for his life on an operating table at the hospital. His mother says he tried to kill her and she tried to stop him. Apparently, he shot himself in the struggle.'

'Do you believe her?'

'Her maid didn't, but I'm keeping an open mind,' Hudson said. 'I'm just praying van Allen comes through so that I can question him. I wouldn't trust that woman further than I could throw her.'

'No, I agree with you. I was just thinking that of the two of them she was the one I would have backed to kill van Allen.'

'You might be right.'

'I thought Lucas Barrett just confessed to killing him?'

'He did, but the man has lost his grip on reality. He is mumbling all the time, but half of it doesn't make sense. I doubt if we will ever get him to trial. They will say he isn't fit and shut him up in some asylum somewhere.'

'Not what you would like in this case?'

'Nah, but it's the way the cookie crumbles. I would like to see the bastard get his just deserts, but he'll probably live until he's old and grey at the State's expense.'

'Well, I'll wish you good luck,' Ben said. 'I'm going to tell Sarah what's happened – that's all right with you, isn't it?'

'Yes, it is. I think she probably guessed some of it long before we did – and I have to admit it was mostly guess work.'

'Good old-fashioned police work, I call it,' Ben said, and grinned. 'Thanks for letting me know.'

'It will be in the evening paper – at least the official version.'

'Thanks again for letting me know.'

'Shall we see you back here again next year?'

'I doubt it. My wife will have my guts for garters when I get back. She expected me days sooner.'

Ben heard Hudson chuckle before he replaced the receiver. He was thoughtful as he went in to tell Sarah that there was a mixture of news. She looked at him expectantly as he sat down in the chair opposite, because with the door ajar she had caught some of Ben's end of the conversation.

'Have they got him? It was Lucy's father who committed all those awful murders, wasn't it?'

'He has confessed to them,' Ben said. 'Hudson had the gun that was used to shoot Annabel. It was the gun that was stolen from the house in Newport after the first Playboy Murders. He said he had considered it a possibility, but it seemed too neat to be true to me. So your feelings were spot on again, Sarah.'

'I couldn't tell you why I thought it might be him, but then I didn't know that they had found the gun at the scene of the shooting,' Sarah said. 'Did I hear you say that he murdered van Allen too?'

'Apparently he confessed to it, but Hudson isn't sure it was him, because he is rambling and not in his right mind,' Ben said. 'I think we might have underestimated Hudson at the start, Sarah. He is a good cop. He looks at all the angles. I thought he was going for the obvious at the start, but he runs deep. He paid you a compliment – said you probably guessed before we did.'

'I only sensed it might be him,' Sarah told him. 'I had no clues, but I just thought the pattern was there.'

'What do you mean?'

Sarah smiled. 'When I went to see Detective Hudson at the precinct he told me that this wasn't one of my cosy village crimes, but I think he was wrong. People murder for much the same reasons whether they live in a big city or a village, in my opinion.'

'Go on,' Ben encouraged with a smile. 'I love to hear you work things out, Sarah.'

'Well, I think he killed those people because they were rich and he was poor. Lucy told me a bit about herself, and Matron told me some things too. I think Lucas Barrett couldn't find work and his wife and small children died, perhaps through lack of proper food and medical treatment. He blamed himself, but he also blamed the man who put him out of work. And then, of course, after he was presumed dead in the riot he would have found it difficult to work anywhere. Mr van Allen must have been his last hope. He went to the van Allen house because he wanted to ask for work, but what he saw there made him angry – those people had all the things he couldn't give to his family. He acted on blind impulse that first time, because he was consumed with jealous anger. Those are feelings anyone might have anywhere in the world in his circumstances. What he saw didn't give him the right to do what he did, but you can see why he felt driven to it. In his eyes it was justice – a different kind of justice and wrong, but a lot of people might feel that way, even if they didn't act in the same way.'

'Yes, you are right,' Ben said. 'It would be easy to understand why he killed van Allen, if he did – and the shooting of Annabel was probably frustration. She made him lose his temper because she wouldn't give him her purse. All the other murders ... well, maybe he discovered he liked having power over others. Just for once he was the one on top.'

'Yes...' Sarah was thoughtful. 'It doesn't explain why he was following me – if it was him, of course – but that doesn't matter now. I'm more concerned about Lucy and what she is going to do in the future.'

'She was with him when the police arrested him. She had fallen or he'd knocked her down, Hudson isn't sure, though Barrett says it was a fall.'

'Yes, I think it would have been,' Sarah said, and looked thoughtful. 'I think he would have been too remorseful over what he did to her face to deliberately hurt her.'

'You're crediting him with some decent feelings?'

'Most people have some, don't you think?'

'Yes, I suppose so,' Ben said, 'though sometimes in this business it makes you wonder. I mean, to kill so many people at that house and then go out and do it again...'

'Yes, I know what you mean,' Sarah agreed. 'But it sounds like raw emotion to me. It certainly isn't organized crime. I think Detective Hudson may have thought it was for a time.'

'Yes, he did mention something on those lines once,' Ben agreed. 'I am glad it is all cleared up, Sarah. We should both have worried about it otherwise.'

'Yes.' She smiled at him. 'We are alike in that way, Ben. When we get hold of a mystery we have to worry at it like a dog with a bone. So Detective Hudson is satisfied it is all finished now?'

'As much as he can be. He isn't sure about what happened between Mrs van Allen and her son, but that is a different crime – nothing to do with us.'

'I agree. None of it was really. I don't suppose I would have got involved at all if it hadn't been for Maura. Mummy is going to invite her here when she is well enough to leave hospital. She was going to visit Lucy too, but I don't suppose she will go back to the home.'

'Where else could she go?'

'Well, she could come here,' Sarah said. 'I know Mummy won't turn her away empty-handed, so I can leave it all to her really.'

'Yes, I am certain you can. And now, if you're ready, Sarah, I imagine we ought to be on our way.'

'Yes, I think we should,' Sarah said. 'I am sure Detective Hudson has it all under control...' She gave a husky laugh. 'He wouldn't thank me for making a suggestion, anyway.'

'Oh, you never know,' Ben said. 'Got something on your mind?'

'Not really,' Sarah said. 'If it was me I would have someone sitting outside Jonathan van Allen's door at the hospital, but I am sure he has thought of that anyway.'

'Bound to have,' Ben agreed. 'Not the kind of thing a man like that would neglect I'm sure...'

Nine

'What do you mean I can't visit my son?' Louise van Allen looked at the police officer sitting outside the small private room she had secured for her son's treatment. 'I have brought him some fruit and flowers.'

'I'm sorry, ma'am,' the officer replied. He put his hand to his hip, touching the gun he had strapped there. 'My superior told me that no one is to go in without clearance from him. You are not on the list, Mrs van Allen.'

'But that is ridiculous!' She glared at him, holding her temper by a thread. 'Your superiors will be hearing from my lawyers. At least you can tell me how he is! Is he conscious yet? Is he recovering, as he ought?'

'I am sorry, ma'am, I can't give you that information.'

'Someone is going to be in trouble for this! He is my son. I have every right to visit him and to be given reports of his progress!'

The officer touched his cap in an apologetic manner. 'Yes, ma'am. I'm sorry. I can't help you. You need to speak to Detective

Hudson.'

'I certainly shall!' she snapped, and walked away, her long skirt twitching like the tail of an angry cat.

How dare they keep her from Jonathan's room? She was furious that she was being treated like a criminal, and even more furious that her son had managed to live despite a wound that ought to have killed him. She was certain that no one could disprove her story – no one but Jonathan if he recovered enough to tell that annoying Detective Hudson the truth.

If she could find some way of getting to him she might be able to make sure that that never happened, but if they wouldn't let her into Jonathan's room there was nothing she could do for the moment. It was only his word against hers, and she was a respectable lady, whilst he ... was like his father.

She frowned as she remembered the things he had said to her – and after all she'd done for him! And all over a little slut who had got what she deserved!

As she left the hospital, Louise was thinking about the slut who had dared to say that Jonathan had promised to marry her. It was a pity she had run off from the home, because it might have been possible to use her against Jonathan.

She had to find some way to get to him, even if it meant making promises she would never keep...

Lucy stood outside the house for several minutes, staring at the imposing front door and trying to gather enough courage to go in. Sarah had told her it would be all right, but she was anxious because she remembered the way Mrs van Allen had looked at her when she dismissed her.

'*You are nothing but gutter trash...*' the words were burned into Lucy's mind in letters of fire. '*You will never marry my son. You are not fit to wipe the filth from his boots.*'

Lucy knew that she was tarnished by her history, even more so now that her father was in the papers, branded as a murderer. She swallowed hard. It was asking too much of Sarah's parents to take her in. Perhaps she should go back to Larkspur House: they would take her in and give her a bed to sleep in, which was more than she deserved.

'Hello,' a voice said at her shoulder. 'Did you want Mrs Harland? Are you looking for a job?' Lucy turned to stare at the handsome young man standing just behind her. She noticed the way his eyes went to her scar and expected the usual look of horror or embarrassment, but instead he smiled. 'I know who you are. Sarah told us you might come. Your name is Lucy, isn't it?'

Lucy nodded, her throat running dry. He was offering her his hand. She hesitated and then gave him hers. His handshake was firm and strong, cool to the touch.

'I'm Brad Harland, Sarah's stepbrother. She isn't here at the moment. Did she tell you she sings on the stage?' Lucy shook her head, fascinated. 'Well, she does and she is on a ship heading for England at the moment, performing twice every night for the passengers.'

'She must be clever...' Lucy offered shyly. Her heart was racing but she wasn't frightened of him somehow.

'Sarah is brilliant. I don't tell her so, naturally, but I think the world of her, and she sings like an angel. Are you coming in? My stepmother will be pleased you've come. I know she has been hoping you would.'

'Has she really?' Lucy stared at him as the first flickering of hope started up in her breast. 'She won't think it's begging or anything like that? Because I am willing to work ... anything...'

'My stepmother is always looking for help in the house,' Brad told her, and grinned, 'but you're too pretty to be a maid. You should be doing something more exciting.'

'Pretty, with my face?' Lucy was about to turn away, because he had to be making fun of her. 'That's cruel...'

Brad held her arm, making her turn towards him. 'I didn't mean to be cruel. You *are* still pretty, Lucy. I know you have a nasty burn on your face and that's awful for you, but you are pretty. You have lovely hair and eyes, and a nice figure. No one is perfect, you know. I have a bump on my nose where it got broken playing football in college.'

'You haven't,' she said, and then looked closer. 'It's only a little bump.'

'Yours is only a scar,' he said. 'You're lovely inside, Lucy. It shines out of your eyes. Having a scar doesn't make you ugly, it's what you are – the real you – that matters.' Tears welled in her eyes. She stared at him as he leaned towards her, kissing the scar so gently that the tears spilled over and trickled down her cheek. 'There, that didn't hurt, did it? Come on in and meet my stepmother, Lucy. I promise she won't bite – or just now and then when she's cross and even then it's only a puppy bite. She's really nice.'

Lucy felt the ice begin to crack around her heart. Sarah had begun the healing process when she had believed Lucy, and this man was making her feel that her life didn't need to be hopeless after all. She wasn't her father and she hadn't done those wicked things. Perhaps she could find a way to make a new life for herself.

'Thank you,' she said. 'It is very kind of you...'

'I am going to be a doctor one day,' Brad said, surprising her and himself, because until now it had been a half-formed thought in his head. He'd almost told Sarah once but he hadn't been sure. Now he was and the idea filled him with excitement. 'And I'm going to specialize in helping people who have scars like you. One day in the future we'll know how to make it much better, Lucy.'

She stared at him for a moment and then she smiled. 'I think you will,' she said. 'I feel better about it already.'

'Then come and meet Ma,' Brad invited. 'I know she will be so pleased that you've come...'

Sarah stared at the envelope the steward was offering her. She sensed that it must be from her mother, and important if she had thought it necessary to send a shore-to-ship telegraph. People did that kind of thing when they wanted to have a murderer arrested, as in the famous case of Doctor Crippen. The ship's captain had recognized him and sent a message to London, and the inspector in charge of the case had taken a faster ship. He had been there when Crippen arrived at what he imagined was freedom to arrest the murderer. But Sarah couldn't imagine what would make her mother go to this much trouble! Her fingers trembled as she opened the envelope and then she gave a sigh of relief. She turned to Ben, who was having coffee with her in one of the ship's lounges.

'Mummy wanted to let me know that Lucy is safe. She has given her a job and says everything is fine at the moment.'

'That is good news,' Ben said. 'I know it

has been at the back of your mind. It is always better to be able to put something like that behind you and clear your mind.'

'Yes, it is,' Sarah said. 'She told me before we left that Maura wouldn't be out of hospital for a week or two so I think I can put it all behind me now.'

'Good.' Ben smiled at her. 'You aren't upset by what happened, are you, Sarah? Only, I've wondered a few times. I know those nasty murders last year affected you.'

'Yes, they did for a while,' Sarah admitted. 'But they weren't the reason I left England, Ben. It was a more personal reason.'

'Ah, I see. I suppose you mean Larch?'

'Yes, I do.' There was a faint blush in her cheeks. 'I was cross with him for backing that show without telling me, but I am over it now. I know he did it as a friend, to help me through a difficult time.'

'He likes you a lot, Sarah.'

Sarah nodded but made no reply. She was trying to decide how she felt about Larch – and Sam. They had both asked her to marry them, but Larch had since withdrawn. He had come to the theatre to bring flowers and wish her luck, but he hadn't been there to wave goodbye when the ship left port. Sarah had felt a bit hurt, though she knew she was being foolish. Annabel needed his help and she would be mean spirited to grudge the time he spent with her — but that didn't stop her wondering if he had regretted asking her to marry him.

As she saw it, she might have two choices. One was to marry Larch and give up singing professionally. He wouldn't mind if she did amateur productions in the village, but that would seem tame after her experiences on the stage of a London theatre. If she married Sam she could have all the excitement of a glittering career *and* marriage ... and she did find him exciting.

Why couldn't life be more straightforward? If Larch had asked her the previous year she would probably have said yes – at least to an engagement. Now she felt as if she were being torn down the middle. A part of her knew deep down inside that despite the attraction she felt for Sam, Larch was the man she had always loved – but did Larch truly want to marry her? And if he did, was she prepared to give up her career to marry him?

It was a difficult decision to make, though she might have found it easier if Larch had been here on the ship as he had intended to be. They could have spent time together after the shows, standing on deck in the moonlight.

Was she looking for romance? Sarah smothered her sigh as she stood up. It was time to leave Ben, because even on board the rehearsals went on. Ellie wasn't a slave driver like Sam, but she had her own way of getting the best out of everyone!

* ★ ★

Lucy had never been so happy. Mrs Harland was kind and a generous employer, paying her as much as she would have got had she been recommended by a top agency for domestic employees. It was like living in another world for Lucy, because she was treated almost as one of the family. She knew her place, of course, and wouldn't have dreamed of stepping over that invisible line, but everyone had a smile for her. Brad often came into the kitchen to chat to her. He had told her that he was going back to school.

'I went to college but I spent most of my time playing football for the team or rowing,' he said with a grin. 'Now I'm going to medical school. Father is thrilled to bits. I thought he might hate the idea, because he would have liked me to work for him in the family business – but he said as long as I was planning on something worthwhile he was with me all the way.'

'You will make a good doctor,' Lucy said. She gave him a teasing look, because she had almost forgotten the scar. Her face didn't matter to the people in this house, and that meant she didn't have to worry about it. They didn't show her pity; she was expected to do her work and she did it well, because it gave her pleasure to repay her kind benefactress. She knew exactly how Mrs Harland liked things kept, because she had paid attention when she was told what was needed, and she worked hard to make the house nice.

'It means years of hard work,' Brad said. 'I shan't have time to play – and I certainly can't get married for years, because I want to pay my way as much as I can, but it will be a good future – don't you think so, Lucy?'

'Yes, I do,' she told him. 'I am very pleased for you.'

'I thought you would be.' Brad gave her his special smile and left her to get on with her work.

Another girl might have thought Brad was hinting at something more than he said, but Lucy just thought he was being nice to her like all Sarah's family. She was glad he had his future planned. As far as Lucy was concerned, her future was here in this house. She felt safe, even cared for, and that was all she wanted for now.

It wasn't until four weeks after she had started to work for the Harland family that she found the old newspaper under the kitchen sink. Hannah kept them to wrap the vegetable peelings before putting them out in the trash, and Lucy was about to start on the potatoes for that evening's meal. The headline caught her eye and she read down the journalist's report, staring at the blurred photograph of Jonathan van Allen.

The article said that he had been injured in a shooting at his home. His mother claimed that he had tried to shoot her and the gun had gone off as they struggled. He wouldn't do that! Her Jonathan wasn't a cold-blooded killer!

Lucy had been hurt when he ran off and left her, but she knew that he hadn't been able to look at her because of what his father had done. It was her own fault for telling him. If she hadn't he might never have gone away. He might have stayed and married her.

She felt her throat tighten, not because she really expected that he would marry her – and it didn't matter now anyway – but she couldn't bear to think of him lying close to death in hospital. She tore out the piece with the name of the hospital and his picture. She hadn't asked for any time off since she started working here, because there was nowhere she wanted to go, but she knew Hannah would let her go for a couple of hours if she finished her work first.

She had no idea if Jonathan was still in hospital or if he had died. She hoped he hadn't died, because she still cared what happened to him. Lucy wasn't sure if she still loved him, because that part of her life was over and done. But she did care what happened to him, and she would like to find out how he was now...

Louise stared at herself in the gilt-framed mirror above the fireplace. It was antique and it had come from her family, an heirloom and something she treasured. It was not a part of her husband's estate. If she did what Jonathan wanted and told the lawyers to go ahead with splitting the estate in two she might be able to keep this house, but it would mean giving in to her son. His letter had made his terms plain. He would tell the police that he had just been messing about with the pistol and it had gone off by accident – and for that he wanted more than his fair share of the cash his father had kept hidden. But he was demanding two million in cash now and she didn't have that much.

She'd had to pay off a couple of her husband's former associates. They had demanded money in exchange for keeping quiet about some of his activities. Louise knew that if the Internal Revenue got involved there could be catastrophic consequences, because her husband hadn't declared even a half of his income, and that would cost both her and Jonathan money, depleting the estate. She would give him the eight hundred thousand dollars she had offered before, but it was all she had. If he continued to be greedy...

Her eyes snapped with temper. The police had kept a guard on his hospital room door while Jonathan played for time. He had been telling them that he wasn't sure what had happened, pretending there was a gap in his memory – but he hadn't asked for her name to be added to the list admitted to his room.

She knew that he was mending well. In another few days he would be leaving the hospital. She couldn't afford to let him live if he was going to blackmail her, but it was too risky to make another attempt at killing him herself. She had found a little book in one of her husband's hiding places. In it was a list of names and the kind of work they did – she had found several who were willing to kill for money. It confirmed what she had always suspected. Her husband had been evil, and he deserved what she'd done to him – but she wouldn't have done it if he hadn't demanded a divorce. She'd had no intention of being cast off with a pittance. She was owed for all she'd had to endure over the years!

Now she was glad of his contacts. She could pay one of them to get rid of Jonathan. It would probably be cheaper than paying him off – but she didn't want to exchange one greedy blackmailer for another. She had to arrange to meet the killer she had chosen, but it needed to be at night, and she would go veiled.

Her plan had flaws, because the killer might realize who she was, and then she would be even more vulnerable to blackmail. She realized that she needed someone she could trust, someone stupid enough to carry a letter of instruction and some money, but she had to choose the right person for the job.

She decided that she would make one more attempt to see her son at the hospital. Perhaps she could reason with him, come to an amicable agreement. After all, she had cared for him once...

'Larch, it is lovely of you to come,' Annabel said. They were outside the hospital standing by her car. She was dressed in a pretty green silk frock with a wide white sash, her shoes, gloves and bag all white leather. On her newly washed and Marcel-waved hair she wore a hat with white veiling. 'I don't know what I should have done without your support these past few weeks.'

'It was the least I could have done,' Larch said. 'I know your car is waiting, but I could not let you go home alone, Annabel. It will seem strange after such a long hospital stay.'

'Yes, perhaps,' she agreed. 'But everyone has been so kind. I am sure I shall have lots of visitors once I am home again – and I feel so much better. The doctors told me they are amazed that I have recovered as well as I have. I think they imagined I should be an invalid for a long time.'

'Yes, they told me that you would need rest and care.'

'I thought perhaps they did.' Annabel looked at him, her eyes intent on his face. 'Tell me the truth, Larch – are you in love with me?' She saw the startled expression in his eyes, the doubts and the denial he could not hide. 'No, I didn't think so. I must admit that I did hope you might be for a while. I believe you know that you are very special to me?'

'Annabel...' Larch was lost, because he couldn't find words that wouldn't hurt her. 'You know I like you. You are a special friend.'

'And you have been a special friend to me while I needed you. I think you love Sarah Beaufort – no, you don't have to tell me, because it isn't my business. I am grateful for all you've done, your friendship and your care – but I think you should get on with your own life now, my dear. If you loved me I should have been happy to marry you, but I know in my heart it is Sarah you want.'

'Sarah understood that you needed someone,' Larch said. 'I wanted to help as much as I could...'

'And you have,' Annabel told him, with a gentle smile. 'But when I marry again it will be to a man who adores me. I value you as a friend, Larch, but I couldn't marry a man who didn't feel the way I did. I believe it is time you stopped neglecting the woman you love for my sake.'

Larch leaned forward and kissed her cheek. 'I told Sarah you were a lovely person, Annabel. I shall take your advice as soon as I can, but she must be in England by now. I know she will be returning with the cruise ship and it is probably best if I wait for her, because if I tried to—' He broke off as something caught his eye. 'What does she think she is doing to that girl?'

Annabel looked in the direction of his gaze and saw a woman and a girl just a few yards away. The woman had hold of the girl's arm, and from the looks of things she was abusing her in some way, because the girl was crying and upset. Larch had already reached them, and the woman could see that he was on the girl's side. It was at that moment that Annabel realized the girl was Lucy Barrett and the woman was Louise van Allen. She walked towards them in time to hear what Louise was saying.

'The stupid, ungrateful girl refused to come with me. I told her I had a little job for her, but she refused me – and most rudely.'

'Lucy doesn't need a job,' Larch said. 'I happen to know she works for a friend of mine. Besides, she has the right to refuse you, Mrs van Allen.'

'I only came to see how he was,' Lucy said, looking nervous. 'I wasn't doing anything wrong.'

'Of course you weren't, Lucy,' Annabel said. 'If you are talking about Jonathan van Allen, I understand he is getting better and should be leaving hospital any day now.'

'Oh, thank you.' Lucy smiled at her. 'You're Mrs Lawson, aren't you? I remember you when you visited Larkspur House.'

'Yes, I am Annabel Lawson. I remember you too, Lucy – but you look so much better. Quite a different person.'

'Yes, I am, thank you.' Lucy's face clouded as she remembered that it was her father who had shot Annabel. 'I am so sorry for what happened to you that day. You know it was—'

'Your father? Yes, I know, Lucy. Don't look like that, my dear. It wasn't your fault.'

'I always knew you came from a bad line,' Louise said sourly. 'If you think my son will marry you now you are quite insane.' She turned away and got into the car waiting for her.

Annabel stared after her with a frown. 'That woman is a she-devil. I never did like her and I shall cut her from my lists. What did she want you to do, Lucy?'

'I don't know,' Lucy said. 'She told me it was for Jonathan's sake, but I was frightened ... she looked so strange.'

'What she said to you was quite uncalled for,' Larch said, and smiled. 'Would you like me to take you home, Lucy?'

'I think I should like to see Jonathan if they will let me,' Lucy said. 'Thank you for helping me, Mr Meadows, but I can manage now.'

They watched her walk into the hospital, her head high. 'So brave,' Annabel said. 'We thought she would never get over it – that terrible scar, and all the rest.'

'I think you can thank Sarah and her family for that particular miracle,' Larch said, and smiled.

'I wasn't aware that you knew Lucy?' Annabel looked at him curiously.

'Oh, I call on Sarah's mother now and then. I knew that Lucy had settled in well, but I didn't expect to see her here.'

'You didn't know that Jonathan van Allen was the father of her baby? She lost it, of course – it was a part of the trauma that made her ill for such a long time.'

'Well, she seems better now. I only hope he doesn't do anything to upset her...'

'If she can handle his mother, I think she will manage Jonathan perfectly well. Besides, she seemed to know exactly what she wanted.'

'Yes, she did.' Larch turned to her with a question in his eyes. 'Are you sure you don't want me to come home with you? I am very willing to do whatever you need, Annabel.'

'I need to get used to being alone again,' Annabel said. 'I have my maid and I shall be perfectly all right.'

'Then I think I'll pay Sarah's mother a visit, ask whether she has heard from her recently.'

'Yes, you should,' Annabel agreed. She left him and walked to her car, waving as she was driven away. It was only when she could no longer see him that she was aware her cheeks were wet with tears. She had sent him away because she knew he didn't love her as she wanted to be loved, but doing the sensible thing didn't mean it wouldn't hurt for a while ... not that she had very long from what the doctors had told her. All the more reason to send Larch away, because she wouldn't want him to see her in the last stages of her illness. She had already arranged to go into a clinic in Switzerland, where she could stay until the last. A few months, the doctors had told her, but she would prove them wrong if she could...

Jonathan looked up as the nurse came into the room. She was pretty and friendly, and he had enjoyed flirting with her once he started to recover.

'Good morning, Jane. How are you today?'

'I'm busy as always,' she replied. 'You have a visitor, Mr van Allen – if you wish to see her?'

He scowled. 'I've already said that I don't wish to speak to my mother while I'm in here.'

'It isn't your mother. It is a young woman by the name of Lucy...' Jonathan sat up, looking as if he might jump out of bed. 'Lucy Barrett. Do you want to see her?'

'Yes, I do,' Jonathan said. 'Ask her to come in, if you will, please.'

He put his hand to his hair, smoothing it over, acutely aware that he was looking less than his usual debonair self. He couldn't believe that Lucy was here after all this time. He held his breath as she opened the door and stood there for a moment. His gasp of disbelief as she walked in made her hesitate; her nervous manner indicated that she was ready to flee again at any minute. He held out his hand to her.

'No, please don't go, Lucy. Who did that to you – my father?'

'No, mine,' Lucy said. She approached slowly. 'I know it is awful. I am sorry if you can't stand the sight of me, but I just found out what happened and I wanted to ask how you were.'

'I am very much better,' he replied, his eyes still on her face. 'Why did he do that to you?'

'Because I wouldn't tell him the name of my child's father.' Tears gathered in her eyes but she didn't let them fall. 'I lost the child before this happened. Father was drunk. He didn't really know what he was doing. I am sure he would have been sorry when he sobered up, but I didn't stay to find out. He is in prison now for murdering people – a lot of people.'

Jonathan nodded: he read the papers. 'I looked for you, Lucy. I wanted to find you but—'

'Now you don't?' Lucy smiled oddly. 'I know my face must be repulsive to you, Jonathan. You liked me because I was pretty. I didn't come here to ask for anything. I have made a new life for myself. Whatever happened between us is over.'

'Yes, it is,' he said, and then realized how it sounded. He hurriedly tried to cover his tracks. 'Not because of your face. We could have got over that, but things have changed. I'm going away, leaving America. I think I shall go to Paris.'

'I'm glad you have plans for the future,' Lucy told him. 'The paper said you had been shot but they didn't say much about what happened.'

'It was an accident,' Jonathan told her. 'I'm glad you came, Lucy – glad you have a new life.'

'Thank you.' Lucy hesitated, then smiled. 'I shall go now, Jonathan. I shan't bother you again.'

'You haven't bothered me,' he lied. 'Look ... are you all right for money? I mean I could get you a couple of hundred dollars if—' he stopped as he saw the look in her eyes. Shame washed over him. 'I'm sorry for what happened. I shouldn't have left you the way I did.'

'No, you shouldn't,' Lucy agreed. 'Goodbye, Jonathan.'

She turned and walked from the room, her head high. Jonathan stared after her, feeling a little sick. Her face was such a mess! He could never have stood looking at her every day of his life, because he found the scar revolting. Yet he couldn't help feeling ashamed of what he'd just done. It was like running out on her all over again, because he was a coward. If he had been braver he would have stood up to his father when he discovered what he'd done to Lucy – stood by her. If he had her face would still be as beautiful as it had once been.

He lay back against the pillows. He hadn't even had the guts to tell the police that his mother had tried to murder him. A shudder ran through him, because he knew he had to face up to what had happened. Louise van Allen was a cold-hearted bitch. He knew that his blackmail wouldn't work, and he would have to force her to pay up – but next time he wouldn't go empty-handed.

Lucy was washing glasses in the sink when Bradley walked in that evening. He was dressed in a smart suit and looked as if he had been somewhere important. Lucy glanced at him but her usual smile was missing.

'Is something wrong?' he asked. 'I haven't forgotten something I promised to do, have I?'

'You haven't made me any promises,' Lucy said. She wiped her hands on a towel and then picked up one of the glasses, beginning to polish it on a soft cloth. 'Why should you?'

'Something has upset you,' Brad said. He took the cloth from her and put it down, then led her to a chair. 'Sit down for a minute and tell me the truth, Lucy. What happened today?'

'I went to see Jonathan van Allen at the hospital. I just found out he had been shot and I wanted to see if he was all right...'

'And was he?'

'Yes, much better.' Lucy made as if to get up but Bradley pushed her shoulder so that she sat down again. 'He offered me two hundred dollars if I needed money.'

'The damned fool! Shall I go over there and punch him for you?'

'No. He is only just recovering from being shot.'

'Serves him right,' Bradley said in anger. 'Why did he offer you that? It was an insult.'

'I think he meant it kindly,' Lucy said. 'He said he had been looking for me but when he saw my face he wished he hadn't found me.'

'He didn't say that?'

'No, but it was there in his eyes.'

'He is a damned fool! I don't know him well, but what I've heard of him makes me think he is a weak coward.'

'Bradley...' Lucy shook her head. 'He ran away after his father raped me. He couldn't bear it – and he couldn't bear to look at me today.'

'I'll thrash him for making you feel like this!'

'No!' Lucy smiled as she saw how angry he

was. 'There's no need, Bradley. Honestly, it was what I needed. It hurt me when he went off and left me, but for a long time I still thought I loved him – but I don't. He gave me pretty things and said he loved me, but he lied. I was so foolish. I should never have believed him. Why would a man like that want to marry a girl like me? It was my own fault. If I hadn't let him make love to me the rest of it might not have happened.'

'His father might still have done what he did,' Bradley told her. 'None of this was your fault, Lucy. I've told you before. You were the victim of evil men. They are to blame, not you.'

'I'm glad I went there,' Lucy said. 'I know he isn't worth crying over now and I can forget him. My face was the reason he wanted me – and it won't happen again. No man is going to want me like this.'

'Don't be a fool!' Brad took her hands, pulling her to her feet and straight into his arms. He looked down at her tenderly. 'I want you, Lucy. I can't marry you until I get through medical school, but then—'

She pulled away from him. 'Please don't say it, Brad! I'm not for you. Your parents wouldn't agree. It would make them unhappy, and they have been so good to me.'

'My father will agree once he knows I am serious. All he wants is for me to settle and make something of myself – and my stepmother isn't a snob. Believe me, when we tell them they will see it is right for us.'

'No.' Lucy shook her head. 'You hardly know me. My face—'

'Is beautiful – at least this side.' He touched her scar. 'It's there and we can't change that, Lucy. If I could I would for your sake – but I don't care. It's you I love. I shall always love you, and one day you will trust me enough to believe it.'

'I do trust you,' Lucy said. She gave him a tentative smile. 'But I can't believe you really want—'

Bradley drew her closer, bending his head so that he could kiss her, softly, tenderly, on her mouth. 'Believe it, Lucy. I'm not proposing to you now. I have a long way to go and so do you – but one day we shall be married. I am making a promise now.'

Lucy touched her lips, a look of dawning wonder in her eyes. 'I want to change, Bradley. I want to be worthy of you. If I went to night school and learned all the things I don't know, became a better person ... maybe then your family would accept me.'

'Do it for yourself if you want to,' Bradley told her. 'But I love you just as you are.'

'But my father—' He silenced her with a finger to her lips. 'Do you think I should visit him? He isn't going to stand trial, because they say he isn't mentally fit. Should I go to the mental hospital? I had a letter telling me where he is now.'

'Do you want to?'

'Yes, I think so.'

'Then I'll come with you.'

'No, I have to do this myself,' Lucy said. 'It's one last door to close on the past...'

'I've enjoyed having you home for a few days,' Sarah's father said as his daughter came downstairs with her suitcase. 'Much too short a visit, Sarah, but I suppose if this is what you want we shall have to make the most of things while you're here.'

'That is what Amelia said.' Sarah laughed and kissed her father's cheek. 'I am not sure what I want, Daddy, and that is being honest with you. I have enjoyed being in the show on board; it was a wonderful experience and I am glad I have the return trip to look forward to, but I think once may be enough.' She hesitated, then, 'I have to make a choice. Someone asked me to marry him, and if I did it would mean living over there – though I should come to England for a visit when I could.'

Mr Beaufort frowned. 'You haven't said anything about this, Sarah. Who is this man – and would I approve of him?'

'Probably not,' Sarah said, and laughed. 'However, I'm not sure that I want the life he has offered me. He wants to make me a movie star in Hollywood.'

'You know I wouldn't approve of that, Sarah.' Her father frowned at her. 'I thought you and Larch might make a go of it one day. You're not still brooding over what he did, are you?'

'No, I'm not,' Sarah said. 'Larch did ask me. He wants me to give up the stage and become a wife and mother.'

'And so I should think,' her father said with a nod of satisfaction. 'Sensible fellow! Make you a good husband, Sarah.'

'I know it would please you and Amelia. She didn't try to persuade me against living in America, but I know the idea upset her. I am very fond of Larch, Daddy, but I like Sam too. Besides, I am not sure if Larch still wants to marry me. He was spending all his time with a friend of his before I left New York. She had been shot and wounded badly ... I told you about it, didn't I?'

'If she needed help it would be like Larch to offer,' Mr Beaufort said, looking at her through narrowed eyes. 'Feeling neglected, Sarah – little bit jealous of the time he is spending with her?'

'Yes, I was just a smidgen,' she admitted. 'It's horrid of me, isn't it? I couldn't help wondering if he really loved me. Sam does, I know – even if he is a bit of a bear at times.'

'Well, don't say yes to either of them unless you are sure of what you want,' her father said. 'Your mother and I were in love once, Sarah, but we weren't right for each other. I hated her for a while after she left me for Harland. I've put the past behind me now. You have to think long and hard before you make up your mind, my darling. All I want is for you to be happy. If being one of those film stars is what you really want, I'll get used to it.'

'Bless you, Daddy!' Sarah hugged her father. 'I do love you, you know. Being with Mummy and Philip was nice for a while, but I missed you.'

'I don't expect you to live in my pocket. America isn't the end of the world. I dare say I could make the trip over now and then if I had to.'

'Thank you. You're a brick, Daddy. I do appreciate you.'

'And I love you, my darling. Is that the last of your luggage? If you're ready, I think we had better get on our way.'

'I'm glad you're coming to see me off.'

'Wouldn't miss it,' he said. 'Whatever you do, Sarah, there will always be a home for you here with me.'

'Amelia said the same,' Sarah said. 'Why can't we have all we want from life, Daddy? I want to do so many things and I know I can't have them all.'

'That's the way life is, my darling. And you have such an appetite for life. It would be a shame if you gave the stage up too soon. Larch may be wrong to ask it. I know it would please me if you came home and married him – but not if it made you unhappy. Why don't you talk to him about it, Sarah? He's a reasonable chap. You may be able to come to some agreement.'

'Yes, perhaps,' Sarah said, and hugged him impulsively. 'I feel better now I've talked to you, Daddy. Things are clearer in my mind.'

'Fathers come in useful sometimes,' he said, and smiled at her affectionately. 'Got enough money?'

'Tons,' she said. 'Besides, I get paid when I get back...'

'Seems an odd arrangement to me,' her father said. 'I wouldn't have stood for it myself.'

'Well, I thought it was a bit much to ask. Some of the girls were stony broke by the time they got here. A couple of them said they would have to do casual work to pay their way until they went back. Sam said it was to make sure they did both trips, but I think it was a little unfair.'

'Are you sure he is the sort you can trust, Sarah? I should be a bit careful if I were you.'

'Sam is all right,' Sarah said. 'I like him.'

She did like him, but she wasn't sure she wanted to spend the rest of her life with him. Actually, she had missed Larch more than she was prepared to admit. She had hoped he might send her a telegram or write, but nothing had come, and she thought perhaps he had gone away somewhere with Annabel.

Ten

'The man I want you to kill is Jonathan van Allen,' the woman said. 'This is a picture of him from a recent press release, taken when he left hospital.'

Jimmy Screamer squinted at her from his right eye; the left socket was empty and covered with a black patch. He'd lost it in a fight on the waterfront years ago. His hair was greasy and lank, his chin unshaven for at least three days. He smelled strongly of alcohol and something more unpleasant.

'I know him,' Jimmy conceded. 'Why d'ya want him eliminated? He ain't long out of the hospital.'

'That is my business,' she said. 'Are you prepared to do it or not?'

'I might be. Depends what's in it for me.'

'Ten thousand dollars.' He grinned evilly, clearly dismissing her offer with contempt. 'What do you want?'

'Double,' Jimmy said, and spat on the sidewalk. 'Half now, half when it's done.' She opened her expensive bag. He saw three bulky packets inside. She selected one and offered it to him without a word. He took the packet from her, looking inside. He was sure the bundles of used notes amounted to ten thousand. He wasn't going to count it now. If it wasn't all there he wouldn't do the job. As he pocketed the packet, he realized that she must have thought he would ask more. He made a mental note to demand extra when the job was finished. Twenty thousand was just the down payment. Afterwards, she would pay more to keep him quiet. She might be dressed in black and heavily veiled, but he knew who she was, and why she had sought his help. She'd got away with attempted murder once; next time the cops would have her inside before she could catch her breath. She knew it and that's why she'd come to him. 'When d'ya want him done?'

'Tomorrow night. He is visiting his mother at the van Allen house – it is the largest of the limestone mansions between Fifth and Madison Avenue. Kill him before he enters the house. He will call at eight thirty.'

'I know the place – it's them big old houses built nearly forty years ago.'

Louise winced at his description of the beautiful mansions, which were a part of the rich architectural history of Carnegie Hill, but she couldn't expect a moron like him to know or understand the way she felt about her house.

'Yes – the largest of them, remember that. I do not want you to shoot the wrong man.'

307

Hardened killer as he was, Jimmy shuddered at the way she calmly ordered her son's execution. Some mother! His own nagged him if he didn't visit her every Sunday like clockwork, but she was more likely to stick a knife in someone who bad-mouthed him than order his murder.

'Sure this is what you want?'

'Quite sure.'

'You got it. You won't get no slip-up this time, lady.'

She made a startled movement, then put her hand up to her veil as if to make sure it was in place, but she didn't say anything.

'I want the rest of my money when I've finished.'

'I'll meet you here the following night.'

'You'd better,' Jimmy said. 'Don't get any ideas about not paying me, 'cos you'll be sorry, lady.'

'You will get your money once I'm sure he is dead.'

Jimmy watched her walk away, her back straight like the fine lady she pretended to be. Cold bitch! Once he'd done the job he would bleed her dry.

The mental institution had iron bars at the windows and looked bleak as Lucy walked up the long drive. Set back from the road and hidden in trees, it was tucked away so that the good citizens who lived less than half a mile away would hardly notice it was there if they didn't already know.

Lucy hadn't found it easy to get a visiting order. She had applied to various people without getting anywhere, and in the end it was Mr Harland's lawyer who had got her permission after Bradley asked him if he could help. She shivered even though it was a warm afternoon as she arrived at the door. Now she was here she wondered why she had wanted to come. Her father probably wouldn't know her, and if he did he would hate her for helping to have him locked away.

Lucy knew it was because she had told Sarah that she thought her father had shot Annabel Lawson that the police had finally traced him. Without her testimony they might never have known who they were looking for. But she didn't regret what she had done. Lucy didn't hate her father anymore, and she hadn't wanted revenge. It was just that he couldn't be allowed to continue hurting people. She hadn't known then that he had killed several victims, and the knowledge confirmed that she had done the right thing, but she couldn't expect him to feel the same way.

She rang the bell. The sound from inside was hollow and made her mouth run dry. She almost turned and walked away, but before she could decide the door opened and a man in a dark suit invited her to come inside.

'You are Miss Lucy Bennett?'

'Yes. I've come—'

'I know why you've come,' he said. 'You are fortunate that the patient is in one of his lucid periods this afternoon. You will be supervised at all times – and one of the female attendants will search you. You are not allowed to give him anything.'

'I know. I didn't bring anything.'

He nodded and stood back. 'You had better come inside then.'

Lucy stepped inside. The smell made her choke. It was the strong smell of disinfectant, but underneath there was something else. The atmosphere was oppressive, and the smell got worse the further into the building they went. Lucy couldn't think what it was, but something in her made her wonder if it was the smell of fear and misery. Or was that just in her mind?

Jonathan decided that he would surprise his mother by arriving early that evening. He had made the arrangement to pick up the money at the house, but this time he had no intention of being on the wrong end of a gun. He patted his coat pocket, feeling the hard shape of the gun he had bought a couple of days earlier. Murder wasn't his style, but he would use it to keep his mother at a safe distance until he had what he wanted.

He glanced around the elegant old houses,

pausing for a moment before crossing the road. He still had his own key to the door and he had no intention of announcing his arrival. The bitch had taken him by surprise last time, but she was going to pay for what she had done to him. He would take what she offered this evening, but he had every intention of forcing the lawyers to sell everything his father had owned to pay him his share. If she wanted to stay in the house, she could pay the full value.

He slipped into the room. She was sitting at her desk, writing, her back to the door. He took the gun from his pocket, cocking the hammer and training it on the back of her head. It was a pity he hadn't the guts to kill her, Jonathan thought regretfully. He could have all of the money then, but he would never get away with it and he didn't want to be executed for murder.

'I hope you have the money ready, Ma,' he said, and smiled as her hand jolted, ink splotching over her work. She was startled, and he saw the disbelief in her face as she swung round to face him. 'I'm a little early, and better prepared this time, as you see.'

'You startled me. There was no need to creep up on me that way, Jonathan!' Her hand moved at her side, her fingers curling and uncurling as if she were tense.

'Don't try anything, Mother, because if you do I shall kill you.'

'You haven't got the guts,' she said, as she

rose to her feet. 'Put that ridiculous thing away, Jonathan. I have no intention of shooting you again.'

'Only because you know you wouldn't get away with it.'

'Oh, I don't know,' she said, her mouth curling in a sneer. 'You are here with a gun, Jonathan. If I shot you in self-defence no court would convict me. You are a greedy, ungrateful son and I think a judge would feel pity for me.'

'No, I don't think so, Ma,' Jonathan said. 'You see, I wrote a letter, which I had a lawyer witness. He will give it to the police if anything happens to me. I've told them what happened last time, and I've sworn testimony to the fact that you want me dead. I think it might look bad for you if I were shot – even by someone else.' He saw the way the colour drained from her face. 'I suspected as much. You had better call him off, whoever he is, Ma – because you'll hang with or without him being found. Mary came to the hospital and told me your behaviour wasn't natural after you shot me the first time. She has testified to that too, and if anything happens to either of us you will be in trouble.'

'What do you want?'

'I want all the cash you have in the house – and I intend selling everything. I want my share of it all. If you try to block me the evidence goes to the cops.'

'That is blackmail!'

312

'Yes, it is,' Jonathan said. 'I could have asked for more, but half of everything should be
enough – and the cash.'

'I told you how much there was,' Louise
said. 'You didn't believe me.'

'I don't now. Where is it?'

'In the bedroom in my safe.'

'I'll come with you.'

'That is hardly necessary. I can't refuse
you now – can I?'

'Not if you want to continue living as you
do.'

'I shall hardly be able to do that once you
have most of the money.'

'Come on, Ma,' Jonathan drawled. 'You
won't be exactly a pauper.'

'Very well, I'll give you what I have,' she
said. 'But it isn't what you think.'

Jonathan followed her from the sitting
room and up the wide sweep of imposing
stairway. He had slipped the gun into his
coat pocket but his hand was on it, ready to
defend himself if he had to. He saw a maid
looking at them curiously from the hall as
they went up. She was new and didn't know
him. It amused him that she might have
thought he was her employer's lover. He
followed his mother into her bedroom.

The room was furnished in dark colours
that he found oppressive. He realized that he
had never liked this room, even as a child.
He watched as his mother moved a picture
aside. She took a key from a chain around

her neck and opened the safe in the wall. Several brown paper packets were inside. She took all but one of them out and laid them on the bed.

'All of it,' he muttered, taking his gun out once more.

'There is only a small amount in that packet. It was my own, not your father's. I need it for something.'

'How much is in the rest of it?'

'One and a half million dollars. You will need something to carry it in.' She pulled out a small case and opened it. Jonathan's finger moved on the hammer, the clicking sound ominous. 'Don't try anything, Ma.'

'I am not stupid, Jonathan. You have the advantage of me this time.'

'I'm glad you realize that,' he said, and grinned. 'Put the money in the case, Ma. I don't trust you.'

'Please do not be ridiculous. I made a mistake, Jonathan. You must have realized that I acted on impulse.'

'Did you?' His grin faded, his eyes narrowing in anger. 'My memory is pretty good, Ma. I might have told the police it was an accident, but I know exactly what happened. That is why I took out insurance.'

'Well, you've won,' she said. 'Your story is foolish. I doubt if anyone would believe it – but I would prefer there was no more scandal. There has been more than enough of that, thank you.'

'And whose fault was that?' He motioned for her to stand back from the bed, then reached for the case. 'I am going now. You will be hearing from my lawyers. I don't expect we shall meet again.'

'No, I don't expect we shall,' she murmured, as he strode from the room.

Louise glanced at the clock beside her bed. It was still only ten minutes past eight. Jonathan would be gone before the killer she had hired arrived. She would meet him as arranged the next night and pay him off. She knew her son had won, because she dare not have him killed now. She went over to the window to look out. Had he walked here? Would he summon a taxicab? She wanted him gone quickly so that the danger was passed.

Across the street a figure moved out of the gathering shadows. She knew at once that the killer had come early. She raised her hand to open the window. She had to shout to warn him not to fire the gun, but even as she moved the killer's arm came up and she heard the shot. Just one. It hit Jonathan in the side of the head and he fell like a stone, face down on the sidewalk. The killer bent over him, hesitated and then picked up the case and walked away as people came running.

Louise went back to the bed and sat down. She felt cold and shivery. Her plan had worked perfectly. Jonathan was dead – and

very soon now the police would come looking for her.

'Are you all right, Lucy?' Bradley walked
into the kitchen. Lucy was at the sink, her
arms up to the elbows in hot soapy water.
She didn't glance round and he knew that
she was crying, silent tears that she had been
holding in all evening. 'Was it very bad?'

A sob broke from her and she turned, the
tears running down her face. 'It was awful,'
she said. 'That terrible place … it smells horrible and there is a feeling … oppressed. It is
like a prison, Bradley, only the inmates are
kept shut up in little secure rooms instead of
cells.'

'You shouldn't have gone,' he said, open-
ing his arms to her. 'Come here and be hugged, my love. I wished I hadn't let you go
there alone.'

'It was best that way,' Lucy said, and shuddered. She let him hug her for a moment,
but then she moved away. 'I had to go,
because I needed to say goodbye to him. He
knew me—' She broke off as a sob lodged in
her throat. 'He was crying the whole time
and begging me to forgive him for what he
did to me.'

'It must have been hard for you,' Brad
said. 'But it is over now. You won't go there
again?'

'No, I shan't,' Lucy said, and shivered suddenly. 'He asked me not to. Besides, the

316

doctor came to see me before I left. He told me that my father's lucid periods are getting less regular. They think he may not have them at all soon.'

'So there is no possibility that he will ever stand trial?'

'None at all,' Lucy said. 'I'm glad it won't be dragged through the courts, because it is all so sordid and nasty, but he has confessed to his crimes and he will never be allowed to leave that place.'

'No, I don't suppose he will. I am sorry, Lucy.'

'Don't be sorry,' Lucy said. 'I am glad I saw him again. I have forgiven him – but I don't want to see him anymore. I'm glad he will stay there, because he has done wicked things. He needs to be where he can't hurt himself or others.'

'Yes, it is for the best. You have to forget what you saw there today, Lucy, and move on. Do you think you can do that, my darling?'

Lucy raised her head, gazing into his face. What she saw there made her smile, and she felt the dark mood that had surrounded her since leaving the mental asylum begin to melt away. It seemed as if she had travelled through a long, dark tunnel, but now she could see the light at the end.

'Yes,' she said, and smiled at him. 'I'm over it now. Visiting my father at that place was the last thing holding me back. The past is gone, finished. I shan't think about it again. After all, I have so much to look forward to now, haven't I?'

'We both have,' Brad said, and bent his head to kiss her. 'And now, my love, I am taking you out.'

'Out?' She stared at him. 'But where – where are we going?'

'To the late show at the cinema,' Brad said. 'We can sit in the back row and hold hands ... and maybe kiss now and then?'

'Oh yes,' Lucy said, and gave a little giggle. 'I should like that very much.'

'Sarah, my darling!' Mrs Harland jumped to her feet as her daughter entered the sitting room, her face lighting up. 'I wasn't sure whether you would get here today or tomorrow. How are you? You look wonderful.'

'I feel wonderful,' Sarah said, and hugged her. 'There's nothing like sea air to make you feel good. I am glad to be back, though. Amelia sent her good wishes, and Daddy says he may come over later in the year. He hopes that you can all meet. He says it is time to talk amicably.'

'Oh...' Mrs Harland looked doubtful. 'Well, I suppose it may be, though I am not sure how Philip will feel about things.'

'It isn't certain,' Sarah said. 'I suppose it depends on where I decide to settle.'

'You haven't made up your mind yet?'

'I have almost,' Sarah said. 'I shan't take

318

on another cruise, though I really enjoyed it – but I don't think I want to go on doing that kind of work. It was an experience, but I would rather be on stage.'

'Yes, I believe I would if I were you,' Mrs Harland said. 'Before I ring for some tea I think I should tell you something.' She paused and then sighed. 'Bradley is going to medical school this autumn – and he is courting Lucy—'

Sarah stared at her in surprise. 'Lucy? When did this happen?'

'I imagine when she came here to work. Yes, it was very sudden. I am not sure how much it has to do with his decision to become a doctor, but Philip is pleased about that and he says if Lucy is the girl Bradley wants we must accept her. She has started to go to night school. She says she wants to improve her education so that she can be a proper companion for Brad when he qualifies. They are not thinking of marriage before that so I suppose we have to applaud their good sense.'

'Yes, well, I liked her,' Sarah said. 'And I think she is very brave to face up to life after what happened to her. You don't disapprove – do you, Mummy?'

'Bradley must make up his own mind. Philip doesn't seem to object so how could I? Besides, she is a pleasant girl – and her father has been locked out of the way. Apparently, he is in no state to stand trial for all those awful murders...' Mrs Harland looked at her. 'Did you hear that he was responsible for the Playboy Murders?'

'Yes, I did read something in the papers, but it was only a few lines. Ben and I thought it might have been him. Poor Lucy, it must have been terrible for her when she found out.'

'She was with him when the police arrested him. I think she had fallen over or something and they thought he might have attacked her, but it wasn't so – and she is fine now. She has settled here very well and I've never seen the house look as nice as it does these days. I asked her if she wanted to find a job elsewhere, but she says she would rather stay here and continue helping me until Brad has qualified. She is comfortable with that, and I am pleased to have her, so for the moment that is the way things are.'

'I am glad you told me,' Sarah said. 'But it makes no difference, because Lucy would have been my friend whatever the situation.' She frowned. 'You didn't mention Maura in the letter you sent me while I was in England?'

'That is because I don't know where she is,' Mrs Harland said. 'I visited her in the hospital and offered her a place here, but she refused. She thanked me but said she had other plans. I went back again another day but she had left and she hasn't been in touch, so I suppose that is the last we shall

320

see of her.'

'Yes, perhaps. She may have tried for another show, Mummy. You know that is what she wants to do with her life.'

'Yes, well, that is her choice,' Mrs Harland said. 'She didn't do her job half as well as Lucy does, but I would still have found something for her had she wanted it.'

'Maura isn't our responsibility. I was anxious about her, because I felt she was in trouble, but that is all over.'

'Oh, you don't know about that...' Mrs Harland frowned. 'Jonathan van Allen was murdered outside his mother's house a couple of weeks ago. The newspaper says it was a contract killing ... and there are rumours that his mother may have been at the back of it.'

'No!' Sarah looked at her in horror. 'Ben thought she might have killed her husband, but...' She shook her head. 'Why would Mrs van Allen want to kill her son?'

'I have no idea,' Mrs Harland said. 'I never liked the woman, but I must say I wouldn't have thought her capable of such a thing. The police haven't arrested her yet, but the papers are saying all sorts of things, and if they are true it can only be a matter of time.'

Sarah shivered. 'It all sounds very unpleasant,' she said. 'Have you seen Larch at all?'

'Yes, he had dinner with us last week,' Mrs Harland said. 'I know he intends to call tomorrow. He would have come this evening but I really wasn't sure whether you would be here.'

'We docked a few hours early,' Sarah said. 'Well, I shall see him tomorrow. I think I might call Sam this evening.'

'Oh, another thing,' Mrs Harland said. 'Detective Hudson brought your necklace back, Sarah. He said they wouldn't need it now. He enquired after you, and asked to be remembered to you.'

'That was nice of him,' Sarah said, and smiled. 'I am glad to have my pendant back, because Daddy gave it to me.'

'Yes, I am sure you are.' Mrs Harland frowned. 'Maura should never have taken it without asking you.'

'No, she shouldn't,' Sarah agreed. 'But I am certain that she intended to return it. She never expected anything to happen that night, I am sure.'

'No, but that still doesn't excuse her,' Mrs Harland said. 'And it wasn't exactly polite of her to go off without a word after I had visited her at the hospital several times.'

'No, that wasn't polite,' Sarah said. 'Just forget her, Mummy. I am sure we shan't be hearing from her again.'

'Why won't you take me out tonight?' Maura asked, looking up at Sam from where she lay sprawled on his bed. She was naked beneath the thin sheet that covered only a part of her, her long red hair spread out on

322

the pillows, her pert breasts shamelessly revealed. 'You promised me we could go to a nightclub.'

'Because I have something else to do this evening.'

Maura's mouth turned down at the corners. 'I hope you're not going to break the other promises you made me, Sam? You said you would take me to Hollywood and make me a star in the movies...'

'Maybe I will.' Sam walked over to look down at her, a frown creasing his brow as he fastened his shirt. She was amusing in bed and she could sing better than a lot of the girls who came to the auditions, but it was her resemblance to Sarah Beaufort that had tempted him. 'But don't whine. I can't stand girls who whine when they don't get their own way.'

Maura got out of bed, wrapping the sheet around her like a sarong. Her eyes narrowed in anger. She had let Sam persuade her into bed, because she had been attracted to him since the first time they met, but she knew deep down that he was only amusing himself with her.

'I'm not a pushover, Sam,' she warned. 'Jonathan van Allen taught me a thing or two about trusting men. Sure, and I went to bed with you because you promised me a great future. Don't let me down. I'm warning you, so I am. I don't take kindly to being treated like dirt.'

Sam stared at her. He wondered why on earth he had got involved with a woman who meant nothing to him. He'd been bored while Sarah was away, and when Maura turned up at the auditions he'd started out feeling sorry for her and he'd given her a spot in the show he was producing. It was when he saw her wearing a dress that would have looked good on Sarah that he had started flirting with her. They had ended up going to bed a few times, and now he was wishing that he'd never seen her.

Sarah was back and she had telephoned him, asking to meet that evening. He knew that she was ready to give him her answer. He also knew that if she ever discovered he had been sleeping with Maura, she would walk out of his life for good.

'I'll give you your chance in Hollywood, Maura,' he promised recklessly. 'But this is over. It was just a fling. It didn't mean anything.'

'You told me I was beautiful,' Maura said, anger hissing out of her as she realized that she had been used. 'You said you wanted me. You can't just walk away from me like that, Sam! I thought you cared about me, so I did. I thought you meant us to be together in Hollywood...'

'I have other plans,' Sam said. 'Look, I'm sorry, Maura. I never intended things to go this far, but they have and I admit I owe you something. I'll speak to a director I know.

He will give you a screen test.' Sam opened a drawer in the chest by the window and took out a bundle of ten-dollar bills. He pulled off twenty and held them out to her, putting the others in his trouser pocket. 'This will get you there and buy you a couple of dresses to help you get noticed. A girl like you can make your own way. Besides, Rod Tibbett likes women with red hair. You can charm him into giving you a part in one of his films, Maura. You don't need me.' He picked up his jacket. 'Take your things and leave. I don't want to see you here when I get back.'

Maura stared after him as he went out. She knew that Sam meant what he said and that he wouldn't change his mind. She began to dress, and then started to pack her things into a valise. She stuffed the money into her purse and then hesitated, looking at the chest. Sam had a bad temper but she would not be around when he got back She walked over to the chest, pulling the top drawer open. There was another roll of ten-dollar bills and lying right next to them a small pistol.

Maura reached out and picked up the notes and the handgun. She flicked open the chamber and saw that it contained a couple of bullets, closing it again before slipping it into her purse. It might come in useful at some time in the future.

She didn't have much to carry, because

most of her things were still at Mrs Harland's house. Maura had been nervous about going to fetch them because of the pendant she had taken without permission, but she was leaving New York and there were a few things she still wanted. She would go round there later this evening and let herself in the back door. She knew it would be open until past ten when the house was locked. If she was quick, she could go in, get her things and be away before anyone saw her.

She would find somewhere to leave her valise for the time being, then have something to eat just to kill a few hours before she went round to Mrs Harland's house...

Sarah looked at Sam across the dining table of the exclusive restaurant. He was just as handsome as when she'd last seen him, but the time away had given her a chance to think, and she knew that her feelings for him were not real. She had enjoyed a flirtation, even considered something more, but she wasn't in love with him.

'Thank you for bringing me here,' she said, smiling at him. 'I think you knew what my answer would be even before we came, didn't you?'

'I guess I've known from the beginning,' Sam said, a rueful look in his eyes. 'You're one classy lady, Sarah, but you're not for me. I hoped that I might kid you into it, but I should've known.' He reached across the table, touching her hand. 'No hard feelings?' Sarah shook her head. 'And I can't persuade you to come to Hollywood and be a movie star?'

'No, I'm afraid not,' Sarah told him. 'I am sorry, Sam. I like you a lot, but you're not the one I want to spend my life with.'

'Pity,' Sam said. 'I know I'm not good enough for you, Sarah – but believe it or not I do love you. I dare say I might have let you down so you're best out of it, but we're still friends?'

'Yes, we are,' Sarah agreed. 'I do like you, Sam, but I can't marry you. I am going back to England. I want to find another show in London if I can – but even if I don't, I believe that is where I belong. My family is there and my heart is there.'

'Then you should go,' Sam said, his eyes soft as they rested on her face. 'I wish you every happiness, Sarah – whether on the stage or as some lucky man's wife.'

'Thank you. I shall always remember you, and the show.'

'Then I guess I should take you home?'

'Yes please,' Sarah said, 'if you don't mind, Sam. I don't want to be too late this evening.'

'Then we'll go now,' he said, and signalled the waiter. 'I'm leaving for Hollywood in a couple of days so I guess this is goodbye.'

'I wish you lots of luck with your new career, Sam.'

'It's in the bag, sweetheart,' he said, and grinned at her. 'Let's get you back where you belong.'

Maura stood across the street watching as some of the lights went off at the front of the house. She knew that the family might be using the back parlour. It wasn't ten o'clock yet and they wouldn't retire for another half an hour or more. It might be best to make her move now, before they locked up for the night. She was about to cross the road but shrank back into the shadows as a taxicab drew up and one of the rear doors opened. A man got out, giving his hand to a woman, who followed him. He paid the driver, who went off, leaving them standing in the street.

Maura felt a surge of anger as she saw who they were. Sam and Sarah Beaufort! It was Sarah he had wanted all the time! The rat! He had seduced her because she looked a bit like Sarah, lying to her, stringing her along until Sarah came back.

Jealousy surged up in Maura. Hot and strong, it tasted like bile in her throat. She was so angry that she couldn't think straight. She took the gun from her purse, moving across the road in a dream, seeing only a red mist in front of her eyes. Men were all the same! They lied and deceived you because they only wanted one thing. The vile old man who had tried to seduce her that evening at the nightclub; Jonathan van Allen, who had pretended he was helping her when he was just worried he might be accused of killing his father – and he might have for all Maura knew. She had thought Sam was different, believed he really cared, but he had used her and dumped her when something better came along.

The gun was in her hand. She was only a few feet away when Sam realized she was there. He swung his head to look at her, his eyes widening with shock as he saw the gun pointing his way.

'Maura!' he cried. 'What the hell do you think you are doing?'

'You wanted her all the time,' Maura said. 'You never wanted me at all. You used me, the way they all do!'

'Maura, put the gun away,' Sam said. 'Don't be a damned idiot. I told you, I'll still help you...'

Maura was past listening. She pulled the hammer back and levelled the gun at his chest, her finger moving down on the trigger.

'No! Maura, don't do it,' Sarah cried, and pushed Sam to one side as she took a step out into the road. 'Don't be silly! It isn't worth it...'

Maura jerked her hand, startled and confused. Her finger came down on the trigger without her meaning it to and the gun jerked, her shot veering off to the right. She gave a scream of fright as she saw that she had hit Sarah, who had fallen to the ground and was bleeding as she lay there in a crumpled heap.

'I didn't mean to do it!' she whispered, her face white. The front door had opened and people were coming out to see what had happened. They were all crowding around Sarah as she lay on the road. Maura's mind was confused as she dropped the gun and backed away. 'I didn't mean to kill her...' She turned and fled into the darkness. 'Oh God, I didn't mean to kill her!'

'Larch, is that you?' Mrs Harland asked as she heard the phone being picked up at the other end. 'Oh, thank goodness! I have been trying to get you for two hours.'

'I've been to a dinner given by the owner of a gallery from Boston,' Larch said. 'He is trying to arrange a showing of various artists. Is something wrong?'

'It's Sarah—'

'What has happened?' His voice was suddenly urgent. 'Please, tell me at once! Is she ill? Has there been an accident on the ship?'

'Sarah has been shot outside the house,' Mrs Harland said. 'We are all at the hospital now. I thought you would want to know.'

'Where are you? I'll be there as soon as I can.'

'Yes, I knew you would come if you could,' Mrs Harland said, a little sob in her voice as she gave him the address. 'I know that you care for her.'

'I love her,' Larch said. 'If anything happens— I'm coming.'

The receiver was hung up abruptly. Mrs Harland replaced her own and turned, walking back to where her husband, Bradley, Lucy and Sam were sitting. She could see the tension in all their faces. Sarah had been unconscious when she was rushed into hospital and taken straight to theatre and as yet they hadn't been told what was happening.

'He is coming straight away,' she said, and sat next to her husband. 'I don't know whether to send her father a telegram...'

'Wait for a bit,' Philip advised her, putting his arm about her shoulders. 'It's hell for us sitting here. Imagine what Beaufort would feel stuck over there with no way of getting here. Let's see if she comes out of this thing before we say anything to him or her grandmother.'

'It will finish Amelia if anything happens to Sarah.'

'If she dies I'll kill that bitch,' Sam said, startling them all. He got to his feet, his face working with anger and grief and something else that might have been guilt. 'I can't stand this! Where the hell are the doctors? Why doesn't someone tell us what's going on here?'

'Because they are too busy treating Sarah,' Philip said. He looked at his son. 'You were the first to the door – what did you see?'

'It was Maura,' Bradley said, and glanced at Lucy. 'We both saw her from the window, didn't we? She had a gun and she was shouting something – at you.' His gaze turned on Sam accusingly. 'Maura was going to shoot you, but Sarah pushed you out of the way and went towards her. I missed the next bit because I rushed to the door. All I saw then was Sarah lying on the ground bleeding. Why was Maura angry with you? What had you done to her?'

'The silly bitch was jealous because she knew I wanted Sarah and not her,' Sam said, but he couldn't keep the guilt from his voice or his face. 'OK, I may have led her on a bit but there was nothing in it.'

'If Sarah dies,' Bradley muttered, 'I'll hold you responsible.'

'Stop that,' his father commanded. 'Go and see if you can find a doctor or nurse who has some news, Bradley. The police will sort out what happened. All we care about is Sarah.'

'I'm going,' Sam announced. 'I can't sit around here waiting like this. I need to get some air.'

'Don't leave town,' Philip Harland warned. 'The police will want to question you about what happened.'

'I've already told you, and the guy who turned up at the scene,' Sam muttered. 'She came at us out of the darkness waving that damned pistol about – she meant to shoot me but Sarah distracted her and I think she fired without knowing what she was doing. The shot could have gone anywhere but it hit Sarah.'

'Well, the police are going to want to question you again to take a statement,' Philip said. 'Be around when they need you...'

Sam nodded but didn't answer, walking off without another glance in their direction. He was clearly suffering from guilt along with a lot of other emotions.

'I'm glad he's gone,' Bradley said. 'He wasn't good enough for Sarah. I don't know what she ever saw in him.'

'Bradley, don't,' Lucy said softly. 'Sam cares about her. You can see that in his face.'

'Yes, he does,' Mrs Harland said. 'Sarah likes him, but I don't think she loved him. I am sure she loves Larch. She was upset when he spent so much time with Annabel. And he loves her—' She broke off, her heart in her mouth as she saw a doctor in a white coat coming towards her. Her hand reached for her husband's. 'Philip...'

Philip took her hand, holding it tightly as the doctor came towards them. They were both on their feet as he reached them, looking at him white-faced and tense as they waited for what he had to say.

'It's good news,' he told them. 'The bullet went clean through her shoulder. She has come through surgery well, and she will be fine in a few days. She was lucky that it wasn't a few inches lower, because it might have been fatal, but as it is she will be out of here in a couple of weeks or so.'

'Oh, thank goodness!' Mrs Harland said, and burst into tears just as Larch came rushing into the hallway. She sat down as her legs went weak. 'I thought she was going to die ... Thank God she is going to be all right. Her father would never have forgiven me if she'd died...'

'Sarah...' Larch said, breathing hard. 'I ran all the way here. It was quicker than getting a cab. How is she? Sarah – is she going to live?'

'She is through the surgery,' Mrs Harland said, tears coursing down her cheeks as she collapsed into her husband's arms. 'She is going to be all right.'

'No thanks to Sam Garson,' Bradley said. 'He's lucky she's going to be all right, because if she hadn't been...' He glared at his father over the top of his stepmother's head. 'Well, you heard him. It was his fault Maura had that gun. He was the one she wanted to kill.'

'Maura did this?' Larch looked from one to the other. 'I think you had better tell me just what has been going on here.'

'I'll tell you,' Bradley said. 'Lucy and I saw it happening from the window. Maura was waving the gun about and yelling something at Sam Garson. I rushed for the door but

334

when I got there Sarah was lying on the ground.'

'Damn him!' Larch said, his eyes narrowed and angry.

'That's what I said. If Sarah had died I would have killed him!'

'You would have had to stand in line behind me,' Larch said grimly. 'As it is I shall have something to say to him another day. I saw him leaving just now but didn't realize he was involved.'

'He couldn't stand the waiting,' Mrs Harland said, disengaging herself from her husband's eyes. 'I don't know exactly what happened, but it sounds as if Sarah probably saved his life by pushing him out of the way.'

'And got shot herself?' Larch frowned. 'That sounds about right. She is always far too reckless! I've told her—' He broke off as the doctor turned away. 'When can we see her?'

'She will sleep for a while, but her mother can go in now. Everyone else will have to wait for a day or so.'

'I'll tell her you were here when she wakes,' Mrs Harland said. 'And I'll ring you as soon as there is any news.'

'Thank you,' Larch said. 'I'll just sit here for a while if you don't mind.'

'I'll come back and tell you how she looks in a while,' Mrs Harland said. She touched his hand. 'It's all right, Larch. She will be fine soon. The doctor told us...'

335

He looked up, his eyes dark with grief. 'I don't know if she understands how much I love her.'

'You will be able to tell her yourself. You just have to be patient for a little while.'

Larch left the hospital an hour later. Sarah's mother had told him that she was sleeping peacefully, and he had been advised to go home by a nurse. He wasn't related to Sarah and he wouldn't be allowed to see her for a few days. The frustration bit into him as he reflected that had she been his wife he might have been there, sitting by her side, waiting for her to wake. He clenched his fists, wanting to strike out at something. He loved Sarah and this was killing him! If he'd given the dinner a miss and gone to her house that evening he might have been there – he might have been able to save her. He would rather have taken the bullet himself than have her go through this pain.

Larch didn't notice the figure leaning against the wall across the street until it detached itself and crossed the road towards him. As Sam stepped into his path, bringing him to a halt, Larch glared at him, anger building inside him.

'What do you want? Haven't you done enough damage?'

'I didn't want Sarah to get hurt,' Sam said. 'You know I care about her.'

'So much that you've been sleeping around with Maura while Sarah has been gone,'

Larch muttered. 'Don't deny it, it's obvious, you bastard! It's your fault she's lying in that hospital bed!'

'I know,' Sam ground out. 'I feel as guilty as hell—' He gave a muffled yell as Larch's fist exploded in his face and he suddenly found himself lying on the ground. He lay there for a moment as Larch towered over him. 'OK, don't look like that. I know I'm to blame. I'm a damned fool...' He rubbed his chin as he got to his feet. 'Don't hit me again!'

'I wasn't going to,' Larch said gruffly. 'I couldn't help myself – and if I ever see you near Sarah again I'll thrash you to within an inch of your life.'

'You won't,' Sam muttered. 'I'll give my statement to the police and then I'm leaving for Hollywood. If it is of any interest to you, I asked Sarah to marry me. I told her she could be a movie star but she turned that and me down. I think it's you she wants. I just needed to ask if there was any news.'

'She will pull through – no thanks to you.'

'Thank you,' Sam said, and suddenly grinned as he rubbed his chin. 'That was some punch. You should have been a professional.'

'I boxed in the army,' Larch said. 'I thought I'd lost my touch, but it's still there. I shouldn't have done it – but you deserved it.'

'Yeah,' Sam said, and laughed. 'I had it coming. See ya around.'

'I doubt it,' Larch replied. He watched Sam hail a cab and get in, then turned in the direction of his hotel. He would have rather been sitting with Sarah, but as that wasn't an option he might as well go back and try to rest, though sleeping was out of the question.

Eleven

Sarah woke up and saw Philip sitting by her bed. She tried to speak but the words were hardly more than a whisper.

'Where's Mummy?'

'She has been here all night,' Philip said. 'She went home to change and rest for an hour or so and I took her place. She will be back soon.'

'Does Larch know I'm here?'

'He came straight over,' Philip said, and smiled. 'He waited for a while, but because he isn't family they wouldn't let him come in yet.'

'Please tell them I want to see him,' Sarah said, and closed her eyes, drifting back to sleep, a single tear sliding down her cheek. She wanted Larch, needed him so badly it hurt.

'So you are awake, my love,' Mrs Harland said, bending over to kiss Sarah's cheek. 'I've brought you some flowers. Philip has gone home now for an hour or two. He told me you woke up earlier and asked for me.'

'Mummy, I'm so glad you're here,' Sarah

said, and yawned. 'I want to see Larch. Why won't they let me see him?'

'He will be here later this afternoon,' her mother said, smiling as Sarah yawned again. She was sleepy but the doctors said she was getting on well. 'He was at the house this morning, and he phoned the hospital to see how you are. We have arranged for him to come this afternoon. You can only have one visitor at a time until you are a little stronger.'

'I feel so tired,' Sarah said. 'I'm sorry, Mummy. All I seem to want to do is sleep.'

'That doesn't matter. It is good for you,' her mother said, taking her hand gently. 'Go to sleep, my love. I shall sit here with you, and this afternoon Larch will be here.'

'Good...' Sarah murmured, drifting back to sleep again.

Sarah opened her eyes. The sun was streaming in at the window and she blinked, putting her hand up to block it out. Someone got up from the chair beside the bed and adjusted the curtains so that it wasn't in her eyes.

'Is that better?'

'Larch?' She could see him now that the sun wasn't blinding her. 'You're here at last!'

'They wouldn't let me stay last night. I wanted to, my dearest one.'

'I know. Mummy told me...' Sarah's hand reached for his. He took it, holding it firmly.

'It wasn't her fault, Larch. She was upset. The gun just went off and I happened to be in the way.'

'She wanted to shoot Sam Garson. He felt guilty about it, but it was his fault for making her think he liked her.'

'Poor Maura. She has been through so much. Please tell the police it was an accident, Larch.'

'I am not sure they will believe me. She shouldn't have had the gun – and why was she there?'

'I expect she came to fetch her things,' Sarah said. 'I shan't press charges against her.'

'You are too generous, my darling, but if it's what you want I'll tell Detective Hudson. He has been here today, but the doctors won't let him near you. I sent a telegram to Ben, asking him to go and see your father. He doesn't want to get this news in a telegram. I've told them there is nothing to worry about. Ben sent his and Cathy's love, and wishes for a speedy recovery by reply. And he has promised to go and see Amelia too – though I am sure your father will want to break the news to her.'

'It's a pity you even had to tell them,' Sarah said. 'I'm not dying. The doctors told me that I should be able to leave here in another ten days.'

'You might,' Larch agreed. 'But your father would string me up if I kept this from him. I wouldn't be surprised if he comes out the first chance he gets.'

'But that is so silly,' Sarah protested. 'We could be home almost as soon as he can get here – or I should say *I* could...'

'You were right the first time,' Larch said. 'After what happened, I am not letting you out of my sight until we are back home. And not then if I can help it.'

'Oh Larch,' she said, and squeezed his hand. 'Are you going to ask me to marry you again?'

'Yes, as soon as you are well enough.'

'Could you please ask me now?'

'Do you want me to go down on my knees?' he asked, with a smile. 'It isn't very romantic. I thought somewhere nice in the moonlight...'

'Please ask me now, Larch.'

He took her hand, leaning closer so that she could look into his eyes. 'Sarah Beaufort, I love you. I haven't said it often enough, and I can't say it often enough, or romantically – but I do love you more than my life itself. Will you marry me?'

'Yes, I should like that very much,' she said. 'I love you, Larch. I should have said yes the first time. I was silly to keep you waiting. Will you forgive me?'

'I will forgive you anything – if you will just say that bit about loving me again?'

'Larch Meadows, I love you,' Sarah said. 'I want to be your wife.'

'Then all you have to do is get better,' he said. 'I think it might be a good idea if I sent your father a telegram inviting him to a wedding. If he comes over we can be married here.'

'What about Amelia?' Sarah asked. 'It might be too much for her. I think we should wait until we get back to England. Mummy and Philip can travel with us if they want – but I should like to be married at Beecham Thorny.'

'If that's what you want, it's what we'll do,' Larch said. He held her hand, turning it over to drop a kiss in the palm. 'What about your singing, Sarah? I know I said I wanted you to give it all up when we married, but if you want to go on with it we could postpone having a family for a while.'

'I shall always want to sing,' Sarah told him with a smile. 'But I think I might be satisfied with joining the choir and singing in the amateur dramatics society shows that your mother puts on now and then.'

'Are you sure that will be enough for you? I really don't mind if you want to go on for a bit longer, my dearest.'

'No, I think I have had enough,' Sarah told him. 'I wanted to show Daddy that I could do it, but it doesn't matter anymore, because I've realized that being with the people you love is more important.'

'I'm so glad you feel that way,' Larch told her. 'I want to take care of you, to cherish and protect you, Sarah. I couldn't do that if I was somewhere in Norfolk and you were on the London stage.'

'Yes, I understand,' she said. 'And I am quite content to give it up now, Larch. I love you and I want us to be together always.'

They both looked towards the door as it opened and a nurse looked in. 'Do you feel up to seeing the police, Miss Beaufort? Detective Hudson has asked to see you.'

'Yes, he can come in if he likes.'

'Just for five minutes then,' the nurse said. 'And you will have to leave soon, Mr Meadows. Miss Beaufort needs her rest.'

'I'll wait until the police have been, and go soon after,' Larch said.

Sarah pulled a face as she went out. 'I would rather you stayed with me longer.'

'We have to do what the doctors and nurses say, my love. I'll be back and we have the rest of our lives to look forward to, Sarah.'

She nodded, still smiling as Detective Hudson walked in. 'Hello,' she said, surprised because he was carrying a basket of fruit tied with ribbons. 'Is that for me? How kind of you.'

'You and Mr Marshall helped with a couple of cases,' Hudson said. 'I just wanted to tell you that Miss Trelawney walked into the precinct today and confessed to shooting you. She says it was an accident.'

'It was,' Sarah confirmed. 'She wasn't

intending to shoot me at all.'

'She came to get some clothes she had left at your mother's house, and got angry because she saw Mr Garson with you. Apparently, he had been stringing her along and she was jealous.'

'Yes, I see...' Sarah frowned. 'Sam should not have done that to her, especially after all she had been through. I knew she didn't mean to hurt me.'

'She is distressed about what she did. We shall have to charge her with malicious wounding and being in possession of a weapon, I am afraid.'

'Must you?' Sarah looked upset as he nodded. 'She has been through a bad time, Detective Hudson. Couldn't you just let her off with a warning?'

'I'm sorry, that isn't possible in this case,' he said. 'But if you want to give her a reference she might get off with a lesser sentence.'

'Yes, I shall,' Sarah said. 'Larch will write it for me and I'll sign it.'

'Well, we'll see what we can do,' Hudson said. 'I am glad that you are recovering, Miss Beaufort. I admire you for several reasons – and now I shall get out of your way and let you rest.'

Sarah was silent as he went out and closed the door, then she gave Larch a wicked smile. 'What do you think of that, then? He actually admitted that Ben and I helped him with his cases!'

'Yes, quite an admission,' Larch said, and grinned at her. 'I think you have made another conquest, Sarah my darling. Shall I have to fight them off all our lives – all your admirers?'

'Oh yes, I think so,' Sarah said, and laughed huskily. 'Shall you mind very much?'

'Not as long as you still love me.'

'I shall always love you,' she told him. 'You are my best friend, Larch.'

'Just your friend?' he asked, and arched his eyebrows.

'No, of course not,' Sarah said. 'You will be my lover and my husband – but I hope we shall always be friends too, because that is something I have valued for a long time.'

'Me too,' he said, and kissed her softly on the mouth. 'I suppose I had better go before I get chased out of here – but I shall be back this evening. I am going to go and buy you a ring – unless you would like to choose it yourself?'

'No, you choose,' she said. 'You have excellent taste, and I like surprises.'

'I'll remember that,' he said, grinned and walked to the door, turning to blow her a kiss.

Sarah smiled as he left her, lying back against the pillows with a little sigh. She didn't mind giving up her stage work, because she loved Larch. Besides, there were other things she could do. She wouldn't mention them to Larch just yet, but an idea had been churning in her head for a while now. She would just let her thoughts ferment in her mind until she was better and they were home.

Besides, she had the wedding to plan. Her father would want a huge wedding with all the trimmings, and her mother would probably want to buy her the most expensive wedding dress in the world. She could just imagine what would happen when they all got together...

Sarah sighed deeply because she was tired. She had to rest and let her strength build up again, but somehow she knew that the future was going to be exciting. She didn't have to turn into a dull housewife just because she had agreed to give up the stage.

Hudson left the hospital. He glanced at his watch and pulled a wry face. He had chosen to do the agreeable thing first. Now he had to carry out a task that would not be anywhere near as simple or as pleasant. He had given himself time to examine the evidence and gather the facts. He knew that a certain known contract killer had recently been picked up with a suitcase full of money. He was pretty certain where the money had come from, though the man was denying it. They had made a search of his home but found no trace of the gun used to kill Jonathan van Allen. However, the letters van

Allen had left with his solicitors had made the job easier than it might have been.

They had the killer locked in a cell, and given time they would break him. There was no way he could explain away that amount of cash – and now Hudson was about to arrest the true murderer. Mrs Louise van Allen would spend the rest of her life in a cell if she managed to escape execution, because she was the real killer, even if she hadn't pulled the trigger.

He could imagine the kind of fight she would put up, but there was no way he was going to let her get away with a double murder – because he was pretty sure that she had killed her husband as well, though he might never be able to prove it. But her son had left letters properly witnessed, and her maid was willing to testify that she had behaved oddly the first time her son was shot. It was unlikely she would walk free, even if she did have a fortune to spend on her defence.

He smiled grimly as he mentally filed away two cases. As it happened, he already had two new ones waiting on his desk, but that was the way it was in this city that he loved. Solve one crime and there would be another waiting. It was the way justice worked: slowly, fraught with difficulty, but sure in the end – if he had anything to do with it.

He thought about Ben Marshall and that girl in the hospital. She was beautiful and clever, and he wished her luck in her future life. Marshall should never have given up the job so early in his career. He was far too good to sit at home with his cats, but it was his choice. Hudson would probably stay in the job until he dropped.

Everyone made their choices in life. In another twenty minutes or so Mrs van Allen was going to be wishing she had made some rather different ones...